Only Work,
NO PLAY

TOUGH GAMES #1

CORA REILLY

Subscribe to Cora's newsletter to find out about her next books,
bonus content and giveaways: www.corareillyauthor.blogspot.de/p/newsletter.html

Cover design by Mayhem Cover Creations
Book design by Inkstain Design Studio

Only Work, NO PLAY

AUTHOR'S NOTE

Xavier's team the Sydney Tigers is born in my imagination.
There doesn't exist a team with that name.
I hope you'll forgive me that artistic freedom.

CHAPTER ONE

EVIE

Fiona's perfectly styled blonde head popped up on the screen. "So how's Dad doing?"

A wave of bitterness washed over me. Fiona had left Dad and me right after high school, and not just to go to college. She'd rounded half the globe to start a new life in Australia. She'd run from us, from her responsibility. From Dad's grief, from mine, perhaps even from her own, only a few months after our mother had died. We'd never been as inseparable as other twins but I'd thought we'd always stay close to each other.

"He's seeing someone."

Fiona's green eyes grew wide. "He's dating?"

I gave a shrug. I'd felt the same incredulity as Fiona when he'd told me. Mom was dead for a little less than three years and Dad had found a replacement. "He is. It's a good thing. He's doing so much better because of it." Part of me knew these words were true, yet the other part childishly held on to the idea that Dad would continue living with only the memory of Mom. It was unfair. He deserved to be happy again. Mom would have wanted him to move on.

Fiona bit her lip, probably not noticing she was ruining her lipstick. "I suppose. He's been so broken up after Mom's death, it's good that he's happy again."

Fiona fell silent. My eyes stung, and I could see hers glistening with unshed tears as well.

"So," she said in a more cheerful voice. "Does that mean you are finally free to live your own life?"

"I've lived my own life these last few years," I objected, but it wasn't true. I'd taken care of Dad since Fiona had fled the States, had chosen a nearby college so I could stay close to him and find time to watch out for him, even if his workaholic tendencies didn't make it easy.

Her nose wrinkled. "You haven't, and we both know it. When was the last time you went out? Got drunk? Partied all night?"

I made a mock thoughtful face. "That would be three nevers."

Fiona pointed her finger at me. She must have practically been poking the camera for it to be this large on my screen. "We need to change that." She paused. "You got your bachelor's in marketing, right?"

I frowned. "Yeah. I just finished." I didn't mention today's dismal job interview, or the many measly paid internships I'd had since I'd finished. Getting your foot into the marketing job scene was tough as nails.

Her smile became wicked, an expression I knew from our childhood days that made me wary. "Fiona," I said in warning.

"I have a job for you."

"A job? Where?"

"Here. In Sydney. In marketing people only care about your work experiences, so you need to get your foot in. I have a job for you that will open

2

every door for you. It's hot."

"Sydney," I said slowly. "You want me to come to Sydney?"

"You always wanted to spend a year abroad. This is your chance. Dad is busy dating, and knowing him, even busier with his job, so it's your turn to do something for yourself. You can live with Connor and me. Our house is big enough."

My mouth hung open in a very undignified way. "You want me to live with you."

Fiona's face became softer, hesitant. It was a look I'd seldom seen in the past. She hated to appear weak in front of others, even me. "We haven't seen each other in more than two years, Evie. I miss you. This could be our chance to spend time together, and your chance to have some fun and gain work experience."

I missed Fiona too, but I wasn't the one who'd left and never returned. I'd always known Fiona was meant for the big city, but I'd hoped she'd choose a city a bit closer to me, not on a different continent. "Who am I supposed to work for?"

"Xavier Stevens." Her lips twitched in a way that made me suspicious. It was a face she'd made when Mom forced her to eat Brussel sprouts.

"You'll have to give me a bit more than that. I don't know who the dude is."

Fiona flashed me a grin. "That's exactly why you are perfect for the job, Evie. Xavier needs someone who doesn't want to kiss the ground he walks on, trust me."

"Okay," I said. "I still don't know who he is. Do I need to Google him?"

Fiona rolled her eyes. "He's a rugby player, of course."

"*Of course,*" I said. Fiona was dating a rugby player of the Sydney Tigers, she was a cheerleader for the same team, and an Instagram star.

"He's a fly-half. Absolute superstar. Everyone knows him, every woman wants to be in his bed, every man wants to be him. He's gone through more assistants than underwear."

A couple of years ago, I wouldn't have had a clue what fly-half meant, but Fiona had been dating Connor for almost two years now and had tried to explain the rules of the game to me on occasion. I still didn't understand them, but I remembered a few terms. "So he's like a quarterback."

"Yeah," Fiona said.

I wasn't into sports. I didn't even grasp football. Why would I bother understanding rugby? "What am I supposed to do for him? I have no clue about sports."

"You don't have to. Xavier needs an assistant. A babysitter, really. You know how to take care of people, and you won't let him boss you around or blow candy up his ass. Those are perfect qualifications."

I wasn't sure how my bachelor's in marketing would come in handy for that, but I supposed a guy like that needed someone for public relations as well. "Did you talk to him about me?"

"Connor is his best friend, and we told him we might know someone who could take over from his last assistant. But you need to come over as soon as possible. Next week. Xavier can't go without an assistant for long."

The guy sounded like a major pain in the ass, but after today's miserable job interview, I actually didn't loathe the idea of trying my hand at being someone's personal assistant. It was less hassle than working in a marketing firm or a company. I'd only have to make sure one person looked good in public. That could be a good start for my career.

"Come on, Evie. Do it for me. You'll love it here. Australia is amazing." She gave me the duck face that had made her get her way in the past. "Or are you worried about Dad?"

Surprisingly, I wasn't. He'd been trying to get me to move out and get my own life for months now. Perhaps out of guilt, or perhaps because he felt uncomfortable taking his date home as long as I lived under the same roof. It wasn't as if he didn't know how to stay busy. Fiona was right. He worked from eight till eight as a litigator and now spent most of his free time with his new girlfriend.

"He doesn't need me anymore." I'd only leave for a year. That wasn't long. And if I was being honest, I wanted a change of scenery, wanted to leave behind the memories that haunted every inch of this house where Mom's ghost still seemed to breathe down each corner.

Fiona smiled. "So you're really coming?"

"I am," I said slowly.

"Do you need me to send you money for the flight?"

"No," I said quickly. I still had some savings in my account, not much, but it should buy me a ticket to Sydney.

When we ended our Skype call, I really let reality sink in. I was leaving for Australia. To become an assistant to a rugby star I had never heard of and didn't know anything about.

That would change now, I supposed.

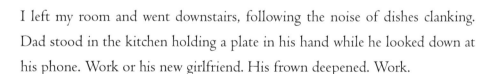

I left my room and went downstairs, following the noise of dishes clanking. Dad stood in the kitchen holding a plate in his hand while he looked down at his phone. Work or his new girlfriend. His frown deepened. Work.

"Hey Dad," I said, as I walked in and took the plate from him. Then filled it with the lasagna I'd prepared yesterday and popped it into the microwave.

Dad gave me a distracted smile, his gray hair all over the place from running his hand through it. "Evie," he said. He didn't ask how my job interview had gone, but I hadn't expected him to. He'd always been too immersed in his job to pay much attention. That had been Mom's job. She had been a stay-at-home mom and taken care of Fiona and me while Dad built his career. Even in the beginning of her cancer it had still been that way, but later Dad had stopped working almost altogether to be at her side.

"Hard day?" I asked him as I leaned beside the counter and put a bite of cold lasagna into my mouth while I waited for Dad's piece to get warm in the microwave.

"This new case is giving me a headache. Large-scale investor who peculated hundreds of millions. It'll take weeks to read all the folders piling on my desk." The microwave binged and I handed Dad the plate. He didn't sit down; instead he started eating, leaning against the counter and reading whatever important email popped up on his screen. If it wasn't for me, he'd probably eat and sleep in his office. When Mom had still been around, he'd tried to spend more time at home.

Eventually, he noticed my gaze. "When do you leave?"

I blinked. "Leave?" Then it dawned on me. "Fiona already talked to you, didn't she?" She had always been a meddler and had acted like a pushy older sister, which was ridiculous, considering we were twins, and I was eight minutes older than her.

He nodded. "She called me in my office this afternoon. I think the idea is great."

"You sure you're okay with me leaving you alone?"

Dad set the plate down and came toward me, touching my shoulders. "I'm fine. I've been feeling guilty for the way you've been taking care of me. That's not your job. I'm capable of taking care of myself. There's takeout and I have Marianne for company."

It was the first time he'd really mentioned her, and he sounded happy. I smiled. "That's good. I'm glad you found someone."

Dad looked away, sighing. "I'll always love your mother, you know that."

"I know," I said, and kissed his cheek. "She'd want you to be happy."

"And I want the same for you, Evie. So go to Sydney and enjoy yourself. Spend some time with Fiona. Go surfing."

I laughed. He had never seen me attempt any kind of sports, or he wouldn't suggest that kind of thing. "I'm going there to work, not to enjoy myself."

Dad chuckled. "You sound like me." He took out his wallet and pulled out several hundred dollars. "Here. For your ticket."

"Dad—" I knew Dad earned enough money, but from an early age he and Mom had taught us to work for our money.

"Take it."

I did. "Thanks."

"And promise me you'll have fun. Work isn't all there is to life."

"I think you should listen to your own advice," I teased.

Excitement bubbled up in me. I was really doing this.

———— ◆ ————

My excitement, however, diminished somewhat when I searched for information about Xavier on the internet and found photos of his former assistants. An onslaught of images hit me. Wow, he was going through assistants fast. Fiona had mentioned that none had stayed very long, but judging by the sheer number of assistants I found on the internet, he couldn't have kept any of them for more than a few months. What was wrong with this guy?

And these women, and all of his assistants *were* women, looked absolutely nothing like me. They were Instagram influencer material. The million-dollar smile, every strand of hair perfectly arranged. All of them had been the fitness model type. Lean, trained, not a gram of fat. I looked down at myself. I was curvy.

I couldn't help but wonder if that was exactly why I had been chosen. I was the safe, less gossip-risky option.

7

XAVIER

Something clung tightly to my back and a too-hot breath hit my shoulder blades. Here we go again. Why did they all have to be clingy? If I wasn't too lazy to throw them out right after sex, I'd never let them spend the night at all.

I unfastened the arm from my waist and swung my legs out of bed, blinking against the bright sunshine filtering in through the panorama windows. What time was it?

I got up, stretched, then turned to find last night's conquest sprawled out on her back with a flirty smile. In bright daylight she looked less tasty than she had last night. Her makeup was smeared under her eyes, and her hair was the fake blonde I absolutely loathed.

"Xavier," she purred. "Why don't you stay in bed?"

Because I'd rather run a grater over my balls than have you touch them again. "I have training." I looked around for a way to find out the current time.

Damn it. I stalked down the winding staircase into the lower part of my loft, looking for my mobile. Where had I left it when I'd stumbled in here with Fake-Blonde glued to my cock?

Something black on the wood floor next to the entrance caught my eyes, and I retrieved my phone from where I must have dropped it when Fake-Blonde had scratched my balls with her fake red nails.

"Fuck," I groaned when I saw that I was already one minute late to training. That made every day since my last assistant had smacked my cheek with a few Russian curses and never returned. One of these days the coach would act on his threats and put me on the bench.

No time for breakfast or coffee. I jogged up the staircase where Fake-Blonde was still lolling about on my bed like a cat in heat. "Hurry!" I snarled as

I walked past her, through my bathroom and into the walk-in closet. I slipped on my gym shorts, no time to look for underwear. My teammates had seen my meat countless times, and so had half of the cheerleaders and a considerable number of Sydney's female population aged between eighteen and sixty-two (a regrettable incident Connor would never let me forget). Grabbing a shirt, I returned to the bedroom, only to find Fake-Blonde still in my sheets, but now she was playing with herself.

I was moments from seriously losing my shit. Did she really think she could convince me to have another go at her only because she fingered herself when I'd already shoved my dick into every opening of her body last night? Usually, I handled situations like this with charm and lies, or rather let my assistants handle them, but I was out of time and patience. "Take your greedy fingers somewhere else, and get out of my bed and apartment. I'm done with you."

Her eyes widened and she sat up, her finger still pushed up her vagina.

Stifling my annoyance, I turned and stalked toward the stairs. "You've got exactly one minute to get dressed and leave, or I'll throw you out naked."

Fifty-eight seconds later, she charged down the staircase and toward me where I waited next to the front door. Her blouse was half open where I'd ripped a few buttons off last night and she was barefoot, pumps dangling from her hand. She stopped in front of me and slapped me hard, pelting me with a string of curses in a foreign language, maybe Polish?

"You ruined my blouse, you bastard! Just so you know, you are the worst lay I've ever had."

I smiled cruelly. "You creamed the sheets you came so hard when I fucked you." I took two hundred dollars from my wallet and put them into the front pocket of her jeans. "And that's for your blouse. Consider the rest my tip."

Her face turned red. I opened the door, nudged her outside and stepped into the corridor as well, then locked the door.

I left her standing there, stewing in her anger and shock. Stepping into the elevator, I hit the button for the ground floor.

I reached the lobby and waved at the desk clerk. The elevator moved back up. "Good morning, Teniel. How's the family?" I asked.

"Good, good. Wife's pregnant with our fourth child." He handed me the keys to my car. "I parked it in front of the entrance for you forty minutes ago."

That's when I should have left for training. "Congratulations," I called as I reached the glass doors. The elevator binged. I threw a glance over my shoulder, seeing a furious Fake-Blonde storming through the lobby. Teniel shook his head with a small frown, but he was used to these kinds of scenes by now.

CHAPTER TWO

EVIE

stepped off the plane, feeling like a train had run me over. Over twenty hours of traveling had completely knocked me out. My mouth tasted as if something had crawled inside it and died.

I pulled my luggage behind myself, my eyes scanning the waiting crowd. I hadn't seen Fiona in more than two years, since she'd run off to Australia on a whim. We'd talked almost every day on the phone, but it just wasn't the same as having her with me. Would I even recognize her in real life?

The second I spotted her, I almost laughed at my ridiculous worry. She stood out as she always had. Tall and thin like a model, with the clothes and smile to match. I felt like a rhino in comparison to her. She rushed toward me, managing to look elegant while running in four-inch heels, and hugged me.

She was about an inch taller than my five foot seven and at least forty pounds lighter. While Fiona showed off her size zero skinny jeans, I was glad for my comfortable size twelve chinos and my loose blue blouse.

Fiona pulled back and gave me a quick once-over. "You look good."

"And you are gorgeous as ever," I said, meaning every word. My eyes went to a tall, muscled man behind her with dark blond hair and a beard. His blue eyes twinkled with mischief and I liked him right away.

"That's Connor," Fiona said, following my gaze. I had never seen her look that way at someone before. Full of adoration and tenderness. She'd been in love with her childhood sweetheart, but that had been puppy love in comparison.

"I know. I Skyped with you both, remember?" I said with a teasing smile. He was taller than I'd imagined and broader. "You are quite a hunk," I told him.

He laughed and pulled me into a hug. Fiona shook her head. "Don't flirt with my man, Evie."

As if I could ever compete with Fiona's gorgeousness. She'd been a cheerleader all her life and now she was also a fitness model. She was perfection, and I was not.

Connor took my suitcase from me and led us out of the airport. The warm summer air greeted us. It was a shock to my system after the freezing cold back in Minnesota.

"You'll love it here," Fiona promised.

Connor drove a black Jeep that fit his size and I slumped into the backseat, feeling like I needed a week of sleep. After twenty hours of traveling, with my clothes crumpled, my hair disheveled and my makeup ruined, I felt even more like an ugly duckling. Fiona was the box of handcrafted Belgian chocolate, and I was the bag of Butterfingers forgotten under the car seat on a hot summer's day in Arizona.

Fiona and Connor were holding hands as he steered the car. I had to admit my heart swelled with warmth seeing her this happy. I couldn't really stay mad at her for running off if it meant that she'd found someone she loved.

"You'll meet Xavier tomorrow," Fiona said from her spot in the front. I'd hoped to get more of a grace period to get my bearings in Sydney, but apparently Xavier really needed a babysitter as fast as possible.

"I read up on Xavier on the internet," I said.

Connor grinned at me in the rearview mirror. "And you're still here. You've got balls, girl."

"I suppose most of it is exaggerated or fake anyway. The press have a tendency to blow things out of proportion for shock value."

Connor and Fiona exchanged a look.

"Right?" I prompted.

"Right," Fiona said, but Connor didn't say anything.

I liked to go informed into difficult situations, and Xavier—The Beast—Stevens seemed to be a difficult situation. Reading up on him had been like a cheap high school drama. He was known for his countless affairs with actresses, athletes, journalists, groupies, pretty much with everything that qualified as female and had a body to die for.

That meant I was safe.

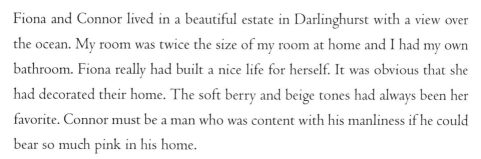

Fiona and Connor lived in a beautiful estate in Darlinghurst with a view over the ocean. My room was twice the size of my room at home and I had my own bathroom. Fiona really had built a nice life for herself. It was obvious that she had decorated their home. The soft berry and beige tones had always been her favorite. Connor must be a man who was content with his manliness if he could bear so much pink in his home.

After a quick shower, I dropped down on my bed, determined to rest for only a few minutes. I was woken much later by a soft knock, and Fiona poked her head in without waiting for a reply. Some things would never change. "Did I wake you?" she asked with a small frown as she slipped in and sank down beside me.

"Yeah," I mumbled, sitting up. "What time is it?" My body was completely confused with the change in time zones.

"Almost six. I thought we could have dinner together. Connor bought so much meat I think he's trying to put the cow back together."

I snorted and hugged Fiona. She might look like a bimbo, but her humor was cutthroat. "I missed you."

She let out a shaky breath and hugged me back. After a moment, she pulled back, as composed as always. "Come on, Connor is probably already massaging seasoning into the beef as if it's my ass cheek. I don't want him to strain his fingers before he gets the chance to put them to use on me tonight."

I shoved her lightly. "Holy shit, TMI, Fiona. I don't want to imagine Connor kneading your ass whenever I eat steak."

She sent me a teasing smile. "Who's marinating your ass, Evie?"

I flushed and stalked past her out of the room. Fiona came after me, laughing. From the kitchen window, I could see Connor manning the barbecue. He looked like a man about to set sail to undiscovered lands. Why did men take their barbecuing so seriously?

Fiona began assembling vegetables and fruit on the counter.

I stifled a smile. She gave me a look. "What? I know what you and Dad enjoyed eating when I was still home. I doubt your greens intake improved once I left. Why don't you help me with the fruit platter?"

She had a point. It wasn't that I didn't enjoy fruits and salads, and I ate plenty, but in the evening I preferred the taste of warm comfort foods like lasagna, mac and cheese, or a good roast.

"I suppose you will change that now," I said.

"I'll try. Not sure I'll succeed, knowing how stubborn you can be," she muttered as she prepared a salad while I arranged a fruit platter.

"I'm not stubborn," I protested, which was a freaking lie. Fiona and I were both mules disguised as humans.

"It'll benefit your health, trust me," she said in the same enthused voice she'd always used when talking about fitness or healthy eating. Fiona truly enjoyed her lifestyle and I envied her for it, and more: for the body that it had given her.

"Maybe I don't want to lose weight," I said as I slipped a piece of mango into my mouth. Another, even bigger lie. Since I could remember I'd bought every magazine that had promised to include the newest, life-changing diet. I'd tried them all and had given up on them just as quickly.

She pursed her lips as she poured dressing over the salad. "I didn't say anything about losing weight. I talked about improving your health."

"Isn't that a synonym for losing weight?"

"No, it's not. You can be healthy and have a few pounds more on your ribs. But if you ate healthy and did sports, you would probably lose weight."

She was probably right, but I wasn't sure if I wanted to be a size zero badly enough to do sports and forgo carbs and chocolate for the rest of my life.

"Don't give me that look," Fiona said. "Like I don't know what I'm talking about because I'm thin. I work hard for it, Evie. We share the same genes, and I gain weight just as quickly as you do, but I get up an hour early so I can squeeze in an additional workout, and I almost never eat carbs even though the taste of bread makes me weep with joy. This isn't gifted, it's earned." She pointed at her body. It was true.

"I know," I said softly. She put down the salad tongs and wrapped an arm around my shoulder. "And my goals shouldn't be yours. We are twins but we aren't the same person. You are beautiful, and I wish you could see it and stop comparing yourself to others, especially to me. I always admired your smarts. You had better grades than me no matter how hard I worked, and for a while it really got to me, but then I realized we have different strengths, and that's okay."

"Fiona, when did you turn so wise?" I teased, then kissed her cheek.

"I'm so happy you're here, Evie." Fiona smiled.

"Me too," I said softly.

"I'm sorry for leaving you alone to deal with Dad, you know?"

I touched her shoulder. "Let's not talk about it. That's the past. I want to focus on the future."

Relief filled her gorgeous face. "You will love it here, Evie."

"I'm nervous about tomorrow," I admitted.

"You will do fine. Xavier is charming and funny if he wants to be."

The tabloids had made him sound like a misogynistic player, so her words calmed some of my worries.

"Can I help you with anything else?" I asked when I was done slicing the fruit.

She handed me a basket with sliced up bread. "Can you take that to Connor so he can put it on the barbecue for a sec?"

"Bread?" I said with raised eyebrows.

She rolled her eyes.

I moved out into the garden, where Connor was turning steaks with a look as if this was a task that required the utmost concentration. Men and their meat. Dad had always made a big deal out of barbecuing as well.

I went over to Connor. "Fiona sent me to give you this."

He took the basket with a smile. He was doing that a lot. He seemed easygoing and relaxed. Perfect for someone like Fiona, who was always on edge. Before he could put the first slice on the barbecue, I snatched one up and took a bite. I was starving. The airplane food had been inedible, so I'd only forced down the dry bread rolls with cheddar they'd served with the main meal.

He chuckled. "Xavier will be delighted to have someone at his side who also likes to eat."

I swallowed and shrugged. Connor with his athlete's body and Fiona with her model measurements probably wouldn't even have bought bread if it wasn't for me.

"What's he like?" I asked. "Fiona wasn't very forthcoming with information about him, and the internet didn't portray a very positive image."

"He's a self-centered, arrogant Casanova… and my best friend."

"Then you should reconsider your life choices," I said with a laugh.

"Touché." Connor's eyes crinkled in amusement. "He isn't a bad guy. He's loyal."

"Not from what I hear. He's changing girls quicker than others do their underwear."

"He does." He pointed the barbecue tongs accusingly in my direction. "I thought Fiona didn't tell you anything about him."

"She mentioned that, but nothing else. And it was all over the press as I said."

"He rucks and fucks. That's about it," Connor said with an apologetic smile.

My cheeks heated. "Ruck?" I'd seen the term when I'd read up on rugby, but I had forgotten what it meant.

"It's when they all cuddle," Fiona said with a glare at Connor as she sauntered over to us. "Watch your language. My sister isn't like me. She has sensitive ears."

I snorted. I was many things but not a delicate flower.

Connor winked at me when Fiona wasn't looking. Then he wrapped an arm around her waist and pulled her against his chest for a firm kiss. I took the basket with the griddled bread and walked back to the table, not wanting to watch them getting it on. Her words about ass-kneading would haunt me for a while anyway.

I sank down on one of the garden chairs, staring up at Sydney's cloudless summer sky.

He fucks and rucks.

Oh man, what was I getting myself into? I closed my eyes, jet lag catching up with me. I needed to grab a few hours of sleep.

Soft steps made me open my eyes again.

Fiona took the seat beside me with an understanding expression. "Don't worry. Xavier won't make a move on you. You're not his type."

I glanced down at my curves and regretted that third piece of bread I'd wolfed down. "Why?"

Fiona delicately put a piece of mango into her mouth—her version of a starter. "Too much work. Xavier prefers his conquests easy and uncomplicated. You are neither."

"How would you know? Maybe I changed?" I softened the hint of bitterness my words held with a smile.

Fiona paused, then looked away and sighed. "I know it wasn't fair to leave you to deal with Dad, but I just had to go…"

The past was harder to let rest than we both wanted. I took a sip of water to gather my thoughts. "You never said why you ran."

"I didn't run…" Fiona's eyes found Connor, who was still manning the barbecue, but slanting the occasional curious glance in our direction. "I caught Aiden in bed with Paisley a few weeks after Mom's funeral."

I choked on the water in my mouth. "Why didn't you tell me?"

Aiden had been Fiona's first love, her high school sweetheart since they were fifteen, and Paisley had been Fiona's best friend.

She shrugged. "I was humiliated. I didn't want people to find out. And you were grieving Mom."

"So were you, Fiona."

"I know," she admitted.

"You went to prom with him."

"Like I said, I wanted to keep up appearances. But after that, I just wanted to leave."

"And you had to round the globe because of one cheating asshole?" I muttered indignantly.

"It was a knee-jerk reaction. I never thought I'd stay for long, definitely not forever, but then Connor came along."

"And now you'll stay."

"Yeah," she said softly, her eyes finding him again. I was happy for her, and the flicker of resentment that I'd still harbored for her disappearance vanished. Even if my new job didn't work out, my trip to Sydney was already worth every last penny.

CHAPTER THREE

EVIE

My jet lag had only marginally improved overnight, but I was excited for this day as it marked a new beginning, and what could be more exciting than that? I walked into the kitchen, where Fiona was already eating an Acai breakfast bowl or whatever the current it-breakfast on Instagram was. It was bright purple with a bit of granola sprinkled on top. She snapped a photo, her brows drawn together in concentration.

"Good morning, sunshine," I said with a smile.

Fiona looked up and shook her head. "Still a morning person."

"You don't look as grumpy in the morning as I remember."

She smiled. "I had to get used to an early schedule to get a workout in before work."

"Isn't working out part of your work?" I asked, confused, as I prepared a breakfast of cereal and fruit for myself.

"It is. But I record my morning workout for Instagram. I can't do that with my other workouts. There's a no-recording policy in place."

I sat down. "I checked the internet for Xavier's previous assistants, and a lot of images popped up. Why did they all run away? Is he a choleric asshole?"

"No, not a choleric one," Fiona said with pursed lips.

I raised my eyebrows.

"He's okay. He isn't an assholey boss if that's what you're worried about. He just can't keep it in his pants."

I froze. "He's a groper?"

Fiona laughed. "Oh, no, Evie. I wouldn't do that to you. Xavier doesn't grope women who don't want to be groped, trust me. He's not that kind of asshole. Women throw themselves at him faster than he can dodge them, not that he's trying. Every single one of his assistants landed in bed with him, and then either Xavier dumped them because they thought it meant something and turned too needy, or the women quit because they realized they were nothing but his fuck thing and didn't want to be his assistants anymore."

"So you think I'm either a lesbian or frigid?"

Fiona snorted. "What?"

"Because I assume you are certain I won't land in bed with him, or you wouldn't have asked me to work for him."

She snapped another picture of her food. "You won't land in bed with him because you have standards and don't do casual sex."

I flushed. I didn't do any kind of sex, much to my chagrin, but I had every intention of rectifying that. Not with a serial womanizer though.

Fiona put down her phone, her eyes searching. "You never mentioned a boyfriend when we Skyped."

I ate another spoonful of my cereal, considering what I wanted to tell Fiona. We had been close once and then we hadn't been, but in the last few months, things had improved. We'd Skyped often and now I was here. "Because there wasn't anyone."

"You never…?"

I shook my head, then shrugged. "Don't give me that pitying look, all right? It's no big deal."

She smiled. "We'll find you a nice guy to date. I could ask Connor if he knows someone."

"Don't," I blurted. "That's too embarrassing. And I've come here to work, not to date."

"Okay. But keep your eyes open. Only promise me that you're not going to fall for Xavier."

"I won't," I said firmly. "Did you show Xavier a photo of me before he hired me?"

Fiona shook her head. "No, he should stop choosing his assistants by their looks."

Great. He'd be in for a nasty surprise if he expected me to look like his former assistants. "See, even if I fell for him, which I won't, there's nothing you have to worry about, because Xavier won't take me into his bed. I'm not model material."

Fiona nodded thoughtfully and finally took a spoonful of her breakfast.

I cringed inwardly. That was a blow. I hadn't expected her to contradict me, but to nod, that hurt even my ego. I guessed I should count myself lucky. I had no plan to make headlines as Xavier's conquests or losing my job, so it was for the best that I wasn't his type.

XAVIER

I drank another sip of my water. Sweat was dripping down my face. Coach had made me run four extra rounds for being late again. He'd probably keep kicking my ass throughout the remaining training if his pissed expression was an indicator.

"Try to be a decent human being around Evie, all right?" Connor muttered beside me on the bench.

I shot him a look. "I'm not paying her an assload of money so I have to cater to her feelings. I'm paying her so she caters to mine."

Connor shook his head. "In moments like this I get why Fiona hates your guts."

The sentiment was mutual. Even an ass to crack walnuts with and a stomach to grate cheese on couldn't make up for her intolerable personality. "You haven't shown me a single photo of her, and I still hired her, so I'm evolving, don't you think?"

Connor raised his eyes to the sky as if he was praying. I doubted anyone would listen to his prayers, not after all the shit he and I had been up to in the last few years—before Fiona. "It was time you chose your assistant based on her skills and not looks."

"I've always based my decisions on their skills... They were all very skillful, trust me."

Connor snorted, then he rubbed his forehead. "If you mess this up, Fiona will kick my balls."

"Doesn't she have better things to do with them?"

Connor sent me a glower. I missed the time when he'd share every fucking kinky detail of his sexcapades with me, but Fiona had him on a short leash.

"So tell me: what is Evie like, what does she look like?" I asked, knowing it would push Connor's buttons.

"She isn't your type, Xavier. Get it out of your head," Connor said, narrowing his eyes. Fiona had trained him well. I could almost imagine her patting his head like a good little dog.

I leaned back with a grin. "She's human and female, right?"

Connor nodded.

"Then she's my type."

He opened his mouth then snapped it shut. "You know what, mate. Never mind. I'm not getting involved in this. I'll be the one to pay for your mess-ups as usual."

"Come on, that one time doesn't count."

Connor gave me an incredulous look. "That one time? You fucked some secondhand gangster's wife and told her my name. That asshole tried to beat me up with his ugly-ass brothers."

"To my defense, I came to your help."

"Geez, thanks," Connor muttered, but he was fighting a smile. He missed our crazy-ass adventures. His eyes moved past me. I followed his gaze and spotted Fiona and a young woman with long strawberry blonde hair. She was much curvier than Fiona and I'd never have pegged them as sisters, much less twins. Which was a fucking relief. If I had been forced to have an assistant with Fiona's face around me twenty-four-seven, I would have lost my shit. My eyes came to a stop on her chest and I released a low whistle.

Connor shot me a glare "Xavier, I swear, I'll hold a pillow to your face while you sleep next time we have to share a room if you mess this up."

I grinned. "At least, I can die happy."

EVIE

Xavier's eyes took their sweet-ass time checking out my body. Surprise flashed across his face, then that was gone. He kept talking to Connor, who looked as if he were sucking a lemon, but Xavier's eyes were fixed on me. To be honest, they were mostly fixed on my breasts. I was a 40 D, and men always noticed, but usually they weren't as unabashed about it. Xavier obviously had no shame. Several of his teammates standing around on the field also threw me curious glances.

Despite my best intentions, heat rose into my cheeks.

When Fiona and I arrived at the bench, he rose to his feet, and holy shit, was he a beast. The photos I'd seen of him hadn't done him justice. That man was six foot six of pure muscle. How he could move that body as quickly as the sport required was a miracle to me. I felt like someone was holding a hair dryer into my face, blasting heat at me full force.

"This is my sister, Evie," Fiona introduced me. The warning in her voice was unmistakable, and her death glare only emphasized it.

I nudged her side with my elbow, not wanting her to embarrass me in front of my future boss. It was endearing that she wanted to protect me from Xavier, but I was more than capable myself.

"You don't look like twins," Xavier said as he took me in then turned briefly to Fiona.

I flushed. I'd lost count of how often I'd heard those exact words. It wasn't even true. I had seen photos of us when we were little girls and we had been almost indistinguishable, only my hair was more strawberry blonde than golden blonde. We shared the same facial features and dusting of freckles, were almost the same height, but later, when Fiona had turned toward sports and I had turned toward reading, people had focused on our biggest difference: our weight.

Deciding not to start off my new job backed into a corner, I made a show out of checking out Xavier. Problem was somewhere along the way, around his ridiculously broad shoulders, or the outline of abs, or that delicious V, it turned into more than a display for him. That man was ripped. Holy mother of too sexy for this world rugby players. "Now I get why they call you the Beast. Can't be easy to find clothes that fit you. Do they have big and tall shops around here?"

Xavier blinked at me, then a slow panty-dropping smile appeared on his face. "I wouldn't know. I have my clothes tailored for me."

"Of course," I said, letting a hint of irony tinge my words, not too much to offend but enough that he'd notice. "Nothing off the rack for you."

"Indeed," he said. He extended his strong, big hand. "I'm Xavier. Your new boss."

I took his hand, squeezing a bit harder than necessary. "I'm Evie, your new babysitter."

Xavier laughed, a deep, low laugh that raised the little hairs on my back. He didn't release my hand and I made no move to pull away. "Oh, I like her already," Xavier said to Connor.

Fiona scowled. "Make sure not to like her too much, all right?"

"Fiona," I hissed, my cheeks growing hot. I couldn't believe her. She gave me a so-what look and shrugged. "What? He needs reminding, trust me."

Xavier smirked and leaned a bit closer. "Don't listen to her. I'm perfectly capable of behaving myself...if I want to."

Good Lord. With that low timbre of his voice, Xavier should do the voiceover in romance novels. It gave me pleasant chills I'd never felt before. "I'll make sure you behave. That's now my job, right?"

Xavier released my hand, but his warmth lingered. "Not yet. You have to sign the contract and a few other documents my lawyer's set up."

I nodded. That seemed sensible, which surprised me a little considering what Fiona had said about him. "When?"

"This afternoon. I can send Connor the details."

I raised my eyebrows. "Why don't I give you my number so you can put it in your contacts? A middle man won't be necessary."

Xavier's smile became more pronounced as he took out his phone. "Here. You'll be quicker."

I took his phone, then keyed in my new number. "There you go."

"First job well done," Xavier said, a hint of arrogance twisting that too gorgeous face.

I snorted. "Are you testing me?"

Xavier smirked. "Nah, the tests will come later."

The way he said it made a mix of nerves and excitement bubble up in me. "I will pass them all."

"I don't doubt it."

"Get your asses over here!" a man in his fifties with a cap that read Coach shouted.

"Have to go," Xavier said, his eyes making a brief detour to my chest again. "See you later."

He turned and jogged over to his coach, followed by Connor. My eyes were glued to Xavier's backside, which his trunks weren't hiding at all. The rest of the team gathered around them. It was obvious that Xavier was the leader of the pack.

"I don't like that look," Fiona whispered.

"I'm only appreciating the scenery."

"Yeah, but don't get entangled in the scenery. It's a thorny, barren land."

I laughed. "Oh, Fiona. I missed your sarcasm."

She flashed me a grin. "I'll have to go too. Enjoy the training."

I took a seat on the benches and watched the rugby team train several tactical maneuvers that made absolutely no sense to me, but the sight of all the tall, muscled rugby players sweetened my time. Only Fiona's occasional warning glance in my direction while she bent her body to her will like the other cheerleaders dampened my mood. She didn't have to worry. I could appreciate Xavier's physical assets without the risk of acting on my urges.

I was used to lusting after the unattainable types. That hadn't changed one bit since high school.

CHAPTER FOUR

EVIE

"Do you think this outfit is okay?" I asked. I had bought the dress shortly before I'd left the States. It was a cream-colored sheath dress with a narrow red belt accentuating my waist. I was a bit self-conscious about it because the dress clung to my curves more than my usual attire.

"You look great, Evie. Perhaps a bit too great."

I rolled my eyes. "I want to look like a businesswoman, as if I can handle anything, even Xavier—The Beast—Stevens."

"If anyone can handle him, then it's you. He won't know what hit him."

"Thanks. I'll try to keep the big guy on his toes." That's what I hoped, at least. I still wasn't entirely sure about my set of tasks, but I hoped Xavier would brief me on the details of my work today.

"I could come with you," Fiona said quickly.

I gave her a look. "If I show up with my twin sister as backup, Xavier will never take me seriously."

"He won't either way because women are only playthings to him. I don't think he sees them as human beings."

"You're exaggerating." Xavier had seemed manageable during our first encounter this morning. A bit cocky, but nothing I couldn't handle. Perhaps he'd be more intolerable if I fit his type, but as it was he'd probably end up seeing me as one of the guys and not so much a female, like every other guy I'd crushed on.

"I'm not. With guy friends, he's loyal and funny, from what Connor tells me, but with women…but you will realize it soon enough." She fixed a strand of my hair that had gotten loose. "Call me if anything happens."

"I'm going to sign my work contract, not take a dip in a piranha-infested river."

"Just make sure you stay away from Xavier's anaconda, that's all I ask," Fiona muttered.

"Fiona!" I hissed. "Now I won't be able to look at him without turning bright red."

Connor was nice enough to drive me to the law firm where I was supposed to meet Xavier. He gave me an encouraging smile when I got out of the car, which only made me more nervous. I waved at him as I headed toward the glass door leading into the sleek office building.

The receptionists pointed me toward an elevator at the end of the large lobby. The moment the elevator stopped on the right floor and I stepped out, a tall, dark-haired man strode toward me. He was dressed in an immaculate dark-blue three-piece suit and was in his early thirties. His face registered surprise upon seeing me. "You must be Miss Fitzgerald?"

I gave a nod and smiled.

"I'm Xavier's lawyer, Marc Stevens." He held out his hand for me to shake. His smile was pleasant but reserved. I wondered if the shared last name was coincidence, but upon closer look he shared a distant similarity to Xavier. Dark hair, same high cheekbones, but he wasn't nearly as tall or broad, and had brown eyes. "Why don't we head into my office so we can go over the details of your contract?"

"Won't Xavier join us?"

"He will, but given the fact that his old assistant left and you haven't started working for him yet, I doubt he'll be on time." He motioned for me to follow him.

His words surprised me. As Xavier's lawyer, I wouldn't have expected him to voice criticism like that. He was definitely family. Brother? Or maybe cousin? "Doesn't he have a watch?"

"Several, and all of them cost more than a small car, but Xavier uses them for their decorating properties, not to read the time. That would be part of your job."

Telling Xavier what time it was and to be on time. He really needed a babysitter.

"Why don't you have a seat?" He motioned toward a massive oval table made from some kind of reddish wood. A stack of papers sat in front of one of the chairs. I sank down on the surprisingly comfortable chair and read the cover page of what seemed to be a long contract.

"Coffee?"

I nodded.

Mr. Stevens took a seat beside me. "Why don't I read it aloud and you will voice your concerns or questions if they arise."

"I assume you used the same contract for Xavier's previous assistants, so even if I had concerns regarding certain parts of the contract, you would be reluctant to change them."

He smiled. "That's correct, but I think you'll find that everything's reasonable."

Most of the contract was reasonable. The only passage that had me a bit worried was the part that stipulated I couldn't stop working for him until I found him a new assistant or six months had passed. I had a feeling that part had been added recently due to Xavier's difficulties keeping his assistants.

Mr. Stevens had read almost the entire contract to me when the door opened and Xavier stepped in. "Am I late?" he asked with a grin, knowing full well that he was.

"You are, as usual," Mr. Stevens said. "We were about to move on to the payment clause."

Xavier sank down across from me. "That's probably the part you're most excited about."

Mr. Stevens cleared his throat and read the next clause. My pulse sped up when I heard how much I'd earn being a mere assistant. My palms became sweaty, and I got a little lightheaded. No matter how nerve-wracking Xavier was, for that much money I would have become the assistant of a serial killer, maybe even helped him dispose of the bodies.

"That doesn't include expenses. They come on top. Whenever you pay for something, let me know and I'll reimburse you."

"How do you manage to drive your assistants away with that kind of payment?" It burst out of me.

Mr. Stevens let out a choked cough that sounded remarkably like he was stifling laughter.

Xavier leaned forward on his elbows, letting the muscles in his arms bulge against his tight shirtsleeves. "My irresistible charm drove them away."

"That brings us to the next point. The non-disclosure clause," Mr. Stevens said with wrinkled brows, sliding a single sheet of paper over to me. Xavier's answering smirk didn't bode well.

Narrowing my eyes, I scanned the clause.

The non-disclosure clause made me snort. "In case of sexual intercourse between the employer and the employee, and any kind of actions that can be classified as such, the employee agrees to keep the details of said acts confidential," I read aloud, then looked up at Xavier. "I think that clause won't be necessary."

And it didn't even make sense. The press reported about Xavier's sexual endeavors with women almost every day. What did it matter if his assistants did too?

Xavier smirked. "My lawyer would disagree with you on the matter."

His lawyer looked up and frowned. "For good reason," he said. Upon taking a closer look at both of them, I realized they looked too related for just cousins. Definitely brothers.

Then he turned to me. "It's a formality, but if you would manage to prove it unnecessary for once, I'd appreciate it, believe me."

I smiled. "Don't worry. Pigs will learn to fly before anything happens between Xavier and me."

"In the Caribbean pigs are swimming around in the ocean. Small step from that to flying, if you ask me," Xavier drawled, winking at me.

And my pulse picked up. He was toying around. I wasn't his type, and I wouldn't let him play with me. "I'm not surprised you know all about pigs." The moment the words were out, my eyes opened wide. I had used all of the money Dad had given me to buy a one-way ticket to Sydney, and even part of my savings. I needed this job.

His lawyer threw his head back and guffawed. He held out his hand. "Call me Marc. I'm the pig's older brother."

A small smile spread on Xavier's face. He wasn't offended, thank God. But his smile made me nervous.

I took the pen and scribbled my signature down on the contract and the non-disclosure clause.

"Good luck," Marc said with a half-amused smile.

"Thank you, but I doubt I'll need it."

Xavier rose from his chair, all six foot six of him, and I had a hard time not risking a peek at his arms again. "Now that you're officially my assistant, why don't I show you my apartment and tell you everything you need to know about me."

I stood as well, thanked Marc and followed Xavier out of the office. He surprised me by holding the door open for me and matching his pace to mine. With his longer legs, I'd have thought he'd make me hurry after him. I slanted him a curious look. He exuded self-assurance and relaxation, as if nothing could get his pulse up. He seemed like someone who could take control of his own life if he wanted to.

We stepped into the elevator and the door closed. Suddenly I felt less sure of myself. Xavier leaned against the wall, tall and muscled, completely at ease. I could feel his eyes on me through the mirrors surrounding us. Resisting the urge to tug at my dress, I tightened my hold on my purse. "Why did you give me the job?" I asked.

Xavier's gray eyes met mine in the mirror across from us. "Connor recommended you. I trust his judgment. Well, apart from his choice in women."

My eyebrows rose. "I assume you mean Fiona. *My twin.*"

His mouth pulled into a smile. "Yep."

"You realize that most people would question your choice in women more than his."

Xavier turned to me so he was looking at me directly. He was a head taller than me even though I wasn't exactly short and wore heels. But next to him I looked almost petite for once, which was a nice experience. "There's a major difference you are overlooking. Connor has chosen Fiona as his girlfriend. My choice in women is only guided by their abilities in the sack."

I was spared an answer, which might have led to me losing my job mere minutes after starting it, by the opening elevator doors as we arrived on the ground floor.

We stepped out into the warm Sydney sun, and I regretted my choice of dress at once. It was sweltering, and I could feel an annoying droplet of sweat make its way down my thigh. "Smile," Xavier said under his breath, his own lips pulling into a million-dollar smile.

"What?" I blurted. "My job description didn't mention that I had to smile."

Xavier chuckled, still with that strange smile on his face, even when he spoke. "You're not smiling for me. Paparazzi are trailing after us. I thought you'd prefer to have your smiling face in every tabloid of the city and not a scowling one."

My eyes grew wide as I glanced around us.

"The deer-in-headlights look will give the assholes a hard-on thinking about all the ridiculous headlines that can go with it."

I quickly masked my face into a pleasant smile, but Xavier shook his head, holding open the door of a black Maserati SUV. Before I got in, he leaned down to my ear, whispering. "Too late. They're going to use your worst expression because it'll give them more ammunition against me."

I sank down into the red leather seat, still considering Xavier's words as he closed the door. My eyes scanned our surroundings and finally I spotted a guy with a camera.

Xavier slid into the driver's seat and started the car. The roar of the engine made me jump. As we drove past the paparazzi, Xavier waved at the man with a twisted smile.

"Maybe you shouldn't provoke the press if you want to be portrayed in a more favorable light," I said curiously.

"They don't want to portray me in a favorable light. Bashing me is their favorite pastime."

"And you've made it your mission in life to provide them with enough ammunition?"

Xavier flashed me a grin. "I give them what they want, and in turn they keep me in the spotlight. Bad press is better than no press, or what do you marketing people always say?"

I wrinkled my nose. That was one of the lines I'd always resented. If you were only out for attention it might hold true, but if you wanted to make a worthy impact it was the wrong approach. "I prefer good news. And you are in the spotlight even without providing gossip. You are a star. You don't need bad press."

"The press will report about me whether I want it or not. My only option is to steer their attention in a certain direction."

His voice held a hint of protectiveness, and I wondered why that was. Why was he turning himself into such a bad boy of the rugby scene?

"Will they start trailing me as well?" I asked quietly, my fingers folding over my stomach to hide the small bacon rolls there. I knew how unflattering photos of me could end up.

Xavier shot me a searching look. "Probably. In the past my assistants provided entertaining gossip material."

I flushed, remembering that he'd landed in bed with almost every single one of his assistants. "I don't intend to give them any kind of gossip material, Xavier," I said firmly.

"I know," Xavier said with a chuckle. "Your sister and Connor told me you were responsible and not out for attention. A nice change from my previous assistants."

"Why did you choose assistants who only wanted to work for you so they could gather media attention?"

"I chose my previous assistants based on their looks."

Ouch. I cringed inwardly at what that implied. I definitely hadn't been chosen because of my appearance.

Xavier's apartment was absolutely breathtaking. A duplex situated in a residence in the heart of the Rocks with a view over the harbor and the harbor bridge. My mouth was probably hanging open as I walked into the loft-like living area. The herringbone parquet was the color of sun-bleached driftwood, and an open kitchen with fronts like Carrara marble spread out on the right side. Gray modern couches, white marble tables and futuristic metal lamps made the room appear like it had been copied out of an interior design magazine. I moved closer to the window and stared at the panorama.

It must be amazing to see the city lights, especially the harbor bridge, at night. But unless I worked late, I'd never get to see it.

Xavier stepped up beside me. "The view is why I bought it."

"It's breathtaking," I breathed, unable to tear my eyes away. Xavier's gaze finally made me take a step back and clear my throat. "Perhaps you can explain to me what I need to know and what exactly you expect of me." I took out a pen and a notebook from my purse.

Xavier cocked an eyebrow. "No fancy iPad to track everything?"

"No money to spare on fancy iPads," I said with a shrug.

Xavier nodded, surprising me by not making a snide comment about my financial situation. For him the concept of not having money for anything was probably foreign.

He led me toward the kitchen and pointed at a massive chrome machine— some sort of coffee maker, I assumed. "This is one of your most important work tools."

I sent him a look. "A coffee maker so I can prepare coffee for you?"

"It's an espresso unit, and you're going to make cappuccino for me with a double espresso shot. Every morning."

I blinked. "You realize I'm not a barista? I don't even know how to turn that thing on, much less how to make a cappuccino. That wasn't part of my bachelor's program." My snide tone wasn't one I would have usually used on an employer, but Xavier's grin pushed all my buttons.

"I'm sure you're a quick learner, Evie."

It was the first time he said my name, and I enjoyed it more than I should have. "Do I have to make you breakfast as well?" I asked, proud for making my voice come out matter-of-fact this time.

"No, I follow a strict breakfast regime to fuel my body for training. I'm not letting anyone mess with my protein shakes."

I wasn't sure if he was shitting me or being serious, but eventually I opted for the latter. After all, he was a top athlete. No muffins and sugary cereal for him. Again I cursed myself for wearing the fitted dress. "Okay. Cappuccino with a double shot of espresso in the morning." I paused. "How am I supposed to know when you want your coffee? I'm not having sleepovers, so I won't know when you're waking up. Or do you have a set time when you need me to prepare a cappuccino for you?"

Xavier smirked. "Let me show you the second floor. It'll all come together soon."

He was toying with me. Narrowing my eyes at his broad back, I followed him up a winding staircase toward a gallery—which was also the huge open bedroom with another heart-stopping view of the Sydney harbor.

The bed, which would have dwarfed any bedroom of a normal size, was positioned against a wall that had been installed in the center of the room. As I walked behind it I found an open bathroom with a massive free-standing bathtub and a floor-level shower as well as a walk-in closet behind another wall. Xavier waited for me in the bedroom as I walked back.

"This is my bedroom, as you can see. A place where you'll spend much more time in the future."

My eyebrows shot up. "This is only work. I'm not going to sleep with you."

"Easy, there," he said with a grin. "I didn't mean it like that."

Of course not. I tugged at my dress, hoping it didn't emphasize my wide hips too much.

Xavier motioned at the bed. "But you are going to wake me up so I'm not late to training or other appointments."

I laughed, then shut up when Xavier raised his eyebrows. He was being serious. Really? He needed a human alarm clock? "You want me to come over to your apartment every morning and wake you?"

"Yes, except on the days you're taking the day off."

Touching the pen to the notebook pages and taking a deep, calming breath, I asked, "When would you like me to wake you?"

"I have training at ten every morning except for the weekend. On the weekend it depends. As soon as the season starts in March, we'll be either traveling to away matches or have games here. It would be best if you synchronized your calendar with mine and just took a look yourself."

I took out my phone and did just that, then also got hold of his work email, and almost fainted seeing the sheer number of unanswered emails. "When was the last time you checked your inbox?"

"I don't. That's my assistant's job, and I haven't had an assistant in over two weeks."

I repeated a little calming mantra in my head. "I'll work through them tonight and sort them according to importance."

"You also need to handle my mail and my social media accounts. I try to handle my own Instagram, but the rest is all yours."

"All right." Besides training at ten in the morning tomorrow, Xavier also had an afternoon appointment marked as beach workout and an event marked NIO party at nine p.m.

"What does beach workout mean?"

"What it says," Xavier said. "I'm doing a beach workout and you're going to film it so we can post it for my fans on Instagram, Facebook, YouTube."

Camerawoman, another job I hadn't expected. "I assume the party isn't my concern?"

"It is your concern. It's Network Ten's party, and I'm supposed to make an appearance to give the party some glamour. You will accompany me, in the background, to tell me about the other guests, their names, their function, and make sure I don't misbehave too much." The panty-dropping grin.

"I don't have clothes that fit the occasion."

"Buy them," he said, then pulled out his wallet from the back of his jeans and handed me a golden credit card. "My birthday is my PIN code. Go to Harrolds or David Jones."

I took the card gingerly. "You trust me with your card?"

"Do you plan on breaking my trust?"

"No," I said firmly. "But you don't know me very well yet. Did you give all your assistants your credit card?"

"No. But I doubt you'll run off with my money. And my former assistants didn't come recommended by Connor."

"Connor only recommended me because Fiona bugged him, you know that, right?"

Xavier chuckled. "Yeah, he's whipped."

I slipped the card inside my purse. I'd have to guard it with my life. I doubted my year's salary would be enough to pay off the debt I'd gather if someone stole the card and went all out with it.

My eyes were drawn to a medal in a frame above the bed. I moved closer. "Clive Churchill medal. Best Player Grand Final 2017," I read aloud. I looked toward Xavier. His expression had changed, had become almost…reverent. "You won the medal as best player?"

He nodded. "Once. But I have every intention of winning it again this year. My team is the best in the league. We need to win the final."

It was obvious by the fervor in his voice and his keen expression that he really lived for his sport, which made his scandalous lifestyle even less explainable. I knew as a fly-half Xavier had a lot of responsibility directing the play of his team, and yet he couldn't be bothered to organize his own life.

Before I left the apartment, Xavier handed me his spare keys. "So you can come in." He said it with a devilish grin. "I'm looking forward to working with you."

CHAPTER FIVE

EVIE

My alarm sounded at six thirty, which gave me enough time to get ready and have coffee before I had to head off to wake Xavier and prepare coffee for him.

I couldn't believe Xavier needed an assistant to wake him. How hard could it be to set an alarm? I drank my coffee in quiet, watching the early morning sun glittering on the ocean from the kitchen window. Fiona and Connor were still asleep, or doing other things I didn't want to think about. Fiona had spent an hour last night interrogating me about my meeting with Xavier. If she kept up the surveillance, even my ridiculous salary wouldn't be worth it.

When I arrived at Xavier's apartment thirty minutes later, I wondered if I should make sure to be as quiet as possible or announce my presence audibly. I really couldn't believe that a grown-up man required waking up. Maybe this was only part of him testing me, but from what his brother and Connor had hinted at, Xavier was indeed too lazy to organize even that small part of his life.

Opting for the quiet option, I pushed the key into the lock and turned it carefully before I slipped in. A low noise, like a groan, startled me. Maybe Xavier was having a nightmare. My annoyance wavered as I considered that he had something that bothered him enough to haunt his nights. Maybe he hid a soft side behind all those muscles and arrogant smiles.

I set my purse down on a barstool at the kitchen island and made my way toward the winding staircase. Another low noise made me walk a bit faster, and I hurried up the staircase, hoping he didn't expect me to serve him coffee in bed. The moment I reached a point at the staircase that allowed me to get a good view at the bed, I froze completely and let out a gasp. Only my hand on the rail stopped a very undignified fall.

Xavier wasn't alone, and he wasn't sleeping. It took my brain a moment to comprehend the scene before me. A woman was lying on her back before Xavier, her ankles on his shoulders, and he was gripping her hips and thrusting into her. That had been the source of the strange groans, which were now accompanied by the slapping of his pelvis against her ass. I really wished she were a screamer, then I wouldn't have headed upstairs.

Both turned my way. Heat rushed into my head.

I whirled around, mumbling some half-ass apology, and stumbled downstairs, my heart beating in my chest. Was I supposed to leave? I could hardly stay while they were at it. The bedroom wasn't really separated by a door from the living area below. What if they kept doing it as if nothing had happened?

But he had told me to wake him, he was *paying me* to do it. Maybe this really was a test. I wouldn't put it past him. Or maybe he just didn't care if someone watched him getting it on? I couldn't believe I'd worried he had a nightmare, couldn't believe I'd entertained a second of pity for his soft side. Soft side. He definitely hadn't looked soft a moment ago.

Furious and embarrassed, I moved toward the espresso machine and flipped the switch. It came alive with a loud hiss and started drawing water. Relieved for the noise filling the apartment, I leaned against the kitchen counter, willing the heat to leave my cheeks. I didn't want to appear flustered when Xavier and his date finally made their way downstairs.

Steps rang out upstairs, but I focused all my attention on the espresso unit. Unfortunately it was still heating up, so I couldn't busy myself preparing a cappuccino, but I moved toward the fridge and took out milk. Did Xavier expect me to make a cappuccino for his date as well? Maybe even breakfast? That would be too awkward. Slowly I realized why he paid so much. Yet I had to admit the very brief glance at his perfectly formed backside had given me a tiny kick. He was magnificent from behind.

In my peripheral vision, Xavier's tall form appeared on the winding staircase, and I couldn't help but risk a full view. Xavier sauntered down the steps, the tall blonde woman behind him. He was wearing only gray briefs, Calvin Kleins, and they did nothing to hide *him*.

If my skin hadn't already been burning up with embarrassment over what I'd witnessed, it would have started now.

Thankfully, the woman was fully dressed, even if her tight dress was wrinkled beyond saving and her makeup was smeared under her eyes. She gave me a curious look when she spotted me in the kitchen area. I recognized her from a few celebrity magazines I'd read in preparation for my job. She'd been part of the last *Bachelor* season but hadn't made it past the first night of the roses. Shannon something or other. I couldn't remember her full name.

"Next time you'd better announce your entry," Xavier said with a cocky grin, his gray eyes scanning my undoubtedly bright red face in amusement. He didn't seem to care that I had seen him with Shannon. He was toying around with me. Shannon didn't seem overly embarrassed about the incident either. I supposed if you took part in *The Bachelor* you enjoyed an audience even while having your legs up a guy's shoulders.

"Good morning to you too," I said to Xavier, not wanting him to get the better of me. Then I turned to the woman and gave her a small apologetic smile. She regarded me as if she was trying to decide if I posed a risk to her, then obviously determined I didn't qualify as Xavier-worthy material and gave me a fake smile before she turned back to Xavier with a much more convincing one.

Forcing down the urge to roll my eyes, I rummaged through the cupboards for cappuccino mugs.

Xavier leaned against the counter right beside me, arms crossed leisurely. I fought the urge to check him out. "Upper left cupboard," he provided in a lazy drawl, one corner of his mouth tipping up in the most annoying way.

I sent him a glare, but regretted it immediately when my eyes dipped lower to that sculpted upper body.

Shannon swayed closer, and walked her manicured nails up from his abs to his pecs. "So," she said flirtingly. "When will I see you again?"

I took down the mugs, wishing I were anywhere else. If this turned into another naughty episode I was out of here, shitload of money be damned.

My temple throbbed as more blood shot upwards. I could have cooked Xavier breakfast right on my forehead. Xavier stared down at Shannon's fingers on his chest like they were a bunch of cockroaches he wanted to squash, then he regarded her with a badly played disappointed expression. "You see, the coach is being really hard on us lately. But if you give my assistant your number, I'll give you a call as soon as he goes easier on us again. So Evie, can you please take…" It was obvious that he had no clue what her name was.

I raised my eyebrows at him with a sugary smile. It was as fake as the disappointed expression on his face.

He cocked one eyebrow in turn, making me want to pluck every last hair out of it.

"Take Shannon's number? Of course," I said sweetly, heading for my purse and taking my phone out.

Surprise crossed his face, then he smiled. "Exactly. Take Shannon's number for me."

Shannon turned to me with an air of importance as she started dictating her number. I keyed it in, then returned to the espresso unit. "So two cappuccinos."

"Unfortunately, I have important matters to discuss with you, so Shannon can't stick around." Xavier touched the woman's back and led her—or rather nudged her—toward the door. "I will see you very soon."

She smiled as she walked out, then he closed the door in her face and turned to me with a shake of his head, looking like this morning had been a terrible inconvenience *for him*. I could hardly look at his shoulders without disturbing images popping up in my head, and he had the expression of a martyr!

"You can delete her number."

I raised my eyebrows. I had a feeling they would make a permanent home high on my forehead if I kept working for Xavier. "Why did you let me write it down if you don't want to meet her again?"

"I don't fuck a girl twice. Well, I do fuck them more than once, but I don't meet them twice." He flashed that infuriating grin as he sauntered closer, every muscle flexing, every inch of him painfully perfect. It was a good thing I liked his character a little less with every infuriating word out of his mouth.

My lip curled. "Why don't you tell them? Why the show of letting me write down her number, Xavier?"

"Because it gets them to leave. They always think they could be the one to make me want to stay." He chuckled. "Idiots."

He leaned against the counter again. "So what about my cappuccino?"

I really wished he would put clothes on. The briefs were awfully distracting.

I supposed I should have expected that with Xavier's ginormous frame, the rest of him would be sized to proportion, but good Lord. I turned toward the espresso unit and put a mug under the nozzles. Xavier was watching me with obvious amusement. "I can't remember the last time I have seen such a ferocious blush. Your face is the color of the lobster in my favorite seafood restaurant. I doubt it can get any redder."

I was going to throw the mug right at his head. Of course, he ate lobster. Rolex, Maserati, lobster, penthouse with a view of the harbor bridge. Xavier not only flouted his conquests for the public, he also flouted his wealth.

"And I have never seen such a shameless act of exhibitionism in all my life. You knew I would come over to wake you, and still you did *this*."

"Then you haven't seen much yet," he said dryly, followed by the lip twitch. I blinked at him, reminding myself of the current state of my bank account and the wondrous number I'd seen in my contract.

"You haven't ground the espresso beans yet."

I shot him a glare as I opened the container beside the espresso unit, which held the beans. Problem was I wasn't sure how to operate the grinder. Xavier startled me when he stepped up beside me, towering over me, and took the container from me. "Pay close attention."

Stifling a remark, I forced my attention toward Xavier's hand, which worked the espresso unit easily. His woodsy manly scent wafted into my nose and occasionally his arm brushed mine. I couldn't bring myself to step away though, even when my eyes kept straying toward the display of muscles right at eye level.

A few minutes later, Xavier presented two perfectly brewed cappuccinos with a beautiful milk foam crown to me. Of course I hadn't paid the slightest bit of attention to the creation of the coffee specialty. "Enjoy," he said. "I hope you remember everything."

"Thanks." I took it, surprised at how flawless the milk foam looked, and took a sip from the hot beverage. It tasted perfect, like a concoction straight from a barista. I had no hope that I would create something that tasty soon. "Perhaps you should make us both cappuccinos every morning," I suggested with a grin over my mug.

Xavier's mouth twitched. "If you pay me as well for it as I pay you."

"Touché." I took another sip, suddenly caught by the surrealism of the situation. I was standing in the kitchen with a half-naked Xavier—The Beast—Stevens, having cappuccino. I drew my eyes to my watch. "You should get dressed. We need to head out for your training in about fifteen minutes."

Xavier set down his mug and raised his arms over his head for a stretch, which made my heart skip a beat. He smiled lazily when he lowered them back to his sides, then shoved away from the counter. "I was wrong, by the way," he threw over his shoulder at me. "Your face could get redder."

<hr />

If I thought having Xavier walk around me in nothing but briefs was distracting, watching him do a beach workout was a new level of insanity. Xavier and I chose a less crowded part of Manly Beach for the recording. I found the name oddly appropriate and wondered if Xavier had chosen it on purpose to shake me up further. It seemed to amuse him greatly to make me blush, which happened a lot. My fair complexion was as much at fault as my lack of experience being around half-naked men.

I had chosen comfy shorts and a tank top for the occasion. The moment my toes dipped into the warm sand, I was in paradise, and forgot that this was actually work. The ocean rolled lazily toward the beach, white and frothy, begging for a swim. But I didn't have a bathing suit with me, and even if I did, there was no way I was going to parade my less-than-perfect body around someone like Xavier.

"Make sure you get me from every angle and don't let the sun blind you," Xavier said as he positioned himself in front of me. His gym shorts hugged the narrow V of his hips and accentuated his strong thighs and shapely butt. Soon Xavier was doing sprints and sit-ups and push-ups, which made his skin glisten with a fine sheen of sweat that accentuated every ripped inch of his body. It was madness, complete and utter madness, and I enjoyed every maddening second of it.

Even though I wasn't moving all that much, I quickly felt hot and sweaty, hoping it was because of the blistering afternoon sun and knowing full well it wasn't. The ocean looked more and more enticing by the second. Perhaps I could go for a quick dip once we were done filming.

"You look flustered," Xavier commented after another round of sprints and sit-ups.

"I need an ice cream. Should I bring one for you?" I nodded toward an ice truck near the promenade.

Xavier shook his head, brushing sand off his glistening chest.

I turned and quickly got myself a cherry popsicle before I strolled back to Xavier. He had sat down on a towel and looked out toward the ocean. I stopped beside him. He shifted to the side, making room for me. Surprised, I sank down beside him. "Thanks," I said then slipped the popsicle into my mouth, and decided this came close to perfection. Sunshine, beach and cherry ice.

Gradually I became aware of Xavier's staring. I turned to him, my cheeks growing hot again. I would have given anything for slow blood circulation at this point. I showed him my popsicle. "You sure you don't want a taste?"

Xavier narrowed his eyes the slightest bit as if he was searching for something. I met his gaze and slowly pulled the popsicle back out of my mouth, wondering what the hell his problem was. "I don't have a sweet tooth," he said eventually, and the late reply threw me off for a moment. His gray eyes flickered over my cheeks and lips.

"How can anyone not have a sweet tooth?" I mused, taking another taste of my icy treat

"Why do you blush so much?" Xavier asked curiously.

Of course, that made me blush more. Sighing, I slid my popsicle back out of my mouth, opting for the truth. I didn't like beating around the bush. It seldom made things easier. "Because you run around half naked a lot and it's making me nervous. But don't worry, I'm sure in a few days I won't even notice it anymore. You'll just blend in with your surroundings."

Xavier tossed me a look, then the lip twitch. He straightened and from my viewpoint down on the towel, he looked even taller. My eyes did the usual head-to toe-dip, and when I finally looked back at Xavier's face and saw his arrogant smile, I knew that man would never blend into the background.

"We need to film the last sequence," Xavier said.

I prepared for a very undignified scramble to my feet when he held out his hand to me. I took it, surprised, and he pulled me to my feet as if I weighed nothing. My stomach did a little flip it definitely wasn't supposed to be doing around my boss.

XAVIER

I dropped Evie off at Connor's house before heading to my penthouse. I didn't have much time to get ready anymore.

The filming took longer than expected, mostly because I enjoyed how flustered Evie got. I had never seen someone blush as much or ferociously as she did.

When she'd started licking that popsicle, I'd thought she'd try to come on to me, but she had been completely oblivious to the effect her sneaky tongue had on me. She was surprisingly pleasant to be around despite being Fiona's twin, and her brand of humor, from what I'd seen so far, would undoubtedly prove entertaining in the future.

When it was almost time to leave for Network Ten's party, I chanced a look down at my Rolex. If we left now, we'd be on time, but Evie wasn't here yet. As if on cue, the keys turned in the lock and the door pushed open. "I'm here!" she called out a warning, and I stifled a grin. The sight of her shocked face this morning had been entertaining, more entertaining than fucking Shannon if I was being honest.

She stepped inside then clapped her hand over her heart as she spotted me close by. She was out of breath and obviously flustered. "Good god, don't scare me like that."

"You're late," I drawled, my eyes drawn to her hand, which was still resting on her impressive breasts.

Guilt flashed across her face. "I'm sorry. It took longer than I expected to find something suitable to wear, get ready and return here. I don't have a car so I have to rely on public transport. It won't happen again."

I didn't really care. I'd hired her solely because Connor had asked me, and had expected the worst knowing she was Fiona's twin. My eyes scanned the rest of her.

She had opted for a classic pant suit in dark blue with a blazer that reached her upper thighs, loose dress pants and moderate heels.

"Pants? Is that what you bought for the party?"

She frowned. "No. I didn't have time to go shopping because of the beach shooting. Why? This is normal business attire. I'm supposed to stay in the background after all."

Why would she hide her curves like that? It made no sense. I held up my tie. "Can you tie this for me?"

She put down her purse on the counter, nodding before she stepped up to me. She took the tie from me and stood on her tiptoes to sling it around my neck, her fingers quick and nimble as she bound the tie, her green eyes trained on the work at hand. My gaze kept wandering, however, over the dusting of freckles all over her nose and cheekbones, over her curved mouth, and her flawless skin despite the minimum of makeup she was wearing. I'd been with enough women who wore makeup like a second skin.

She patted the tie, and my chest once, looking up. "There you go." We were quite close, so her sweet scent wafted into my nose.

She took a step back. "We should really hurry or we'll be late."

"Fashionably late," I corrected.

"Late is late, there's nothing fashionable about it," she said with pursed lips. Was there anything she agreed with me about?

"How do I look?" I asked, more to annoy her than anything else. I knew I was a hot piece of man-candy in the form-fitting dark blue Ermenegildo Zegna suit, and I'd have my fair share of willing women to choose from.

Her eyes trailed over me slowly, taking their time as if she, too, was trying to make a point. "Well," she said neutrally. "For a man your size you make the suit work quite well."

I had to stifle laughter. "I've never had an assistant who chose to wear pants to a party like this," I countered, nodding toward the atrociously loose-fitting fabric over her curvy butt.

She blushed. "It's not my party. Like I said, I don't want to draw attention to myself."

I gave her a doubtful look. "You're the complete opposite from my previous assistants, that alone will make you the center of attention, and these clothes probably won't do you any favors, knowing the furies that parade around as journalists nowadays."

She tugged a strand of hair behind her ear, with a look that suggested she was considering to hide behind me all night.

"Don't worry. I'll make sure to be extra scandalous to keep all the attention on me."

Her mouth quirked. "I don't think you need any prompting to be scandalous."

"True," I admitted, suddenly not in the mood for the party and all the attention-whores waiting to be my next conquest.

She peered down at her slender silver watch. "We should really go now."

I decided to humor her and arrive at a party less than two hours late for once.

The second we arrived at the party I could already feel my patience slipping. Photographers began circling me like vultures, and the women were only marginally better. Evie tried her best to stay several steps behind me and let me be in the spotlight, but I caught a few photographers taking photos of her.

For some reason it annoyed me even more because I knew she hated the attention. I spotted Connor and Fiona at the other end of the party, chatting up one of Network Ten's hosts whose name I couldn't remember.

As I made my way through the crowd, shaking hands and exchanging necessary pleasantries, Evie stayed close by and whispered the names of the people heading my way, so I'd know who they were. She did so without prompting as she knew I didn't know a single name. I couldn't care less about most of these people. They took what they wanted and needed, and I took what I wanted in turn.

After an excruciatingly long chat with a group of middle-aged women who flirted unabashedly with me, we finally arrived at the bar. I leaned over to the bartender waiting for my order. "One sparkling water with a slice of lemon, a slice of cucumber and ice." Then I turned to Evie who hovered beside me, glancing around herself self-consciously. She needed to drop the deer-in-the-headlights look in public. I wasn't sure why she had trouble showing her feisty self in a situation like this, when she was already giving me fire even though I was her boss—not that I minded. "What do you want?"

"A beer," she said without hesitation.

Surprise washed over me, and it must have shown because she frowned. "Or does that convey the wrong image? I can take a glass of white wine or a water if that's what you prefer."

"Drink whatever you want as long as I don't have to haul your drunken ass home later."

She narrowed her eyes, nodding toward my glass of water. "I'm not the one with the gin and tonic."

I grinned. That was exactly what everyone was thinking. I held the glass out to her, challenge in my eyes, and she took a hesitant sip.

"Water," she said incredulously.

"I don't get drunk in public, or at all. I'm an athlete."

She blinked but I turned to the bartender and ordered a beer, then handed it to Evie. "Thanks," she said, watching me closely. "Do all women fawn over you as if you're the second coming of Jesus Christ?"

I leaned back against the bar. "Not all, but many."

She rolled her eyes and took another sip. Another flash blinded us, and Evie stiffened beside me. "I hope I'm not in any of these photos."

She would be in all of them.

I made small talk with a few more Network Ten personnel when Evie excused herself to go to the restroom. Connor joined me at the bar a moment later. "So mate, how's your new assistant fairing so far?"

"I have no complaints except for her choice in clothing," I drawled.

"She's a bit self-conscious about her figure." He grimaced. "I shouldn't have said that. Fiona will kick my ass."

I could see how Evie was self-conscious about her body in an environment like this. The women surrounding me had turned starving into a competitive sport. I twisted my glass around in my hand as I searched the crowd for my fling of the night. I was in the mood for something spicier than the bore from last night. "Why does she blush so much? It's like she's from some hicktown behind the woods and has never been around a naked guy."

"You were naked in front of Evie?"

"Not really. She caught me in bed with my last fuck. Got a good look at my backside, maybe more."

Connor shook his head. "This will cost me my balls, I can see it coming." He emptied his glass. "Seeing you banging someone would have disturbed anyone."

"She's kind of adorable," I said to get a rise out of my best friend.

"Evie is a good girl, Xavier," Connor muttered, narrowing his eyes.

I turned my attention to him. "How good?"

"Too good for you," Fiona said in warning as she came up behind us. Her sneaky tendencies grated on my nerves. "Don't even think about making a move on her, you hear me? Evie spent the last few years taking care of our dad after our mom died. She doesn't need additional crap from you."

"And where were you?" I shot back because I didn't like her tone.

She blanched, turned on her heel and disappeared in the direction of the ladies' room as well.

"Great," Connor snarled. "Was that really necessary?" He left me standing there as he stormed off after his girlfriend. I smirked into the camera lens pointed at me from across the room. Soon a woman with chin-length black hair in a tight black jumpsuit sauntered over to me, introducing herself as Maya Nowak, as if her name should ring a bell with me. I assumed she was a journalist from one of the sketchy tabloids that made millions with my scandals. I supposed it was only fair that I got something in return, so after an hour of shameless flirting and the second time her knee accidentally rubbed my cock through my pants, we made our way to an empty meeting room where she sucked my cock with so much eagerness you'd think she was a starving dog gifted a bone. After I'd banged her on the meeting table, I zipped up my pants, threw the condom in the bin and turned to leave.

"Hey!" she called. "Don't tell me you're leaving just like that?"

I didn't look at her. "What else am I supposed to do? I don't do a pussy twice. Bye, Marie." I knew that wasn't her name, but for some reason I wanted to piss her off. She'd probably let me fuck her for the very reason to write an article about me—might as well give her the necessary fodder.

Back outside, I returned to the bar for another glass of water. The night was still young; maybe there was more pussy to discover. When I didn't spot Evie anywhere, I checked my phone and found a message from her.

Fiona told me you were busy, and I quote, getting head, so I decided to take a taxi home. Charming women's panties off is your job, not mine.

I shook my head with a smile. She was something else. When I looked back up, I was hit with Maya's scowl. I had a feeling she'd savor her revenge even more than she'd savored my dick.

CHAPTER SIX

EVIE

I grabbed a few newspapers on my way to Xavier's apartment and let myself in with enough noise to waken a hibernating grizzly, then headed into the kitchen area. I listened for strange noises from upstairs, but it was quiet. Was Xavier alone?

Choosing not to risk another embarrassing incident, I turned on the espresso maker, which came to life with a satisfying hiss. As I waited for it to heat up, I perched on a barstool and spread the newspapers out in front of me, and immediately wished I hadn't. Xavier having left the party with another woman who had been in the last season of *The Bachelor* was worth only a side note. His new assistant, aka me, filled up the rest of the article.

As I started reading and scanned the photos, I could feel the color draining from my face. The first photo was the deer-in-the-headlights look as Xavier had called it, but that wasn't even the worst. Somehow they had chosen the perfect angle to show the two half-moon-shaped sweat stains on my too tight beige dress right under my butt cheeks. I must have sweated while reading the stupid non-disclosure clause. The subtitle logged a lump in my throat. "Never heard of antiperspirant? You need it for your butt."

The next photo was a close-up of me on the beach in my shorts with a nasty comment about my missing thigh gap. The last few photos finally showed me at the party. The dark blazer and pants with the white blouse made me look like a penguin in the photos as I skulked a few steps behind Xavier. Even worse than the photos, which seemed hardly possible, was the accompanying article. It speculated that Xavier had chosen me because his advisors had forced him to pick an off-putting assistant for once. They called me fat, mousy and boyish. I had been submitted to my fair share of mockery in high school and convinced myself that comments about my appearance couldn't hurt me anymore, but this article got to me. Despite my best efforts, tears burnt in my eyes. I couldn't believe the press chose to attack me, but I should have expected it. Xavier was a constant guest in the tabloids and I was a new piece of gossip. Even if I didn't want their attention, they wouldn't allow me to stay in the shadows. It was what Xavier had warned me about I could only decide on what kind of scandal they focused.

"What kind of bullshit did they come up with today?" Xavier drawled from behind me.

I jerked on my stool, not having heard him approach. Before I could cover the embarrassing article, Xavier stepped up beside me, once again in those infuriating Calvin Kleins, and started reading. I slid off the stool and busied myself with the espresso unit, hoping my face didn't give away how much this got to me. It was ridiculous.

"Usually they attack me," Xavier said quietly.

The strange note to his voice made me turn to him. His eyes scanned my face, lingering on my own eyes, which still felt a bit prickly. "I guess I should ask for a bonus. After all, I'll be your shield from the nastiness of the press now." My voice came out surprisingly flippant, for which I was glad.

"You aren't supposed to be," Xavier muttered.

I gave a small shrug as I prepared the milk foam, then poured it on the espresso. It wasn't as fluffy as Xavier's foam had been, but for my first attempt it wasn't too bad. I handed him the cup. He leaned back against the kitchen island and regarded me as he sipped his coffee. "You should ignore them. If you show them that what they say bothers you, they will attack even worse. They want to get a rise out of you, or me."

"It doesn't bother me," I said. Both Xavier and I knew it was a lie. My voice betrayed me, and my eyes did too.

Xavier's mouth pulled into a daring grin. "We could prove them wrong, you know?" He raised his eyebrows in a suggestive way. "Have a nice public make-out session. Give them a little show."

I laughed. "Yeah, *right.* Not going to happen."

Xavier chuckled. I doubted he had any kind of interest in me. He'd tried to lift my spirits, which was surprisingly nice, and yet felt like a letdown. It wasn't that I wanted to sleep with Xavier, but it would have been nice if he showed at least the slightest interest in me. I had seen how he undressed pretty much every woman at the party with his eyes. That he didn't look at me that way was a worse blow than the stupid articles, even though it shouldn't be.

"So what's on today?" Xavier asked eventually.

"Training, and a meeting with a local sports label that wants you as their poster boy, literally. Apparently they want to create an exclusive Xavier line of sports fashion. They need to take your measurements, and have you choose the designs and fabric for the clothes."

Xavier nodded. "Sounds like fun," he muttered.

"It's better publicity than you usually get," I said, remembering the horrid articles.

"True."

"The meeting is right after training so you won't have much time to shower."

"If you give me a helping hand, I'm sure the shower won't take as long," he drawled.

As if I needed the image of Xavier lathering his Adonis body in my brain.

———— ◆ ————

Xavier took longer to shower than he was supposed to and I considered heading into the changing room and dragging him out personally when one of his teammates, a broad guy with blue eyes and blond hair, stepped out and extended his hand with a warm smile. "Hey, I'm Blake and you are Evie, right?"

I smiled as I shook his hand. He wasn't as tall as Xavier but like all rugby players I'd met so far, he was above average. "That's me. Did Xavier tell you about me?" I hoped he didn't tell any embarrassing stories.

"No, but everyone knows who you are. Xavier's victims can't really fly under the radar."

"Victim," I said with a frown. "It's not like that."

He shook his head with an embarrassed look. "I mean because you have to work for that slave driver. It can't be easy."

I shrugged. "Could be worse." I didn't want to talk badly about my boss in front of his teammates.

Xavier finally sauntered out, dressed in dark-blue jeans and a white polo shirt, looking surprisingly dapper. His eyes zeroed in on Blake, who gave him a curt nod before he excused himself.

"What did he want?"

"He introduced himself. Some people have manners, Xavier."

"Sure. Manners are the reason why guys approach girls." He slung his sports bag over his shoulder and raised his eyebrows. "Ready, if you are," he said in the same voice Hannibal Lecter had used in *The Silence of the Lambs.*

"I love that movie," I said as I followed Xavier toward his Maserati SUV.

He cocked a dark eyebrow. "You recognized the quote."

"I've watched *Silence of the Lambs* at least ten times. Of course, I do."

Xavier held out his keys to me. I stared at them. "You can drive. I want to catch a quick shut-eye."

I took the keys hesitantly. "The drive won't take that long. And I've never driven on the wrong side before."

Xavier shook his head. "It's not the wrong side. It's the left side, and around here it's the right side."

I rolled my eyes. "You are a smart-ass." I snapped my mouth shut. *Evie, he's your boss, for heaven's sake!*

Xavier's eyes twinkled in amusement. "Takes one to know one, right?"

"Right," I said, relieved.

I got behind the steering wheel, swallowing nervously. "It's a shift."

Xavier slanted me a look as he leaned back in the passenger seat. "It's a Maserati, a sports car, of course it's a shift."

"It's an SUV."

"Drive, Evie."

I turned the ignition and the beast came alive under me with a soft purr. I got used to driving on the left pretty quickly; shifting, however, was a struggle. We arrived eventually, after I'd stalled the engine or mis-shifted about one million times.

"I think in the whole company history of Maserati none of their cars have ever taken longer for five miles," Xavier drawled before he got out. I unclasped my hands from their tight grip on the leather steering wheel. Cold sweat ran down my back and into my pants. I could only imagine what kind of pictures the paparazzi would take of me today. I needed to change my approach, and my wardrobe, or find a chill pill that worked its magic.

The cold sweat turned into a hot sweatiness when the tailor took Xavier's measurements in the company's office in one of the heritage buildings in the Rocks, not too far from Xavier's apartment.

Xavier was in his Calvin Kleins as a feminine young man measured almost every part of his body. I could tell that there was one part in particular he would have loved to measure as well, but which wasn't on his list of tasks.

Xavier noticed the admiring glances of the tailor as well and winked at me.

I rolled my eyes as I returned my gaze to the myriad of fabric samples spread out on the table before me. Xavier came up to me once the tailor was done, still only in his Calvin Kleins so his privates were on eye level with my head, which made for a very bothersome distraction.

A few members of the design team soon joined us, and they didn't seem bothered by Xavier's almost nakedness. I supposed it happened a lot in the business. Xavier propped his arms up on the table, scanning the samples. "What do you think?"

Surprised, I looked up but quickly put my professional face back on, considering the patterns. I pointed at few uni-colored ones, then at a few more daring patterns and at last at one with red lips all over it.

Xavier smirked. He pointed at a few more, but took every single one I'd suggested.

I had a feeling he and I would get along well.

CHAPTER SEVEN

EVIE

After four weeks of working as Xavier's assistant, he and I had fallen into a comfortable routine. I woke him by making excessive noise when entering his apartment so he got the chance to stop banging whoever shared his bed that morning, got him to training in time, which made his coach love me like crazy, took care of his emails and social media, but otherwise stayed in the background. There had been a few more parties Xavier had attended alone, and that had ended in him embarrassing himself by not knowing who he was talking to or offending more people than was acceptable even for him.

I needed to put on my big-girl panties and accompany him to these events to protect him from himself, even if that meant more unfavorable articles. Due to my lack of public appearances, they had been rare, but a few times they had gotten me anyway, and of course they'd always commented on my weight and choice in clothes. Worse was that they had started to bug Fiona. They kept asking her about me or made snide comments that compared her to me. Knowing her, it was only a matter of time before she lost it and caused a Xavier-worthy scandal.

Taking a deep breath, I stepped onto the terrace where Fiona was doing a Pilates sequence for her Instagram followers. The second she was done she turned to me. It was my day off, so I didn't have to wake Xavier for once.

"No work today?" she asked, surprised. "You've worked every single day since you came here."

"So do you," I said. Fiona was a total workaholic. She was driven in every aspect of her career; it was admirable, really.

She smiled guiltily. "We could spend the day together?"

"That's why I'm here. I got my first paycheck from Xavier, and I want to use it to buy new clothes."

Fiona's eyes lit up. "You want to go shopping with me?"

"Yeah," I said hesitantly, regarding her size zero gym leggings. "Don't get too excited. This girl doesn't fit into the clothes you love."

Fiona frowned, crossing her arms. "You are being ridiculous, Evie. You have curves, so what? You've got great hips, a big, nicely shaped butt and big tits. You've got the golden package if you don't hide it under boyfriend jeans and ugly T-shirts, or those horrendous old lady blazers. Not every guy wants size zero."

I stared down at my boyfriend jeans and the loose-fitting blouse. "All right."

"Let me give your wardrobe a once-over, and the press will shut up once and for all."

I was wary of Fiona's idea of a once-over, but she had amazing taste in clothes so I decided to trust her. Still I knew nothing short of a miracle would stop the press from bashing me as long as I was Xavier's assistant.

Three hours later, more than half of that month's salary had been invested in new clothes, and none of them were anything like what I'd owned before. Tight pencil skirts, glittery tops, form-fitting dresses. Every piece accentuated at least one of my "big three assets", as Fiona put it: ass, tits or hips.

On our way home, Fiona's mobile beeped. She risked a quick peek at it, then frowned. "Connor says Xavier's coming over for barbecue tonight. We're supposed to bring everything for a salad and dessert." Fiona pursed her lips. "Is that okay? Him coming over?"

"It's your house and Xavier is Connor's friend, so of course. Why wouldn't it be?"

"Won't it be weird to have your boss over?"

I frowned. So far the time Xavier and I had spent together had been strictly work related, but it wasn't like we usually worked in an office. I woke him, drove him to meetings, filmed his workouts, and catered to his every whim. "I don't mind. Xavier is funny."

Fiona slowed the car as she shot me a look. "Funny? *Evie.*"

"Don't give me that look. I'm not into him, and he's definitely not into me, but he's not hard on the eyes and he's easy to be around. He doesn't make my life hell like I expected."

"Really? That's not what I heard from his past assistants."

"I didn't let him trample over me. I talk back. He seems to enjoy my snarky comments. Maybe he just needs someone who kicks his ass now and then."

"Maybe." Suspicion tinged Fiona's voice.

I decided to put on one of my new outfits. The least extravagant ensemble of the lot, a tight white tank top and jeans that hugged my curves more than my usual chinos or boyfriend jeans. I arranged my hair in soft waves around my shoulder and applied some makeup, then left my room barefooted.

Xavier's deep voice rang out downstairs, and for some reason I felt suddenly nervous. Putting my big-girl panties on, I walked down the stairs and followed the voices into the kitchen, where I found Xavier and Connor, bottles of that disgusting low-carb, non-alcoholic beer in their hands, and a pile of meat on a tray in front of them.

Xavier brought the bottle to his mouth but paused when he spotted me. His eyes scanned me from head to toe, lingering on all the places Fiona wanted to accentuate. Though, I was fairly sure her intention wasn't to draw Xavier's interest toward them.

"Connor! The barbecue started blowing up smoke!" Fiona shouted from outside.

Connor's gaze darted between Xavier and me, as if he was unsure if he should leave us alone, but at a glare from me he grabbed the tray and hurried outside.

"Hey," I said awkwardly. Funnily enough, Xavier was wearing a similar outfit to me. Dark jeans and white shirt. "Didn't know we agreed on matching outfits."

His mouth tipped up, then his eyes did the quick scan again. "You look better in it than me."

"Let's agree to disagree." A second too late I realized what I had blurted out so carelessly. My God. I hovered in the doorway, unsure of what to do with myself, and worse, how to act around Xavier, especially now that he was giving me such an intense look.

"Kind of strange to have my boss over for dinner," I rambled, which wasn't the reason for my sudden awkwardness but Xavier didn't need to know that.

"I can ask you to make me a coffee if that would make you feel better," Xavier said, taking a long sip from his beer.

I laughed. "No, thanks."

He shrugged, grinning. "Let me know if you change your mind. I'll boss you around whenever you need it."

"I'm good, trust me," I said with a grin of my own as I walked into the kitchen and toward the fridge. "Do you want a real beer? The two lovebirds don't want to ruin their bodies, but maybe you're up for it."

"A real beer?"

"Yes, you know, the kind with too many carbs and calories and alcohol in it," I said with a small shrug. "I don't follow the same no-carbs routine like most girls."

Xavier's eyes slid over my curves, and I had to fight the urge to cover myself. I had chosen this new style, now I needed to own up to it.

"So what about that beer?" I asked, opening the fridge and glancing at Xavier over my shoulder. He was still watching me with a strange expression. It was making me increasingly self-conscious. Beer would definitely help.

"I eat and drink carbs if the occasion requires it, so hit me with your beer."

"And this occasion requires it?"

"Definitely," he murmured.

I hid my smile behind the open door as I grabbed two bottles.

XAVIER

My eyes were drawn to Evie's butt, which she didn't hide for once. It was round and bigger than that of any girl I'd ever been with, and I couldn't stop wondering how it would feel to squeeze my cock between it.

"I hope you like craft beer. These are two Indian Pale Ales from a local microbrewery," Evie's voice tore me from my inappropriate thoughts. She turned back to me with the bottles. It took me another moment to register what exactly she had said, and then another to trust my ears.

My eyebrows climbed up my forehead. "Okay," I said slowly. "Those were the sexiest sounds I've ever heard from a woman." And I had heard every moan, groan, scream, screech and gasp imaginable.

I had never been around a woman who enjoyed drinking beer, much less knew what the hell a microbrewery was or an Indian Pale Ale. Evie was a surprise package all over.

She pursed her lips, her blonde brows pulling tight. "Are you mocking me?"

"I wouldn't dream of it," I said, stifling laughter. Whenever she gave me that stern look, I felt the urge to grin. With her strawberry waves, freckles and cute little mouth, the stern expression just didn't have the desired effect.

She opened one bottle by wedging the cap of the other bottle under its cap and twisting up, then handed the now open bottle to me. I was so stunned, I could feel my jaw dropping to the fucking floor.

Evie flushed and snorted. Two of her favorite pastimes. "What?" she muttered as she leaned against the counter, propping her ample hip up against it in a way that accentuated her curves even more—and I knew she wasn't aware of it.

"Nothing." I raised the bottle to my lips and took a long sip. The taste was amazing, and hit me with its fruity and bitter notes. "Wow. That tastes great." I checked the bottle, but I didn't recognize the name of the brewery. "Never heard of that brewery before, though I've visited a few local breweries."

Evie looked surprised at my admittance. Just because I didn't have alcohol at home didn't mean I didn't enjoy the occasional beer, if it didn't interfere with my training routine. "They are pretty new. I hear they have great tastings and tours through the brewery."

I glanced at Evie. "You didn't do one?"

She gave a small shrug. "I didn't want to go alone, and I don't know anyone except for Fiona and Connor yet. You are a slave driver who stops me from having a social life."

For an insane moment, I considered asking her if she wanted to do a tour with me. I loved them, and Marc was busy with his kids and work. But I'd never gone out with a woman like that, just because we enjoyed the same things that didn't involve getting nasty between the sheets. It would have crossed a border I shouldn't cross with Evie. And I really didn't want the press to get photos of me spending quality time with my assistant. That would lead to a new onslaught of speculations Evie didn't need. For some reason I wanted to protect her from the shit the press threw my way, and it wasn't only because Fiona could be threatening as hell where her twin was concerned. Evie had been broken up after the last few nasty articles. She really didn't need additional abuse thrown her way, and not just because Fiona would kick my balls until they were different shades of blue and violet.

My attention shifted back to Evie who used a spoon to open her own bottle, then took a swig and let out a small moan. But that sound wasn't what made my mind drift off to another level of inappropriateness again. A droplet of water had fallen from the cold bottle and landed on Evie's neckline, and was now slowly making its way down the crevice between Evie's ample tits. My God. She had never worn a low neckline before, and I had a hard time—in more than one sense—not looking at it.

I took another deep pull from the bottle, hoping the cold liquid would clear my head. It didn't.

Evie frowned, her perfect nose wrinkling. "You okay?"

I forced my eyes upwards. Too late, of course. Evie followed my gaze and rolled her eyes. Then she took a step toward me and punched my shoulder. I took a step back, utterly startled by her reaction. She had never done anything like that before. "Eyes on my face, Xavier."

I made a show out of rubbing the spot. "You realize hitting your boss isn't your best idea."

"You are in my home, and I'm not on duty, so at the current time you aren't my boss, only a very rude visitor."

I flashed her a guilty grin, then clinked my bottle against hers. "Don't worry, I like it when you manhandle me."

"If I manhandle you, you'll know it," she said with an answering grin. When Evie smiled it always took hold of her entire face. It wasn't the cautious kind of smile, the smile women used so they would still be pretty. Evie showed her emotions without holding back, without worrying how it would make her look, and it was a breath of fresh air. I didn't need to guess how she felt. She showed it plainly or told me outright. No female subtlety that drove me up the walls. Evie was like one of the guys, but with curves that gave my dick ideas that would make Fiona choke me to death if she knew them.

Speaking of the evil twin, Fiona entered the kitchen, her eyes darting between Evie and me with a suspicious expression. "What's going on here? I thought we would have dinner together outside, not do a standing party in the kitchen."

"We're getting drinks," Evie said, holding up her bottle.

Fiona narrowed her eyes at me as if she thought I was doing nefarious things to her sister. If anyone needed protecting, it was me. Evie could pack quite a punch for a woman. "Is that beer?" she asked. "You realize you've got training in the morning?"

"It's one beer and I'm a big guy. I can handle it, *Mom*."

Fiona turned to Evie. "You shouldn't encourage him to act like this. As his assistant you need to make sure he eats healthy."

Evie burst out laughing. "You want me to tell Xavier what to eat, Fiona? I consider a carrot cake a nutritious start to my day."

"Maybe you should change your eating habits then as well," Fiona said with a sigh.

Evie's cheeks turned red, but Fiona didn't notice. She was busy grabbing water and a salad from the fridge. Evie wrapped one arm over her stomach and scowled down at the beer in her hand. The second Fiona left, I leaned down to Evie and whispered, "Eat all the carrot cake you like, as long as you stay as cool as you are and don't turn into a stuck-up bitch like your sister."

Evie laughed and took another sip. "She isn't a bitch."

I raised my eyebrows.

Evie shrugged. "Most of the time."

I grinned. "Now come on, before Fiona orders Connor to get us. He can be a nasty bugger if provoked."

Evie followed me, a smile on her face that set me oddly at ease.

Two hours into the barbecue, Evie and I were in a full-blown discussion about Marvel movies.

"*Amazing Spiderman* was a complete fluke. They should keep their hands off the old movies. Every time they try a new take on Spiderman, they ruin the story a bit more," Evie argued, her cheeks flushed, her chair turned toward me.

"Tobey Maguire was a shitty Spiderman," I said, slinging my arm over the backrest of my chair to turn fully to Evie. "I didn't buy his interpretation of the bad guy for one second. That guy's too much of a goody-two-shoes."

"And Andrew Garfield isn't?" Evie muttered.

"Did you know they were nerds?" Connor interjected.

Fiona shook her head. "I knew Evie enjoyed a good book or movie more than actual human interaction. But this...no."

Connor shook his head at me. "What's wrong with you, mate?"

"Now come on, you watched the Spiderman movies."

"I did. But that doesn't mean I can spend hours discussing the merits of the Marvel universe."

"Don't listen to them," Evie murmured. "They don't even like Pale Ale."

71

I chuckled. "One of these days we'll have to do a movie night where we binge-watch all Spiderman movies, and then we'll have that discussion again."

"Deal," Evie said.

Fiona cleared her throat. "Evie, I doubt movie nights are part of your job description?"

"She needs to cater to my whims," I said with a shrug.

Fiona gave me a scowl that could have frozen over hell before she turned to her sister with an expression I couldn't decipher, but Evie could and sighed.

Before I left, Fiona cornered me in the entryway, her manicured nails digging into my forearm. "Listen, Xavier, I don't know what kind of game you're playing, but stop the charm offensive on my sister, all right? She won't have movie night with you. She doesn't do overnight hours, especially not the kind you want."

I withdrew my arm from her tight grip, stifling my anger before I said something nasty that would make Connor kick my ass. "You aren't Evie's guardian, nor mine, Fiona. Why don't you keep your nose out of our business?"

"Because I don't want you to hurt my sister, and that's the only thing you're good at—hurting women."

I scowled. "Evie's my assistant. If I decide that includes hours watching movies together, then that's what she'll do, understood?"

"You're such an asshole."

"And proud of it," I muttered. "Say bye to Connor and Evie from me. I've had enough of your bitchiness for one day."

If it wasn't already late and if I didn't know that Evie would be kicking me out of bed in the morning no matter how long my night had been, I'd have headed straight for a bar to pick up a fuck for the night. Instead, I returned home like a good little athlete, and fell asleep with the image of Evie's butt giving me the boner of a lifetime.

CHAPTER EIGHT

EVIE

The day after the barbecue Xavier was in a sour mood. I wasn't exactly sure why. After making sure he was on time for his training, I took Xavier's car toward the office of the sports label to pick up the newly designed briefs so Xavier could try them on in the afternoon. I was still in awe that Xavier let me drive his Maserati for tasks like that. Despite his soft spot for anything that could be classified as luxury, he wasn't very attached to any of his possessions. Sometimes it felt like they were a necessary evil for him. Who wouldn't like a Rolex and Maserati as their necessary evil, really? His knack for flouting his wealth didn't bring him lots of good press, however, and had led to more than one investigation by the National Rugby League to see if his salary didn't surpass the salary cap after all.

His mood had improved considerably when I picked him up from training in the early afternoon, as it usually did.

"Good training?" I asked as he flung himself into the passenger seat. Sometimes I felt like a chauffeur. Not that I minded. After my initial problems with the shift and the left-side traffic, I enjoyed driving around Sydney, despite the annoying traffic.

"Things are coming together. We need to make it to the Grand Final. We need to win."

"When's the first game again?" I asked.

"Second week of March. But the pre-season kicks off next week."

"Yeah, I know. I saw that. Central Coast Stadium against the Sea Eagles." It would be my first live rugby game. I had never even been to a football game, so I was curious if I'd enjoy it at all.

Xavier's expression was focused and eager. No cockiness or flirtiness, only fierce determination. "This is our year."

Back at his apartment, I sent him upstairs with the package with briefs so he could see which ones he liked best while I fixed us lunch. A huge salad with avocado, chicken, and feta cheese. Xavier, of course, got three cooked eggs and another chicken breast on the side to reach his protein goals for the day. I'd have never thought that I'd become a master in macronutrients, but being around Xavier and Fiona, it was inevitable, not that it had any impact on my own figure. I had lost a couple of pounds without trying, however, because of all the running about for Xavier and the forced healthy regime in his and Fiona's company.

I put down the cutlery beside the two salad bowls when Xavier came down the winding staircase in one of the briefs. Low-rise trunks hugging his body like a second skin in subdued olive green. I could feel warmth traveling up my throat and face when Xavier turned so I could see him from every angle. I wasn't sure why the label wanted Xavier as the face and body for their campaigns, as if anyone would pay attention to clothes in this underwear ad.

"What do you think about the color?"

"It's nice," I got out.

"Green's not my favorite color, though it matches your eyes."

I snorted. "Your underpants aren't supposed to match my eyes."

His answering grin was devilish, and I raised the fork still in my grasp in warning. "Whatever you're about to say, don't. I'll poke you with this fork and not in a girly, teasing way, all right?"

Xavier raised his arms and backed away slowly. "So that's a no to this model?"

He turned around, giving me a premium view of his defined ass and back. I grabbed a glass of water and took a few desperate gulps.

Things didn't improve from there. With every new model that Xavier presented, the temperature in the room seemed to rise until I wished for panty liners so I could wedge them under my armpits to prevent another embarrassing sweat incident.

"Oh this is my favorite," Xavier shouted, then laughed.

I perched on a stool, my elbows propped up on the kitchen island, as I snuck one bite of avocado and chicken into my mouth after the other, and almost choked to death when Xavier came into view. This model wasn't a trunk. It was a slip, and even that term didn't do the thing justice. The bright purple fabric didn't cover much.

I coughed. Xavier's grin grew, and then he turned around, and I was fairly sure my legs would have given way if I hadn't been sitting. It was some sort of thong that revealed Xavier's perfectly shaped butt, with two strange strings under his ass cheeks. He turned back to me. "What do you think?"

Not much. Any sane thought had fled my mind. My head was moments from raising a fire alarm. I sat up slowly, trying to form an articulate reply despite Xavier's grin. "What is that?"

"A jockstrap. Have you never seen one?"

"Until you I wasn't around jocks all that much," I muttered, trying very hard not to look at how the jock thingy accentuated Xavier's *thing*. But it was really really difficult not to risk the occasional peek because that man wasn't only ripped, he also had every reason to be cocky as far as I could tell.

Xavier was enjoying this far too much. I bet he wouldn't have tried on every single piece of clothing if it wasn't for my reaction. "Yay or nay, Evie?"

"To be honest, I think ninety-nine-point-nine percent of the male population shouldn't even be thinking of wearing something like that."

Xavier strolled over to me. Did this man not have any kind of shame? "But I should?"

"God no," I said, forcing my gaze to rest firmly on his annoyingly cocky face. Of course, the reason why Xavier shouldn't be wearing a jock strap was an entirely different one. It was to preserve the last shreds of my sanity because seeing him in his Calvin Kleins was already bad, but this?

"Why not? Share your thoughts with me." He crossed his arms over his chest.

"I don't think it's very manly if guys wear thongs."

What I really thought was that if Xavier didn't start wearing more than briefs around me soon, the non-disclosure clause would be useful after all.

"Sure. That's why," Xavier said, then turned to head back upstairs. I wasn't sure, but I thought he flexed his butt cheeks to give me an additional show.

"Only one more," he informed me a couple of minutes later.

"If it's got less fabric than the last, I'm out, Xavier. I warn you," I called up.

His answering chuckle made me smile stupidly. To my relief—or disappointment, it was difficult to determine at this point—the last model was another low-rise trunk with the red lips pattern.

"This is my favorite pattern," he announced, standing on the last step.

"Why?" I asked suspiciously.

"I like lips on my junk," he said as he strolled over and sat on the stool beside me.

"Of course."

Xavier glanced down at his salad, then at mine. "Where's your chicken and avocado?"

"Your show made me hungry," I said without thinking about it.

Xavier's expression made me lift the fork and poke his side with it.

I narrowed my eyes. "Last warning."

"I wasn't going to say anything," he said, rubbing his side.

"Your expression did."

We spent the remainder of the afternoon going through several interview questions for online magazines and *Rugby World*, as well as a few fan emails that required a more thorough reply.

It was almost seven when I glanced at my watch. "It's later than I thought."

Xavier looked up from the last fan letter. Thankfully, he'd by now changed into jeans and a gray shirt. "Why don't you make good on that Spiderman movie marathon you promised me."

I frowned. I had really liked the idea, but after seeing Xavier half naked the majority of the day, I wasn't sure anymore if it was safe to be around him after work as well. *Don't be ridiculous, Evie.*

Even if Xavier's body gave me all kinds of fantasies, my body definitely didn't have that effect on him. In the month that I'd worked for him, I'd seen him with twenty women, all of them tall, thin, fit, and breathtakingly gorgeous. I could bind myself to Xavier in my birthday suit and it wouldn't get his pulse up. "Why not," I said.

Surprise flashed across Xavier's face, and then he smiled. Not the cocky, the challenging, the arrogant smile. A real smile. One I'd never seen on his face before, and my pulse rate doubled.

"Since I don't have training tomorrow, why don't we treat ourselves to some ribs and French fries from my favorite fast-food joint?" Xavier asked, getting up from the barstool to grab his phone and a takeout menu.

"Sounds perfect," I said.

After Xavier had put in his order, he opened the fridge and took out two bottles of beer that didn't look like the low-carb dishwater he called beer. "Got a few craft beers in preparation."

I hopped off the stool and joined him in front of the fridge, surprised. "You didn't know I'd agree to a movie night."

He shrugged. "You're working late all the time, might as well have a beer you enjoy when you're here."

I blinked up at him, but he drew his eyes away with a small frown. I scanned the inside of the fridge, finding beer bottles of different sizes and forms. All of them craft beers. "What's your rec for the ribs?" I asked.

Xavier held up the two bottles. "Oatmeal stout from a brewery I visited with Marc a while back. They sell their beers in a small craft beer shop in the Rocks."

He opened the bottles then handed me one. We clanked bottles. "Cheers," I said.

"Cheers."

For some reason, the atmosphere shifted slightly. Maybe it was because it was the first time we were in his apartment without it being work-related. I took a sip of the stout, and smiled around the bottleneck. "That's what I call beer."

"It's one of my favorites."

"If Fiona knew I wasn't stopping you from having an alcoholic beverage, she'd blow a gasket."

"I don't think that's what would piss her off the most about this."

I frowned. "Did she say something to you at the barbecue?"

"She doesn't want us to spend time together."

"We work together."

"Outside of work. She thinks I have ulterior motives."

"And? Do you?" I said with a laugh.

He grinned. "Always. But you don't have to worry. You aren't the focus of any of them."

Ouch. I took another sip. "Does it make sense to start with the movie?"

Xavier nodded.

We settled on the sofa together, which felt strange. We'd sat there before when we'd worked, but not like this. Xavier made sure to keep an arm-length between us when he sank down.

Luckily the food arrived soon and together with the movie managed to relax me. Xavier and I quickly resumed our banter while drinking beer and eating the most delicious ribs I'd had in a long time.

"You are the only girl I know who enjoys drinking and eating as much as I do," he said with a laugh.

I flushed. That was because I wasn't a size zero. I stared down at my upper thighs, which were touching. No thigh gap for me. Ever.

Xavier leaned back again, his eyes returning to the movie but now his arm was stretched out on the backrest, his hand behind my back. For some reason it was awfully distracting.

"You can't possibly prefer him as Spiderman," Xavier said when the famous kissing scene flashed across the TV screen. "He kisses the girl as if he's a limp dishrag. There's no passion. Nothing."

"For me the kiss looks okay," I said with a small shrug, but discussing kissing techniques really wasn't on my agenda when alone with Xavier, or at all.

Xavier turned to me. "Then you've never been kissed properly. Trust me, if I kissed you, you wouldn't let me disappear—you'd rip my bodysuit off and fuck me in that alley."

I swallowed because I had a feeling he was right. His gray eyes held mine with an intensity I hadn't seen in them before. I nodded toward the screen. "Spiderman isn't about kissing," I said, my voice a bit breathless to my ears.

After that kissing was off-limits and we found less awkward topics, though I had a feeling I was the only one who felt uncomfortable. Xavier was cool as a cucumber as usual.

After the second movie, I prepared to leave. "Should I drive you home?" he asked as he brought me to the door.

"Usually I'm your chauffeur," I teased.

"True. But we've both had a couple of beers, but I'm much bigger and can hold my liquor better."

"I doubt that," I said with a laugh. "I'm not the one who usually drinks light beer."

"It's late, Evie. You shouldn't be out alone."

I rolled my eyes. "I'll be fine. I'm not the only woman taking public transport from this house. It's only midnight. And you can't risk being caught behind the wheel with alcohol in your system. The Rugby League might ban you for a few games."

He grimaced. "Then let me bring you to the bus station."

"Okay," I said, grabbing my purse and following Xavier out of his apartment. We walked in comfortable silence toward the station, where an older man and a young woman were also waiting for the bus to Bondi Junction.

"This was nice," I said quietly when the bus finally approached.

Xavier looked down at me. "Yeah." I couldn't quite pinpoint his expression. He looked almost...apprehensive.

I got onto the bus. Xavier watched with his hands stuffed into his jeans pockets, and my heart thudded a bit quicker in my chest.

CHAPTER NINE

EVIE

Even Fiona's interrogation couldn't dampen my mood after the movie night with Xavier. I enjoyed his company, even if she couldn't understand. I knew he could be a major prick, but he wasn't to me.

The chances of me misinterpreting his motives were blown right out of the window when I entered his apartment two days later to wake him for training as usual. A female voice sounded upstairs.

My smile dropped and I headed for the espresso unit and flipped the switch, announcing my presence.

For a moment, the woman quieted down, but then her voice rang out again. I didn't listen, didn't want to, too worried by the realization that for the first time it really bothered me that Xavier had a girl over to bang her brains out. I'd seen him do it from the start, so what had changed? And more importantly, how could I return to my previous indifference?

I grabbed the pitcher, filled it with milk and began to froth it. From the corner of my eye, I saw Xavier make his way down the staircase, looking royally pissed. Behind him one of the women who'd tried out for a position in the cheerleading team, a lithe girl with long black hair, followed, talking to him without pause.

"We could work out together. I'm sure you can show me a few new moves."

Xavier stopped next to the kitchen island, in his usual Calvin Kleins. "Listen—" he began, then paused.

He looked at me. He didn't know the girl's name. Of course.

I fought the urge to let him get through this situation on his own, but it would embarrass him less than the girl. Xavier was lucky I had a good memory, and that Fiona had bitched about the candidates almost nonstop while she'd watched the tryouts on repeat at home. Still, I wavered between two names. Samantha or Cameron.

Cameron, I mouthed at him.

"Listen, Cameron, our coach is kicking our asses right now, but if you give my assistant your number, I'll give you a call as soon as I have time."

Never.

The girl told me her number and I put it into my mobile. Xavier led her out of his apartment with his hand on her lower back. She stole another kiss from him that turned my stomach into ice before he finally closed the door. And just as quickly, he would have forgotten all about her. I deleted her number from my phone again.

"What's on today?" he asked me.

I paused, resisting the urge to ask for the name of the girl just to make a point. He had already forgotten anyway. "You have a fan meeting in the afternoon, and please don't land in bed with any of them. The press will tear you apart if you do."

"They do anyway. But I don't take fans into bed on general principle."

I frowned. "Xavier, you sleep with everything that qualifies as female."

"No," he said firmly, almost angrily. "Not fans. They fall for me because they think I'm someone I'm not. I only fuck women who don't care who I am, only what kind of attention I can bring them. There's a difference."

I tilted my head. "Don't bang any journalists either for a while if possible. I'm really trying to improve your image here. The season is about to start. You have your first test match in two days. You should focus on what really matters, not meaningless flings with women who take advantage of you."

Xavier touched my shoulder. "Are you worried about me, Evie?" he teased in that deep rumble his voice took on in the morning. His strong, big hand was warm even through the thin material of my blouse. "You really don't need to be. I'm taking as much advantage of those women as they do of me. It's a symbiotic relationship."

"Most of those women leave your symbiosis hating your guts."

"I don't care if they hate me or love me. They are not the people I care about."

"Who do you care about?"

Xavier's expression became guarded, but he answered anyway. "Connor, you, my family."

Despite the giddiness his mentioning of me had given me, I said, "You never talk about your family. And they haven't come to visit."

"I don't want them here where the press circles over my head like vultures. My mother and sister live on a farm in the countryside, near the Blue Mountains. I visited them two weeks ago."

"When you were gone for two days?" I said as I poured the milk foam on his espresso and handed the cup to him.

He nodded.

I'd thought he'd been on a sexcapade trip with one of his conquests, but the truth sat much better with me.

"How old is your sister?"

"Willow is seventeen," he said, and I could practically see his protective brother mode snapping into place and I had to stifle a smile. It was a side of Xavier I hadn't seen so far, but one I liked. He was eight years older than his sister, so it was normal he wanted to protect her.

"I bet her friends ask her about her superstar brother all the time. What does she say to your scandals?"

He set down the cup. "Willow is being homeschooled. And she doesn't read the tabloids. She knows who I really am."

Sometimes he let me see that side of him as well, and in the last few days, it had become more frequent. Like during our movie night or when he'd bought me a cherry popsicle when we'd filmed his second beach workout. And it was a side of him that posed a bigger threat to my resolve than any jock strap ever could.

◆ ◆

I had premium seats for the first test match of Xavier's team, right behind the coach bench, and I was oddly nervous. Not just because it was the first time I'd see Xavier in action, but also Connor and Fiona. I had seen Fiona's cheerleading skills in high school but never cared much about it.

After the referee tossed the coin and pointed at the guy from the opposing team who got to choose which half his team would play, Xavier grabbed the ball and positioned himself in the middle of the halfway line. He looked incredibly hot in his rugby uniform. All these men had muscled thighs to die for, muscled everything. But Xavier...he stole the show. When the referee gave the sign, Xavier did the dropkick, sending the ball flying the length of the field as his teammates charged forward. A member of the opposing team caught the ball, and then both teams clashed and then there was a big huddle. It was wild and confusing, and with the cheers and screams of the crowd, utterly intoxicating.

I didn't understand all the details of the game, but I cheered whenever Xavier and his teammates cheered, and shouted obscenities when the crowd around me did.

I had a splendid time, and when Xavier's team did their little victory dance at the end, I felt like dancing myself. Fiona waved me down, then jogged over in her cute little cheerleading costume and told the stewards to let me through. I climbed down onto the edge of the field and hugged my twin. "I'm not part of the team," I protested. "I belong on the bleachers."

"For making sure Xavier is on time, you deserve to be here," Connor said as he jogged toward us, sweaty, muddy, and disheveled. He kissed Fiona and pulled her tightly against his side.

My heart did a stupid little loop when I spotted Xavier heading our way. He was smiling, a huge smile, an honest one. He clapped Connor's shoulder in passing, then shocked me by wrapping his arms around me and lifting me off the ground for a moment. My fingers clutched his shoulders, my eyes widened and I let out an embarrassing cry. When he released me, he and I both hesitated a moment. Fiona and Connor were watching us with wide eyes but fortunately a few teammates joined us, stopping Fiona from a comment.

XAVIER

I didn't hug girls after games like many of the other guys. Not a girlfriend because I'd never had one, and not the cheerleaders because half of them wanted to clamp my balls in a vice. And I definitely didn't talk about my family, not with my teammates, except for Connor, and definitely not with any women of the past, but with Evie my guards seemed to be crumbling and I didn't even mind. I knew she wouldn't sell me out to the press. She had absolutely no ambitions to gain attention, and she was responsible and loyal. I liked having her around. With my previous assistants they'd worked from home, not in my apartment. I'd spent as little time as possible with them, but with Evie I found myself giving her tasks just so she'd have to be in my penthouse more often.

"I can't imagine you on a horse," Evie said during our next movie night after I'd told her my mother and sister lived on a farmstead with stables, a place where I'd spent part of my youth. "What kind of poor creature can carry your body?"

"Horses are strong. They can carry a lot of weight, trust me."

She looked doubtful. "Still. I can't really imagine you as a cowboy."

I chuckled. "I'm not wearing a cowboy hat or cowboy boots when I ride, if that's what you're thinking."

She tilted her head in that thoughtful way where she wedged the corner of her lower lip between her teeth. It was fucking distracting. "Now I want to see you on a horse," she said with a shake of her head and a laugh.

"Why don't you come with me next time I visit my family?" I hadn't considered asking Evie, but oddly enough I realized I wanted her to see where I came from, and meet my family. Marc was already completely enthralled by her, and from the few things I'd let slip to my mother, she was too.

Evie blinked. "Really? Wouldn't they wonder why you're bringing your assistant along for family time?"

"You're more than that, and they'll be ecstatic if I bring any woman home."

"You've never brought a girl over?"

"No," I clipped. "Never dated, never will. I didn't want any of the women I slept with to go anywhere near my family."

"So you're bringing a woman you don't sleep with," she said with a twitch of that pink mouth. "Ask your family if it's okay. I really don't want to impose."

"You won't." I had a feeling both my sister and mother would enjoy Evie's quirky nature.

Evie regarded me for a couple heartbeats before she let out a small sigh. "My mom had breast cancer," she said softly.

I angled my body toward her, but didn't say anything. She was searching for more words.

"Fiona and I were fifteen when she was diagnosed with stage three. At first it looked like she could beat it, but then it flared up again and..." She swallowed, her green eyes sad and teary, and I reached out and touched her shoulder, rubbing it with my thumb.

She gave me a small smile.

She was soft and warm to the touch, and smelled of that mix of honey and a hint of cinnamon. "How old were you when she died?"

"Seventeen. It was in my last year of high school."

"That must have been hard."

"It was," she admitted. "It would have been easier if Fiona hadn't left right after graduation. I'd needed her at my side."

"Why did she leave anyway?"

"That's Fiona's story to tell," Evie said. That was another reason why I knew I could trust her with personal information.

She wiped at her eyes, then squinted with an embarrassed smile. "I didn't mean to ruin our movie night with an emotional outburst."

"I asked," I said. "How about something funny like *The Hangover*?"

"Why did I know that was a movie you'd like?"

"Connor and I experienced something very similar when we were in Las Vegas a few years back."

She perked up. "Do tell."

"I think I'll pass. Don't want you to get the wrong impression," I drawled with a wink.

"It's a little too late for that, Xavier."

I realized I was still touching her shoulder and removed my hand, then turned back to the TV and searched for the movie. Evie curled her feet under herself and leaned her head against the headrest with an expression I had trouble reading, so I didn't bother.

We were halfway through the movie when Evie's head slumped forward and her breathing deepened. I let her sleep. When she didn't wake before the end of the movie, I decided to let her sleep here. It was already past midnight and we'd have to get up early. If Evie still needed to return home, she would hardly get any sleep at all. I carefully rose then grabbed a folded blanket from the second sofa, unfolded it and covered Evie with it. The position she was in looked slightly uncomfortable, so I lowered her gently to her side. For a moment, I regarded her peaceful face, then her lit-up mobile screen caught my attention. The sound was off.

Fiona.

I picked it up and went upstairs before taking the call so I didn't wake Evie.

"Where are you?"

"She's with me."

Pause. "Xavier?" Fiona asked, sounding caught off guard.

"The one and only."

Pause.

"It's late. When will she be home?"

"Evie will spend the night."

"I warned you to keep your hands off her!" she muttered. I could hear Connor's deep voice in the background, probably trying to calm his crazy girlfriend.

"She fell asleep on the sofa." I was too tired to annoy Fiona with a half-truth, just to see her outburst.

"Don't do kinky stuff to her while she's asleep."

Fury burnt through me. I'd never touched a woman who wasn't one hundred percent willing and conscious. Connor spoke again.

After several moments of silence, Fiona said, "Sorry. That was out of line."

"Yeah, it was. Good night." I hung up.

I set the alarm, a new experience, then with a last glance down the landing at the sleeping woman below, I went to bed. This was the first time a woman spent the night in my penthouse without spreading her legs.

Evie got to me in a way I couldn't quite understand.

CHAPTER TEN

EVIE

A loud hiss tore me from sleep. I woke with a stiff neck, disoriented. Staring up at a high ceiling, it took me several moments to gather my bearings. When I sat up and my surroundings came into focus, I realized where I was. Xavier's apartment.

"Good morning, sunshine," Xavier said.

My head whirled toward the source of the sound. Xavier was propped up against the counter beside the espresso unit in his underwear, foaming milk.

I untangled myself from the blanket and jerked to my feet. "What time is it?"

"Six forty-five."

"You woke by yourself," I said, surprised, as I tugged my shirt back in place, wondering what kind of bird's nest my hair created at the moment.

"You were sound asleep."

"Waking yourself, making coffee. Does that mean you will fire me?" I teased.

"No chance in hell am I letting you go."

My heart did that stupid lurch it had adopted only recently.

Xavier poured the milk foam into the two cups on the counter, then came over to me.

I held up my palm. "Don't come closer. I haven't brushed my teeth yet."

Xavier cocked one eyebrow. "I wasn't going to kiss you. I'm giving you coffee."

Keeping my lips shut, I took the cup from him. *I'd prefer the kiss.*

Oh Evie, you big fool.

"Thanks," I mumbled then took a deep sip, hoping it would banish the foul taste in my mouth. I could imagine what kind of undignified sight I'd provided lying on the sofa like a stranded whale; I didn't need to make it worse by smelling like a dumpster.

"Should I write down my number now and delete it later? Since that's your modus operandi when women spend the night?" I joked.

Xavier flashed me a grin, moving closer, too close, because his manly scent and the sight of all the muscle wreaked havoc with my body. "My usual *modus operandi* includes hot sex. How about that?"

He was joking, playful and teasing, so I forced out a laugh, even if heat washed down my spine. "Sorry. This coffee is the only hot thing you'll get."

———— ◆◆◆ ————

After Xavier left for his training, I drove home where I found Fiona in the kitchen. She stood the moment I entered, narrowing her eyes. "Have you lost your mind?"

I blinked, putting my purse down on the table. "Excuse me? What crawled up your ass?"

"Xavier did."

"Ew. That's an image I really don't need so early in the morning, or ever."

Fiona didn't crack a smile. "You spent the night."

"Yes, I did. I'm twenty, Fiona, not twelve."

"But you're letting Xavier charm his way into your pants."

"He isn't trying to charm his way into my pants, trust me. I'm not his type, as you very well know."

"Maybe he wants to try something different for once."

"He doesn't, Fiona. Xavier doesn't have the slightest interest in me in that regard. I don't think he sees me as a woman."

"And you?"

"I know I'm a woman. I see the proof every time I undress or curse the fact that I can't pee standing up during a road trip."

Fiona sighed. "You know what I mean."

"Yes, and I also know that I can take care of myself. I'm Xavier's assistant and maybe his friend, but nothing else, okay?"

"Okay," Fiona conceded, but I knew she didn't really believe me—and who could blame her when I didn't believe it myself.

XAVIER

I was supposed to visit home tomorrow and had yet to make the call Evie wanted me to make. I knew how my mother would react if I as much as mentioned bringing a woman with me. I picked up the phone and called her.

"Xavier," Mom said before I could say a word.

"Hey Mom, just wanted to let you know that I'm bringing someone over tomorrow."

"Someone? What kind of someone?" she asked curiously.

"A female someone—"

"Oh Xavier! That's wonderful. I thought you'd never settle down—"

I interrupted her before she started making wedding plans. "Mom, it's not like that. I'm bringing my assistant Evie."

"So she's only your assistant, but you want us to meet her?" Confusion rang clear in her voice.

"Evie is a friend, not just an assistant. " I paused, realizing it was true. In the past six weeks Evie and I had become friends. She was funny, and kicked my ass in the kindest way possible.

"Okay," Mom said slowly, trying to sound nonchalant, but I caught the hint of excitement in her voice. I'd never brought a girl home and she would make a big deal out of it, I could just tell, and so would the rest of my family.

◆◆◆

Not even thirty minutes later, my mobile rang and Marc's name appeared on the screen. Here we go. "Mom called you, didn't she?" I said by way of greeting.

There was a short pause on the other end, then a chuckle. "She did. Can you blame her? It's the highlight of her year."

"She doesn't need to get too excited, all right? Evie is a friend and my assistant."

"She is. Did the non-disclosure clause come in handy yet?"

I hung up.

Five minutes later my mobile flashed with a message from Milena, Marc's wife.

I can't wait to meet your "assistant". ;-)

I didn't reply. Maybe introducing Evie to my family gave the wrong message, but I wanted her to come with me even if my family was intent on driving me up the walls.

I was glad for my plans to meet Connor for a kick-ass workout later. I really needed to blow off steam.

Of course, I should have known even my best friend wouldn't give me a fucking moment of peace.

"You're spending a lot of time with Evie," he said twenty minutes into our workout.

"She's my assistant," I told him as I put more weight on the barbell for my next set of deadlifts.

Connor shrugged, regarding me curiously. "Sure. But with your previous assistants you didn't do movie nights."

"Because they grated on my nerves trying to blow candy up my ass."

"You didn't take them to visit your family either."

"So Evie told you about it?"

"She let it slip. Fiona is a bit suspicious about your motives toward her sister, to be honest."

I grunted as I pulled the barbell up, then finished the set before I answered Connor. "I don't have any motives. Evie's never been outside of the city since she's come here. She has never even been in a saddle. I want to rectify that."

"There are other things she hasn't done. I hope you won't rectify them as well," Connor mumbled as he took my place in front of the barbell.

"What's that supposed to mean?"

"Nothing," Connor bit out between deadlifts. "I'm not getting involved in this."

"For not getting involved you're asking an awful lot of questions, mate."

He straightened, looking me square in the eye. "I don't want you to fuck Evie over. Or fuck her at all. Period."

My eyebrows climbed my forehead. "I have no intention of fucking Evie over."

Connor's eyes narrowed. "And fucking her?"

I didn't say anything because I didn't like to lie to my best friend. Though the term *fucking* didn't sit well with me when I thought of Evie.

Connor touched my shoulder. "Just do me one favor: *don't*, okay? Not with her. Keep your dick in your pants for once."

"Don't worry. I enjoy being around Evie, that's all," I said, and it was the honest truth. She was the first woman except for my mother and sister whose company I enjoyed.

EVIE

Xavier picked me up that morning from home under the watchful eyes of my sister and Connor. They didn't say anything, more because of my warning glare than anything else, but Fiona's expression told me all I needed to know about her thoughts regarding the road trip.

In the car, I asked again, "You asked your mom, right?"

"I did," Xavier said with a grimace.

"You don't look very happy. I don't have to come."

"You have to come. My family's already planning the wedding."

I choked on a laugh. "Just so you know, if you propose, I expect the full package: falling to your knees, bling, red roses, violins and fireworks."

Xavier bared his teeth. "I have the full package—what else could you want?"

Heat blasted through my body like a pyroclastic flow. "You are *full* of yourself, that's all."

Xavier shrugged. "I guess you'll never find out."

I scowled out of the side window. I guessed he was right.

Despite Xavier's words, or maybe because of them, I was inexplicably nervous about meeting his family. It felt like being introduced to your boyfriend's parents for the first time, not that I had any experience in that regard. Not that Xavier was my boyfriend. I was his assistant.

I slanted him a look, still surprised that he'd asked me to come to his family home with him. "Are you really sure your family will be okay with me staying the night as well?"

"Of course," Xavier said without hesitation. "Maybe with you being there they won't be on my back all the time about my manwhore ways."

I snorted. "So I'm your safety shield?"

Xavier gave me a grin. "I fear you will join in their bashing of me. I know what you think of my manwhore ways."

"You act like a caveman and pig to women, Xavier."

His fingers around the steering wheel tightened ever so slightly. "They know what they're getting when they come home with me. I never lie beforehand. They come freely despite what they can read about me in the tabloids."

I was surprised by the serious note in Xavier's voice. "I know. They are grown-ups, Xavier."

He relaxed. "I don't act all caveman around every woman. I never do around you."

My lips twisted. That was true, and for some inexplicable reason it bothered me. I was Xavier's assistant, his friend, and definitely not his type, and that was for the best. Xavier's eyes flickered to me again. "Or do I?"

The hint of doubt in his voice was almost adorable.

I gave him a small smile. "No, you are surprisingly tolerable around me."

The corner of his mouth tipped up in that annoying way that made me want to slap and kiss him with equal fervor.

Xavier's family home was a beautiful white farmhouse with a faded red roof. It was surrounded by pastureland for the family's horses. Stables spread out to the left of the building, and in the distance I could make out the first signs of the Blue Mountains. "This was my grandparents' home, but it was pretty desolate before my mother had it renovated a few years back. The stables are new. My grandparents had sheep, not horses."

Two dogs shot toward the car the moment Xavier turned off the engine, ginormous creatures with reddish fur and slightly darker muzzles. I wasn't afraid of dogs, but their deep barks made me jump briefly. "Sherlock and Watson are big pussycats. You don't have to worry."

"Sherlock and Watson?"

Xavier's mouth curled in that sexy way. "My sister is obsessed with the series, and she got to name the dogs."

"What are they?" I asked as I watched the dogs prowl around the car.

"Rhodesian Ridgebacks." Xavier got out of the car and I followed after a deep breath. The dogs were busy greeting Xavier but the second they were done they trotted toward me, wagging their tails slightly. I stiffened when they nudged me with their muzzles and Xavier stepped up to me, taking my hand. "Come on, Evie. You usually handle me. You can handle two dogs."

I sent him a look, trying to ignore how good his hand in mine felt. "With you I don't have to worry about having my fingers chewed off."

"I wouldn't mind nibbling at certain parts of you," he drawled, and we both stiffened at the same time.

My eyes flew up to his, my cheeks flaming. Xavier had never flirted with me like that, not like he meant it, but this had sounded like something he'd say to someone who wasn't me. From the look on his face, he hadn't meant for the words to slip out either. I supposed it was habit.

"Do I have to put you on a leash?" I said to lighten the mood.

Xavier winked. "I'm not into that kind of kink, I'm afraid."

Thankfully, the door opened at that moment and a thin, tall woman in her early fifties opened the door. She was dressed in jeans and a loose checkered shirt, her dark hair pulled up in a messy bun. The dogs rushed back into the house.

Nerves hit me hard, which was ridiculous really. Xavier released me when his mother came down the steps. She didn't greet him first; instead she pulled me into a tight hug. "It's so good to meet you, Evie. Xavier hasn't been very forthcoming with information." She drew back with a warm smile. "I've been waiting for this day for a very long time. Finally Xavier brings a girl home."

"Doesn't Xavier get a hug as well?" Xavier muttered.

His mother stepped back from me and up to her son, touching his cheek. He bent down to kiss her cheek, and she gave him a slight clap on the chest, a silent reprimand. "I read that last article in the *Daily Mail*."

Xavier frowned. "I told you not to read that bullshit."

She pursed her lips. "It's easier to get information about you than from you." She nodded toward the house. "The rest are already inside, eager to meet your girl."

"Xavier and I, we aren't together," I said hesitantly, worried she might have forgotten that small detail.

She shook her head. "Call me Georgia. Now come in."

I slanted Xavier a confused look. "They know I'm your assistant, right?"

"They do," Xavier muttered as he took our bags out of the trunk. "But that doesn't mean they'll treat you that way."

I followed Georgia up the stairs, noticing a ramp leading up to the porch. The moment I stepped inside I knew why it was there.

A teenage girl with dark hair and gray eyes like Xavier's waited in the entrance hall in a wheelchair. Her face broke into a blinding smile when she spotted Xavier. After dropping our bags, he went straight toward her, leaned down and hugged her before he kissed the top of her head twice and straightened. Sherlock and Watson tiptoed around Xavier and Willow excitedly, wagging their tales.

"This is my sister Willow," Xavier introduced the petite teenage girl. His voice rang with protectiveness and his eyes held a flicker of apprehension, as if he thought I'd freak out because his sister was disabled.

Willow smiled shyly. I had a feeling she didn't get visitors very often out here.

I smiled in return, walked up to her and extended my hand. "I'm Evie. It's so nice to meet you."

Her gray eyes flitted between Xavier, who stood beside her with a hand on her slender shoulder, and me, then she shook my hand. Her grip was light but her smile brightened. "Nice to meet you too."

"I love your dress," I told her. It was a cute, frilly flower dress that fit her slender figure perfectly but would have made me look like an exploded flower bouquet.

Xavier's eyes softened and his stance relaxed. I sent him a look. He should know me by now. Steps rang out, and a second later a kid barreled into the entrance hall and latched on to Xavier's leg. It was a little boy of perhaps three years. Shortly after, Marc and a woman with brown wavy hair, carrying an infant, stepped into view. Their eyes zeroed in on me.

Marc's wife stepped up to me and held out the hand that wasn't holding the infant. "I'm Milena. Xavier's sister-in-law. This is Sarah." She nodded toward the little girl who was staring at me with huge eyes. "And you are Evie, Xavier's. . ."

"Assistant," I provided to prevent any misunderstandings.

"Assistant," she said with an amused little smile. She squeezed my hand, then moved on to Xavier. He took his niece and kissed her chubby cheek before he gave Milena a one-armed hug.

My ovaries ignited a spectacular firework at the sight. Damn it. Why did he have to be cute with kids, and protective with his sister? I was so done for.

Marc stepped into my line of view and held out his hand. I shook it, glad for the distraction. "Good to see you again, and for keeping your promise so far."

I flushed, realizing he meant my comment about the non-disclosure clause.

"What promise?" Willow asked curiously.

"Nothing," Xavier and I said at the same time.

Willow frowned. "I'm not a little kid."

Xavier tapped his finger against her nose. "You will always be my little sister."

She rolled her eyes and wheeled herself into the next room—a combined living and dining room, I realized as I followed the rest of the family inside. The table had been set with rustic stoneware and silver cutlery. A fresh bouquet of what looked like white and pink wildflowers perched in a clay vase in the center.

"I hope you like meat?" Georgia asked me.

I never got the chance to reply because Xavier beat me to it. "Evie loves meat. I've never seen a girl who enjoys her steak as rare as she does."

"The cow died once—it doesn't need a second death," I countered.

"True, but if you eat your steaks any rawer, it'll start mooing."

"Says the man who's obsessed with sushi because it's better for his figure."

"Keto-sushi," Xavier corrected.

"Cauliflower doesn't belong in sushi, Xavier. Take my advice and don't mention your strange sushi habits in public, or you'll be taken into custody if you ever try to enter Japan."

Xavier flashed me a grin. "I know someone who'd bail me out."

"After a few days to let you rethink your transgressions."

"A few days won't be enough for that," Xavier drawled.

"As if I don't know it."

I grinned and Xavier grinned right back.

Suddenly I realized everyone was staring at us as if we'd each grown a second head. Marc and Milena exchanged a meaningful look. Willow's mouth was slightly agape and Georgia smiled widely.

I cleared my throat, feeling a bit on the spot.

"I made lamb roast and potato bake," Georgia said, and with a last lingering glance at Xavier and me, she disappeared from view. Watson and Sherlock rushed after her, probably hoping for a treat.

"Why don't you show Evie to her room, Xavier?" Milena suggested.

Xavier frowned briefly at his sister-in-law, then motioned for me to follow. He grabbed our bags and led me upstairs. "They are amazing," I said.

"Wait till they start being annoying."

His voice held affection despite his words.

I stifled a smile. Xavier opened the first door to the right, a small, cozy guest bedroom with a checkered rug and a narrow wood bed.

Xavier put my bag on the round table next to an armchair before he turned to me. "Nothing fancy."

I shrugged. "I love it here. I bet it was wonderful to grow up in this house."

Something dark passed Xavier's face but as quickly as it had come, it disappeared. He didn't give me a chance to ponder his reaction. "I'll take my bag to my room, then we should return to my family. They're probably up to no good."

Suppressing my curiosity, I nodded. Together we walked back into the dining room.

The moment I caught Milena's eyes, she winked at me.

I wasn't sure why she did it, but I had no intention of asking. I didn't want to make a fool out of myself in front of Xavier's family.

The lamb roast was amazing, and I complimented Georgia several times for it, until she asked if she could adopt me. Her words briefly lodged a lump in my throat, reminding me of my mother, and I excused myself under the pretense of having to go to the toilet. It only took a couple of minutes to gather my bearings and when I stepped back out of the guest bathroom, I was surprised to find Xavier waiting in front of it. "My mother didn't know about your mom," he said quietly, his eyes scanning my face.

I smiled embarrassedly. "It's no big deal. I got emotional for a moment, but I'm fine now."

"You sure?"

The worry in Xavier's expression warmed my insides. "Absolutely. Now come. I need another bite of that roast."

"You aren't one of the girls who have qualms eating fluffy baby animals, are you?" He grinned.

I snorted. "They aren't fluffy and cute anymore when I eat them. If I had to butcher my meat, I'd become a vegetarian."

We headed back toward the dining room table, and again received a few curious glances.

After dinner we talked for a long time, mostly about my time in the US but eventually we moved on to funny stories from Xavier's childhood. I quickly noticed that everyone skirted around a certain topic: Xavier's father.

I had a feeling it wasn't because the man had died and everyone grieved his absence. As I knew from experience, the silence surrounding the gaping hole a beloved person left behind felt different—not as resounding, more lingering. I hadn't seen a single photo of a man in the entryway or living room, even though there were plenty of family pictures.

It was close to midnight when Milena and Marc went upstairs where their kids were already sleeping. Willow had fallen asleep in her wheelchair, her dark hair covering her face. She reminded me of Snow White in a tragic way. Then I felt guilty for the thought. Just because she was in a wheelchair, that didn't make her a tragic figure. She had a loving family.

Georgia got up and moved toward her daughter, but Xavier rose from his chair. "Don't wake her. I can carry her upstairs," he whispered.

Georgia nodded, then mouthed good night before she headed upstairs as well.

Xavier scooped up his sister carefully, as if she was the most precious thing he knew. Her head dropped against his chest and she looked fragile and small against his tall frame. He raised his eyes, catching me staring at him.

And in that moment, I realized what I had been denying for a long time: somewhere along the way I had fallen for Xavier. Not for the brash manwhore or the arrogant asshole, but for the glimpses of the kind, funny Xavier that he so rarely showed to the outside world.

Oh, Evie, you idiot.

"Do you need my help?" I asked in a whisper.

He nodded and walked toward me. "Can you open Willow's door for me?"

"Of course."

We headed upstairs in silence, Xavier carrying his sister as if she weighed nothing, and me carrying my feelings like a stone weight shackled to my ankle, dragging me deeper into the depths of the ocean.

I stayed in the doorway as Xavier lowered his sister into her bed and covered her with a blanket before pressing a kiss to her forehead. Sherlock and Watson curled up on the rug beside the bed. I stepped back and Xavier walked out, closing the door.

For a moment neither of us said anything. Xavier's warm scent surrounded me, and I could feel my body answering to it. My eyes lingered on Xavier's mouth.

"Good night, Xavier," I murmured, my voice catching in my throat.

"Good night, Evie," Xavier said somewhat gruffly.

A small shiver passed through my spine, and I quickly disappeared into my bedroom.

CHAPTER ELEVEN

EVIE

Horse riding was scheduled for the late morning. So much for not making a fool out of myself in front of Xavier's family. But seeing Xavier in faded jeans and an equally faded unbuttoned jeans shirt with a tight white wifebeater beneath it, a brown cowboy belt and boots, made up for it. The Marlboro Man would have wept tears of jealousy seeing Xavier, not that Xavier would go anywhere near cigarettes.

When Xavier led me toward the stables and I caught sight of the five huge beasts, my pulse sped up. Georgia, Marc and Willow were already waiting for us while Milena stayed back to watch over the children. I wished that could have been me. I knew many girls dreamed of owning their own horse and riding every day, but I had never been one of them. The idea of being at the mercy of an animal that weighed more than many Asian car models just never struck me as something desirable.

"Xavier," I whispered as we arrived beside the animals. "I told you I've never in my life sat on a horse, and to be honest their size terrifies me."

Xavier's eyes flashed. "Being around me all the time, size shouldn't bother you anymore."

I rolled my eyes and shoved his shoulder. He grinned.

I could feel everyone's eyes on us and flushed. Marc and his mother exchanged a look, and Willow looked like she was about to freak out from joy.

"You'll be fine, Evie. I'll stay close," Xavier murmured.

"You'd better."

Xavier moved toward his sister. To be honest, I was surprised that she'd join us. I didn't know much about horse riding, but I hadn't considered it a possibility for someone who was disabled. The saddle on her horse, a harlequin beauty, had additional straps and props for her thighs.

Xavier lifted his sister out of her wheelchair, her arms coming around his neck, and again my heart did the flip that began to scare me senseless. He hoisted her up on the horse and helped her strap herself in. I wondered how she could steer a horse without her legs. Maybe only through the reins. Xavier patted her horse before he returned to me. The only thing missing for him to become the star of a Western romance was a cowboy hat, and the only thing missing from me turning myself into the star of my own embarrassing soap opera was if Xavier realized that his charm had the same effect on me as on every other woman on this planet.

My God, Evie, get a grip, will you?

"You okay? You have a strange look on your face," Xavier said as he led me toward two majestic horses with dark brown fur while his family trotted ahead.

"I'm fine. Only nervous."

He pointed at the bigger of the two beasts. "That's my horse, Adobe. And your horse is Cinnamon."

My mouth twitched. "You're giving me a horse named after food."

Xavier chuckled. "I didn't choose Cinnamon because of that. She's the calmest of the lot. She's a good beginner's horse. But it's fitting. You smell like cinnamon."

"Probably because I love cinnamon buns," I said.

"Probably," Xavier murmured. He tore his eyes away from me and nodded toward the horse. "Let's get you in the saddle."

"Okay," I said uncertainly, peering up at the huge animal. She had beautiful dark brown eyes with long dark lashes. That horse was prettier than most people. My gaze was drawn to her back. How was I supposed to get up on the saddle? "What do I do now?"

Xavier took my hand and lightly pressed it to the side of the horse's neck, then moved our hands over the soft coat. "Show her your touch is good," he said quietly, his eyes on the horse.

I shivered at the feel of Xavier's gentle touch and his closeness. His eyes met mine and for a moment my breath caught. Then I cleared my throat. "She's beautiful."

Xavier nodded. Slowly he looked back to our hands pressed up against the horse's neck. He dropped his hand. "Why don't you try to mount her?"

I huffed out a laugh, couldn't help it.

Xavier grinned dangerously. "You have a dirty mind, Evie."

I blushed but pushed past Xavier and glanced up at the saddle.

"Grab the horn," Xavier instructed.

I automatically looked toward the horse's head as if it had sprouted a horn like a rhino. Xavier chuckled, the deep rumbling awfully distracting. He touched a small knob at the front of the saddle. He, being a giant, would have no trouble mounting the horse, but I was neither fit nor a lightweight. I was glad that Xavier's family had gone ahead and wasn't still watching.

I gripped the horn.

"Put your foot into the stirrup," Xavier said.

That proved already a small challenge. I couldn't remember the last time I'd had to move my leg that high up. "Don't you dare laugh," I muttered when I saw Xavier's expression.

"I wouldn't dare."

I sent him a glare but had to stifle a smile.

"Now pull yourself up."

As if it was as easy as that. I tried to use my hand on the horn to pull me up, but with the angle my leg was in I had no way of getting up. Heat rose into my cheeks. Xavier was a professional athlete, and all the women he usually dealt with were fit, and I couldn't even hoist myself onto a horse. I didn't even want to think of the way my butt looked in that angle.

"I can't," I said, and cringed at how my voice wavered. I wasn't a teenage girl anymore who hid in the restroom after gym classes, damn it.

Xavier stepped up close behind me and put his hands on my waist. Tension shot through my body at the unexpected closeness, at the way my body responded to it. Then another thought struck. What did Xavier think of the soft feel of me? I wasn't all muscle and bone.

He released me with a small frown. "I wanted to help you. I should have asked first."

He sounded regretful, but there was a darker note to it. I searched his face, but it was closed off.

"Don't be ridiculous. I was only startled. You have touched me before." Not on my waist, not anywhere near it, and heaven have mercy, I wanted his touch back despite my worry about his opinion of my soft body. "I need your help. But I doubt you can hoist me up."

Xavier shook his head. "Don't be ridiculous, Evie," he threw my words back at me with a confident smile. His hands returned to my waist, big warm hands, hands I wanted to feel everywhere on my body. "On three, you pull."

"Okay," I said quietly.

"One…two…" His fingers on my waist tightened, sinking into my softness, but before I could feel self-conscious about it, he said, "Three," and lifted me. I quickly pulled at the horn while pushing against the stirrup at the same time, and suddenly I was on top of the horse, safely positioned in its saddle. I stared down at Xavier with wide eyes.

Xavier was a beast. All muscle, all strength, all man. God have mercy.

"See?" he said smugly.

I swallowed as I stared down into his cocky gray eyes and handsome face. This was getting dangerous. "Thanks," I said with a shaky smile.

Xavier stepped closer. "Are you okay up there? You look scared."

I was scared, very scared, but not of the horse or the riding. "I'm fine. It just takes some getting used to being up so high," I lied.

"You will get used to it quickly." He touched my knee briefly, lightly, like a friend, but the contact zapped through me like electricity. Xavier pulled away, walked to Adobe and swung himself up as if it was the easiest thing in the world, then he grabbed the reins in one hand and straightened leisurely in the saddle.

My eyes trailed over his muscled thighs pressed up to the horse, up over the ripples of his stomach that his shirt didn't hide, to his flexing arms. He patted his horse lightly, then steered it toward me. He grabbed the reins of my horse as well. "I will lead for now because you haven't done this before. If you feel confident on top of Cinnamon you can take over the reins, all right?"

I nodded. There were so many things I hadn't done, and wanted him to take the lead in. He clucked his tongue, tugged at the reins and Cinnamon began trotting beside Adobe.

I let out a startled gasp and clutched the horn as if my life depended on it, my thighs clinging to the horse's belly.

"Straighten your back. Don't just hang there like a limp dishrag," Xavier instructed.

I stiffened my spine with a glare, but Xavier only laughed and turned back to the front. Eventually I started to feel more comfortable on Cinnamon. She followed Xavier and Adobe obediently, and Xavier oozed enough calm for the both of us. He looked at peace, as if this was who he truly was. That he let me see this side of him meant something. Problem was, I didn't know exactly what.

After about thirty minutes in which I got magnificent views of the rugged hilly landscape of the Blue Mountains, Xavier handed the reins back to me. "You can do this," he assured me when I gave him an uncertain look. "It's like riding a bicycle."

I didn't mention that I'd always hated riding a bike and hadn't done it in years. The beautiful landscape made up for my fear of dropping to my death from the horse. I'd have to visit the Blue Mountains National Park when Xavier and I weren't on a family visit. Even from a distance the forested rock formations were breathtaking.

I clutched the leather reins and clucked my tongue like Xavier had done while pressing my thighs against the horse's sides. Cinnamon started trotting at once. Xavier stayed close by the entire time until Georgia fell back and led her horse alongside us. "Why don't you talk to Willow for a bit?" she suggested to her son.

"Don't interrogate Evie," Xavier muttered before he twitched his thighs and Adobe sped up.

"There's really nothing interesting I could tell you about Xavier, nothing you can't read in every tabloid in the country," I told her when she fell into step beside me.

"I don't care about gossip," she said quietly. For a while she didn't say anything, only let her gaze stray over the surrounding greenery and distant mountains, glowing bluish and gray on the horizon. "This house was up for foreclosure a few years ago."

I slanted her a curious look.

"Marc was still paying off his tuition, and Xavier had only just started playing for his team. There was no way I could have paid off the bank. I had made peace with the fact that I'd lose my home, but Xavier took out a loan to save the estate. Without him I would have lost the farm of my parents and grandparents."

Why was she telling me that? "I know Xavier is a good man. The tabloids report about a side that he allows them to see, a side he wants them to see. But he's much more than that."

She gave a terse nod. "He needs a woman who makes him believe in his goodness."

"It's not like that between Xavier and me. I'm his assistant and friend. He doesn't see me as more than that. I'm not his type, for obvious reasons."

Her eyes did a quick scan of my body. I didn't have to elaborate. We both knew I was about forty pounds and one million sit-ups away from being Xavier's type. "I have eyes, and I know my son," she said cryptically. "I have a feeling you might be the one to crack through his shell."

Xavier prepped the bed of a massive Ford pickup truck, cleaning it of clutter and putting sleeping bags inside. Xavier and I were supposed to head out and watch the stars. Milena had suggested it after we'd returned from the ride, and everyone had been absolutely enthusiastic about the idea, especially Georgia and Willow.

The idea had seemed good at first, but the longer I thought about it the less I was convinced that alone-time with Xavier was safe. Georgia's words had rattled me. That combined with my evolving feelings for Xavier made a romantic adventure seem less desirable, even if it wasn't supposed to be that.

"Ready?" Xavier asked. "We have only about thirty minutes left until sunset."

I nodded and got into the front of the truck. Xavier joined me a moment later and steered the car away from the house. We drove in silence. Xavier had been oddly quiet since our ride, and I wondered why that was. Had his mother said something similar to him? I hoped not. I didn't want her to push us together when it was obvious that Xavier wasn't interested in me that way. And to be honest, I wasn't sure if I should even consider following my feelings at all. Xavier's lifestyle didn't really favor a woman like me at his side.

Xavier eventually stopped the car in the middle of nowhere, and we got out and climbed on the truck bed.

The air was getting surprisingly cold as the sun set, and soon goose bumps covered my skin. My chinos and the thin sweater didn't really keep out the cold. I dragged the sleeping bag up to my chest as I stared up at the night sky in awe. Despite the chill, I could appreciate the sparkling beauty that nature had to offer.

"Are you cold?" Xavier murmured, startling me. He hadn't spoken since we'd left the farm. It was unsettling seeing him so quiet.

"Yeah," I admitted.

Xavier shifted a bit closer and wrapped an arm around me lightly. "I can be your personal space heater." He paused, regarding my face. "Is that okay?" He squeezed my arm.

"Yeah," I said breathlessly. His scent surrounded me and the soft fabric of his jeans shirt brushed my neck. Every nerve ending in my body stood at attention from his proximity.

Xavier was a womanizer. I had seen how he made a move. He was never restrained. Of course, with those women he wanted them in his bed and they made it clear that they wanted to be in his bed too, so he knew his touch was welcome. I supposed it was a good thing that he didn't want me in that way, and even better that he didn't know I wanted what all these women did. "What did my mother want from you? Did she try to meddle?"

It took my brain a heartbeat to process his words. My synapses were on a break. "Nothing important. And no, she didn't." I wasn't sure why I was lying to Xavier because I was almost certain that Georgia had, in fact, tried to meddle.

"That doesn't sound like my mother. Meddling is her favorite pastime when it comes to me."

"That actually sounds a lot like Fiona."

I laughed, peering up at Xavier, and suddenly our faces were too close. Xavier's breath became my breath as we stared at each other. *Pull back.*

But my body was frozen in time and space, because I couldn't stop looking at him, at those gray eyes, at that mouth, which spewed self-assured bullshit half the time but the rest of the time, it said funny and heartwarming bullshit that made my stupid little heart skip a beat. And heaven have mercy, I leaned forward. That was all the encouragement Xavier needed because suddenly there was no air left between us and he kissed me, and there was nothing restrained about Xavier in that moment.

And yet, it wasn't a Xavier kiss, not like the ones I'd witnessed.

Not the let's-get-this shit-going kind, or the this-should-shut-you-up kind. It wasn't impatient. He cupped my cheek and kissed me, consumed me, with his lips and tongue. I was lightheaded from his taste, his warmth, his touch. I had never been kissed like this, not anything close to it, hadn't thought it possible to lose myself in a kiss, in the feel of someone like that.

His other hand touched my back and he pulled us closer until his warmth was everywhere. The fabric of my shirt might as well not have been there at all. My body responded, eager and hungry for his touch. I wanted Xavier. My body did, but so did my heart. What did this mean to him? His palm moved away from my back to my ribs, the touch gentle. I stiffened. I needed to stop this now.

But Xavier did before I could.

When he pulled back, I blinked at him, stunned. Xavier, too, looked almost surprised. For a while neither of us said anything. I cleared my throat and brought a bit more distance between us, but stayed in Xavier's arm because it was too cold to leave his warmth. My eyes were drawn back up to the stunning night sky, trying to get distracted by the sight, trying to ignore the fireworks in my body and the way Xavier was still watching me.

This kiss could ruin everything.

Xavier's warm manly scent clung to me, and I could still taste him on my lips, still feel him. I tried to think of something to say, anything, but my mind drew a complete blank.

Xavier finally looked away and up at the night sky as well. He was tense. My gaze was drawn to his hand, which was resting in his lap, and my eyes grew wide. I jerked my head up. There was an unmistakable bulge in his pants.

I had done that to him.

I, Evie, the dumpling. I had to resist the urge to drag him closer and continue the kissing.

Eventually, Xavier sighed. "Will this make things awkward?"

"We don't need to let it get awkward. We are two adults who can handle the situation in a grown-up way, right?" My voice was strangely rough and breathless.

Xavier glanced my way, and I swallowed. "Yeah," he rasped, and his eyes darted back down to my lips.

Awkwardness galore it was.

"Maybe we should head back," I said. I had a feeling neither Xavier nor I were in a state of mind to make responsible decisions at this point.

He nodded and removed his arm from around me. I quickly slid off the truck bed and walked around the car, my pulse still racing in my veins. Xavier and I didn't talk as we drove back through the darkness.

It only got worse when we entered the dark house. Only Sherlock and Watson greeted us. The rest of the family was probably already in bed. We walked up the stairs together, Xavier close behind me. I could feel his presence and wondered what he saw when he looked at me. A sum of imperfections? Had this kiss been a fluke? Had he been horny and kissed me because there was nobody else around to make a move on? Maybe his family's meddling had gone to his head after all. Whatever had prompted the kiss, it wasn't for the same reasons I had enjoyed it.

I stopped in front of my bedroom door. Xavier was closer than I'd thought, towering over me, staring at me with a look I couldn't read. "Good night," I said quickly, before I did something stupid like ask him in.

"Good night, Evie," Xavier said quietly as I slipped in and closed the door in his face.

I leaned against the door and closed my eyes. What had I done?

Regret over the kiss was only a small part of my feelings, but it was the worst—because more than the kiss, I regretted that I hadn't allowed Xavier to take things further.

XAVIER

I leaned against the wall for several minutes, stunned by what had happened. I'd kissed Evie. I'd kissed so many women, and pretty much every one of my assistants, but for some reason this felt different.

Evie wasn't a girl I'd ever considered my type. Yet Evie's personality would have made her attractive even if she were ugly.

But she was gorgeous, perfect with all her imperfections, and despite her amazing breasts and squeeze-worthy ass, that wasn't the reason why I had kissed her. When I was close to her, silences didn't feel like missed opportunities to leave my mark; they weren't loaded or awkward. We could sit beside each other in comfortable silence, content in each other's company, and moreover, content being ourselves. Fuck, I sounded like a fucking psychological love horoscope.

I dragged myself over to my room, reliving the kiss. Of course, my cock sprang to attention as I remembered Evie's taste, her scent, the breathy moan she'd released, the way her breasts had brushed my arm. I couldn't remember the last time a make-out session had left me this desperate for more, along with the crushing realization that there would never be, could never be.

Evie had kissed me like she meant it, like she too wanted to take things further, but she had stiffened, a fucking wake-up call if I ever needed one. I couldn't sleep with Evie. I didn't want to lose her, and sex would make that outcome inevitable.

Things remained awkward between Evie and me the next morning and of course my family picked up on it, exchanging questioning looks, and whispering behind our backs when they thought Evie and I weren't paying attention.

To my surprise, neither my mother nor Marc or Milena interrogated me about it, but shortly before it was time to leave, Willow used our goodbye to speak her mind. I crouched in front of her, my hands cradling hers as she regarded me with a soft smile. "I really like Evie. She's funny, and nice."

"She is," I agreed, chancing a glance at the rest of my family, who were hugging Evie as if she were the long-lost daughter they couldn't bear leaving.

"Will you bring her over again?"

I sighed, pressed a kiss to Willow's palm and straightened. "I don't know."

"I wish you were dating her."

"I don't date, Willow, and what's more important, I don't discuss my love life with my little sister." I bent down and kissed her forehead to soften my words. Willow clung to my arms, forcing me to meet her eyes. "I'm not a little girl anymore. Being stuck in a wheelchair doesn't mean I don't see things. And I see how you're looking at her, and how she's looking at you."

Willow had a point. I often ignored the fact that she'd soon be a grown-up but she was wrong about everything else. Whatever she saw, it was born of wishful thinking on her part. At least, that's what I told myself as I hugged my sister goodbye.

CHAPTER TWELVE

EVIE

have a feeling that you might be the one to crack through his shell.

I'd occasionally entertained the idea that maybe Georgia's words could be true, that the kiss meant something, that there could be more between Xavier and me.

That proved what kind of idiot I was.

One day after our return, I entered Xavier's apartment only to hear a woman screaming her head off in obvious ecstasy.

That was the answer I wanted and the wake-up call I needed. The kiss we'd shared had meant nothing to him. It shouldn't have mattered because it had only been one kiss. Nothing to write home about, right? But that kiss...the memory still gave my heart palpitations.

For a moment I considered turning around and leaving. He was already awake and knew how to get to training. And maybe he'd forget and be late.

Then the coach would put him on the bench for the next test game. The start of the season was only three weeks away, so he was less tolerant when it came to Xavier's bullshit.

But I was Xavier's assistant and even his friend, and being petty wasn't in my nature, so I turned on the espresso unit so he could finish his business without me overhearing every second of it.

Taking a deep breath, I waited for Xavier to be done with his woman of the night and busied myself sorting through his mail. The only appointment, except for training, was something Xavier had added to the calendar only yesterday evening after he'd dropped me off at home. It said only "W.S. afternoon," and I had no clue what to make of it. But the more pressing problem was that I needed to get Xavier to training in exactly forty minutes, and he was still busy banging his date.

My mouth twisting, I took out the milk and cups, and made myself a cappuccino. I sipped at it when more screaming rang out above, only this time it sounded angry, and a woman stormed onto the landing, half-dressed and looking royally pissed. Usually women left Xavier's bedroom with a dreamy little smile or a look of sick infatuation. The anger came later, when he didn't call them back. "You're an asshole."

He was.

Xavier stepped out of the bedroom, in his white Calvin Kleins, looking like a wet dream come true. "Listen—"

She interrupted him. "What's my name?"

He grimaced.

He rubbed his head, eyes finding me. I had no clue who she was. She wasn't someone I knew from the tabloids, so he couldn't hope for my help in this case. I smiled at him over the rim of my cup as I took a leisurely sip of my coffee.

One corner of his mouth tipped up. He didn't even care that he didn't remember the woman's name.

"You don't remember, right?" she hissed. "I can deal with that, but calling me by a different woman's name? Really? You are a dickhead." The woman stormed down the remaining steps. Xavier followed without hurry. I lifted the lever of the espresso unit and the dark liquid poured into Xavier's cup. I added one cube of sugar how he liked it. It was pretty much the only sugar he allowed in his meal plan.

The woman's eyes landed on me, recognition flashing in her eyes. It was difficult to stay in the background as Xavier's assistant. Her gaze darted from Xavier to me. "Let me guess, you are Evie?"

I frowned. "Yes. I'm Xavier's assistant."

She shook her head, then she left without another word.

"What was that?" I asked, handing Xavier the cup.

He took it. "The usual," he said, then added quickly, "What's on today?"

I paused. Xavier never asked about his appointments on his own accord. He needed ass-kicking and reminding twenty-four-seven. "Training in thirty-five minutes so you need to get your ass moving, and something you marked down as W.S. but I don't know what it is. You never told me."

Xavier downed his coffee and looked almost uncomfortable when he said, "It's short for women's shelter."

"Oh," I murmured. I hadn't expected that. "What do you want there?"

"They asked me to pay them a visit."

"Okay. Who of the press will be there?" I asked, taking out my phone to jot down the names and gather information on them. I needed to make sure Xavier didn't say something politically incorrect. I was actually surprised he'd come up with the idea to improve his image by visiting such a facility. It wasn't his usual style.

"No press," Xavier muttered. He put down the cup without another word and headed back upstairs to get ready, I supposed. He emerged ten minutes later in his training attire. His expression was closed off, so I didn't bug him about the women's shelter despite my curiosity. Maybe he was still pissed because of the incident with his conquest, though usually that never got to him.

Once we were in Xavier's car, I asked, "Will you go alone to the shelter?"

Xavier shook his head slowly as he steered the car onto the street. "I want you to come with me."

"Okay," I said. Somehow this was a big deal for him.

We made it to training with five minutes to spare. Coach Brennan came toward me and gave me a high five like he'd done every day for the last couple of weeks. "Seven weeks on time. That's a new record. You deserve a prize, young lady."

"She's allowed to see my pretty face every day. That's a prize if there ever was one," Xavier drawled as he threw the rugby ball from one hand to the other.

I rolled my eyes at him, then smiled at the coach. "I deserve accolades from the queen, if you ask me."

Brennan laughed. "I love her."

Xavier regarded me with slightly narrowed eyes, still playing with the ball. Then Connor bumped into him, and the two of them began shoving each other in jest.

Xavier was oddly quiet on our way to the women's shelter in the afternoon. These strange silences had become more frequent, and not just since the kiss.

"Why isn't the press invited to this?" I asked. "If you'd let me know in advance, I could have arranged something. You could really use that kind of positive publicity Xavier."

"It's nobody's business what I do in my spare time."

I huffed. "Xavier, you flout pretty much every aspect of your life for everyone to see. People know about your women, your party escapades, your morning, training and evening routines."

He parked the car in a narrow side street in Yennora, a suburb of Sydney where I'd never been, apparently one of the poorest neighborhoods in the region. Many of the houses were run down, and Xavier's car drew unnecessary attention toward us. "That's business."

I tilted my head. His family had never been in the press. He hadn't even mentioned them in interviews except for very general references. "How are your sexcapades business?"

Xavier grinned cockily. "They keep me on everyone's lips."

The way he said it held more than a little innuendo.

Of course he couldn't leave it at that. "And in everyone's mouth."

I snorted. "You *are* a dickhead."

That wolfish grin twisted my insides into a spitfire-hot knot. "I'm giving people what they want. The press, women, even the team's marketing people."

"And what is it you want?" I asked curiously.

Xavier didn't say anything, only stared out of the windshield, leaving me to stare at his striking profile. My fingers itched to reach out and rake my nails over the dark stubble. The air became stuffy and hot inside the car. I shook the collar of my blouse to cool down. Xavier's eyes darted down to my chest. I released the fabric, swallowed, and met his intent gaze. "We should get out. It's getting too hot."

Xavier's mouth twitched and I narrowed my eyes at him, but then quickly got out of the car before things could get even hotter.

I glanced around. There wasn't a sign anywhere that hinted to a women's shelter, but I supposed that was necessary for protection. "Are you sure this is the right address?" I asked.

Xavier nodded. "I've been here twice before."

As if on cue, a door in the three-story house in front of us swung open and a small, round woman with salt-and-pepper hair in a pixie cut stepped out. Like the other houses in the street the paint was peeling off the front and the dumpsters were spilling over.

Xavier headed toward her and shook her hand. "This is my friend Evie, as I mentioned in my call."

The woman nodded and greeted me with a firm shake of her hand.

She led us through the shelter, which was organized like a residential community with a common living room and kitchen, and several bedrooms for the women and their children. The inside was in a much better condition than the outside. "I can't show you all the rooms because some women don't want to be seen by anyone. They are worried."

Xavier nodded. "I know. You don't have to show me everything."

"We want to make sure you see that your money has been used to do good, Mr. Stevens. We don't get nearly enough support through government funds, so without your money we couldn't have done this renovation. There are so many women who need a safe place, and we appreciate that you help us give it to them."

Xavier nodded, but didn't say anything. It was surprising to see him this... serious. We moved into the communal part of the shelter with a huge kitchen and several dining tables. A few women and children had gathered in the room. I had to stifle a gasp when I noticed a woman whose face was swollen, her skin red and blue, one arm in a cast. Two girls were with her. The older of the two had a bruise on her cheek. My heart clenched tightly seeing it, but Xavier's reaction drew my attention toward him. He looked murderous. I had never seen that kind of anger on his face. His expression changed the second the girls turned to him, becoming gentle and kind.

The older girl rushed toward Xavier, a book clutched to her chest. He got down on his haunches at once as she smiled shyly at him and held out a friendship book. "Can you write in it?"

Xavier's eyes flickered to the bruise on her cheek and he gave her a gentle smile. "Sure. It's my pleasure." He took it and she stepped close to his side, wringing her hands nervously. "What's your name?"

"Millie. Emilia. But my friends call me Millie," she said. My heart burst with warmth seeing Xavier's kind expression, the way he made himself small for this little girl.

He could be the biggest egocentric, arrogant prick sometimes, but for this I would cut him some slack in the future. And damn, if the sight didn't set my heart and panties aflame all over again.

———— ◆◆◆ ————

A few days after the shelter visit, Xavier and I found ourselves at his dining-room table, where we went through a few interview requests as well as two advertising contracts, one for some fancy protein powder, the other for a new razor. Considering that Xavier almost always sported dark stubble, I found the choice curious, but they paid enough that Xavier would survive a thorough shave for once. It was approaching six o'clock when we were finally done.

"I need a relaxing evening and tomorrow's no training, so how about a movie night?" Xavier asked, sounding nonchalant. There hadn't been any cozy evenings between us since the truck bed incident.

"I'm up for it," I said with a smile. I wanted things between Xavier and me to return to how they were before the unfortunate kiss. We were grown-ups and the kiss had been a slip in judgment, nothing more.

Xavier seemed to have forgotten all about it, after all. He had already kissed God only knew how many women since then, though I was probably the only one whose name he remembered.

"What movie do you have in mind?" I asked as I slid down from the barstool and shook out my stiff legs. This had been a long day. Most days with Xavier were, but they never felt like a chore.

"Today I thought we could go for a classic. *Alien*," Xavier said, cocking an eyebrow challengingly.

"*Alien*?"

"Or is it too bloody for you?"

I snorted and patted his shoulder. "Bloody is right up my alley, as you should know by now."

"Still difficult to believe there's a woman out there who doesn't enjoy dramas and chick-flicks."

"I resent that name," I muttered. "And I have enjoyed the occasional drama or chick-flick, like *The Color Purple* or *The Devil Wears Prada*, but I prefer action to sappy romance or tearjerkers." I pulled my sweater over my head because it was simply too warm. Xavier's eyes scanned my tank top and I resisted the urge to cover up again.

Xavier shook his head again, watching me with an expression I had trouble reading. Deciding not to bother before I ended up misinterpreting it, I grabbed a bottle of water and moved toward the sofa where I made myself comfortable.

"What's for dinner, honey?" I piped as I threw my nylons-clad feet up on Xavier's table.

Xavier shook his head, but the same strange expression remained on his face. "How about burgers?"

"Sure. I'm taking whatever you're having," I called, then turned the TV on.

Xavier, of course, didn't order just any kind of burger. He ordered a keto-friendly burger without bread with a side of avocado fries and salad from some organic café around the corner. He came over with the low-carb non-alcoholic beer I'd grown used to when I was in his apartment. Craft beers were almost never allowed in his strict diet, much to my disappointment.

"Of the two of us, I eat like the man," I muttered, accepting the bottle from him.

Xavier chuckled. "I need to reduce my carb intake and up my protein if I don't want to sport a paunch soon." He clapped the six-pack that even his shirt couldn't hide.

I narrowed my eyes. "Yeah, you're really getting plump around the middle." I shook my head. "Just so you know, I'm offended on behalf of all less than perfect people on this planet."

Xavier sat down beside me, his arm brushing mine. "First of all, my body is my capital. And second, you are perfect in your own way."

I paused with the bottle against my mouth, my eyes darting to him. Had he really just said that? And what the hell did it mean?

Xavier was frowning at the TV as he searched for the movie. How could he just return to acting normal after saying something like that? He could go right back to screwing random girls after kissing me, so why was I even surprised?

He started the movie, and soon any kind of awkwardness was forgotten. "That's my favorite scene!" I gushed when the first alien burst out of a chest, splattering blood everywhere.

Xavier closed his eyes with his deep rumble of laughter. "Evie, something's seriously wrong with you."

"What?" I said, only half offended. "You were the one who suggested we watch *Alien*."

His eyes opened, full of amusement and warmth. "How many times have you watched the series?"

"The first three movies about ten times each, the others only once. They aren't as good as the old movies if you ask me, and don't get me started on *Alien vs. Predator*."

Xavier nodded, but I wasn't even sure he had listened to a word I'd said. His eyes lowered to my mouth, but the ringing of the doorbell spared us another misfortune. I paused the movie while Xavier headed for the door to get our food. He returned a couple of minutes later with the compostable food bags that contained equally compostable boxes with our burgers.

Only the salad was served in a plastic box, but that too was probably biodegradable to some degree. I shook my head with a small smile. Xavier handed me my box. The two meat patties were sandwiched in grilled portobello mushroom halves. "To think that I'd ever eat burgers without bread," I murmured as I took a big bite.

Xavier had already wolfed down half of his burger, plus it was already his second burger. "Admit it, they are delicious."

"They are," I agreed, "but I still like bread."

"I like bread too, but it's full of empty carbs and doesn't sustain the body for long."

I fell back against the backrest and groaned. "You and Fiona could have been the dream couple if you didn't hate each other's guts so much."

"I don't hate her guts. She's annoying. And I don't want your sister. We don't have anything in common except for our dietary convictions."

I took another bite from the burger, then snatched up an avocado stick and dipped it in the spicy dip. "That's more than many other couples do."

Xavier frowned. "You and I have far more in common."

He said it matter-of-factly, but it wreaked havoc on my insides.

"We do," I agreed. "We're like brother and sister without the bickering."

Xavier gave me a disbelieving look.

"Okay. With more bickering."

"I don't see you as a sister, trust me, Evie," Xavier muttered.

I paused with an avocado fry against my lips. It slipped to the side, smearing the corner of my mouth with dip. I stared at Xavier. *Blink. Blink.* He reached out and brushed the stain away and my lips in the process, then put his finger in his mouth with a look in his eyes I had never seen directed at me. *Blink. Blink.* Ovary-explosion-in-process.

He drew his eyes back to the TV and turned the movie back on, as if I could still focus on an alien going rampage after what just happened. Xavier didn't share my troubles, obviously, because he leaned back against the sofa, cool as a cucumber, low-carb beer perched on his muscled stomach, and stared intently at the screen.

I put the avocado fry back into its box and took a deep gulp of cold beer, trying to make sense of his words and actions, but as usual drawing a complete blank. Deciding to play it cool and get a grip on my hormones, I relaxed against the backrest, and focused on the movie. Sometime close to the end, Xavier stretched his arms out to both sides of him as he often did, but this time the presence of his muscled biceps so close to my shoulder blades was the additional distraction I really didn't need.

I glanced down at myself, making sure I didn't sport a muffin top over my skirt, then shifted slightly so my legs looked leaner.

"Everything all right?" Xavier asked curiously.

"Sure," I said, and finally accepted that no matter what position I adopted it wouldn't make me look like the size-zero models Xavier usually took to his bed.

When the closing credits rolled down the screen, I considered faking exhaustion and leaving quickly, but then Xavier spoke up.

"My mother tried to get into a women's shelter with us when I was a kid," he murmured.

I turned to him, caught off guard by this admission. "Because of your father?"

He had never mentioned him, but it had become apparent that the man was a dark presence in his family's life.

Xavier nodded. I didn't push him. It was obvious that he wasn't going to divulge more information for now. For some reason I wanted to stroke his chin, feel the stubble there, and press a kiss to his cheek to show him I appreciated that he allowed me to see this side of him.

"Only Marc knows I'm helping shelters," he continued in the same detached voice.

I bit my lip and touched his shoulder. "Thank you for letting me be part of this. It means a lot to me."

He nodded, twisting his body away from the screen and toward me. His arm on the backrest shifted and his fingertips lightly grazed my bare shoulder. I wasn't sure if he did it on purpose, but he definitely didn't pull them away. I exhaled, shivering, my body exploding with heat under the soft touch.

Xavier leaned forward, bringing us even closer. He cupped my face, eyes locked on mine, his fingers sliding into my hair. I held my breath, and then his lips were on mine, softly, questioningly.

And I responded to his kiss, my body coming alive with a rush of adrenaline and longing. I moved closer, gripped his shirt, needing to feel his heat and strength. I'd wanted this for so long, still wanted it after that first taste on the truck bed.

Xavier's kiss became less restrained, demanding, all-consuming.

His hands roamed my back and sides, stroking and tugging, and I had trouble keeping up, even as my own hands tore at his clothes. I had never felt like this, never longed for someone with such abandon.

Xavier's hand slipped under my tank top, and before I could clamp up with worry, he cupped my breast through my bra. He groaned against my mouth and

I kissed him even harder, trying to match his eagerness and skill. Good Lord. That man.

"This is a bad idea," I whispered between kisses as I slid my hands under his shirt and over Xavier's stomach, feeling the hard lines, the soft hairs. His skin constricted under my touch.

"It is," he agreed before his mouth latched down on my throat, finding a point that I could feel right between my thighs. His fingers cupped my nipple, and he gave the smallest twirl that had me moaning wantonly into his mouth. I didn't know my breasts were this sensitive, much less that I could make these sounds.

He pulled back and removed his shirt, and I was done for. I knew it then. His lips reclaimed my mouth and his finger my nipple. I pressed my thighs together, needing friction. His eyes flashed up to my burning face. "I want you," he rasped.

I didn't know how long I'd wished for those words, and they tore down my last wall, obliterated my final sliver of doubt. "Then take me," I whispered, a thrill shooting through me.

Xavier growled against my mouth. "Upstairs."

I nodded, half delirious with want, half terrified. Xavier pulled me to my feet and kissed me again. Somehow we stumbled our way upstairs, kissing and touching.

The glow from downstairs was the only light source, for which I was glad when Xavier pulled my tank top over my head, leaving me in my bra. I didn't get the chance for worry because his hands were already on my skirt, opening it quicker than I had ever managed, and then his mouth was back on mine and his fingers slipped into my panties.

Oh holy mother of goodness.

Xavier groaned deeply when his fingers glided between my folds. "Good Lord, Evie, you are so fucking wet."

Nobody had ever touched me there. I didn't get the chance for embarrassment, because Xavier began stroking the small nub that soon became the focus of my existence. I gasped into his mouth. He drew back to watch me and I ducked my head, my cheeks heating. My hand brushed his bulge curiously and it seemed to be the last straw, because Xavier helped me out of my skirt and nylons and backed me up toward the bed, removing my bra in the process. I fell back, and he was out of his pants and completely, breathtakingly naked before I had time to process anything.

His mouth was hot on my knee as he kissed my skin, then his fingers gripped my panties and pulled them down.

At the back of my mind, I realized I should warn him. Not just for myself, but also because maybe he would like to know. But then Xavier molded his strong body to mine for a kiss that obliterated any sane thought.

CHAPTER THIRTEEN

EVIE

His kisses were heat and power. I could hardly keep up. His hands roamed my sides and back until he cupped my ass and squeezed, his fingers deliciously close to where I ached. I gasped into his mouth.

He sat back, reached for something. In the dim light from downstairs I made out a flat bright red wrapper. A condom.

This was really happening.

He made quick work of the condom package, ripping it open with a tug of teeth. With practiced ease, he rolled it down his erection; he was long and thick, good God.

Tomorrow morning I'd be just another girl he'd banged. Another notch on his belt. I'd watched him kick one woman after the other out of his bed. The only difference was that tomorrow morning, no assistant would be waiting to write down my number, only to delete it moments later.

Xavier.

My undoing.

He climbed back on top of me, muscles flexing, expression hungry and eager like that of a famished wolf. His weight felt perfect on top of me, like it was meant to be.

But this meant nothing to him. One fuck like thousands before. In and out. Then he moved on.

"I've wanted to do this for a very long time," he rasped.

I caught his gaze. It was hungry, eager, possessive. What did this mean to him? I wasn't someone he could ignore after the deed. I was his assistant. But would that even bother him? Fiona had said that his last few assistants had left exactly for that reason. He'd fucked them and then moved on. But was I even only his assistant? It hadn't felt like that to me in the last few weeks.

He positioned himself between my thighs. All muscle and glory. That man was too gorgeous for words. He could have any girl and he knew it; he *enjoyed* it. Why would he want someone like me?

He supported himself on one arm, gripped my hip with his free hand, then pressed his tip against my opening. His gaze was intense, full of desire.

Evie, last chance.

The words climbed up my throat.

Xavier shifted his hips, thrusting forward, but he didn't get very far.

My butt arched off the bed, my fingers digging into the bed linens. I squeezed my eyes shut, trying to breathe through the pain. Good God. My muscles clamped down on his erection, my body obviously very averse to taking him in.

Xavier froze. "Evie," he whispered. Suddenly he shifted, causing a sharp pain that had me wincing. The overhead lights came on and I blinked to get accustomed to their bright glare.

I peeled my eyes open. Xavier was propped up above me, perfectly still, perfectly handsome. Almost too perfect to bear. His gaze bored into mine, searching, confused, incredulous. I'd never seen that look on his face.

"What—" he began. "Tell me this isn't..."

His gray eyes looked almost like they were begging me. For what exactly?

He shifted slightly, and I released a pained breath. So far losing my V-card wasn't what people made it out to be.

"Fuck," he breathed out before he lowered himself slowly, upper arms flexing, and pressed his face into the pillow beside my head. He was still in me, but his hips weren't pressed up against mine. He definitely wasn't all the way in yet. *Size matters.* I had to agree. But right now small would have been my preferred choice. Of course, nothing about Xavier was small.

I lay unmoving beneath him, not sure what to do. He wasn't moving either, only breathing harshly into the pillow beside me. I was pretty sure this wasn't how he usually went about sex with girls. I waited a few seconds but was starting to feel awkward.

"Xavier?" I asked quietly, embarrassed.

"Hmm," came his muffled reply. Slowly he lifted his head. "You should have told me," he said, voice and eyes full of regret.

"Why? It's not as if it matters."

He smiled like I'd made a joke only he was in on. "You know it does."

"So what," I said quietly. "You took my virginity. It had to happen at some point."

The words sounded almost like they were true. But my heart told a different story. Perhaps Xavier could see it, because he shook his head. "I haven't yet. Only my tip is in. And it's up against your barrier." He grimaced. "That's what I think. You are getting tighter and I'm nowhere near in so it has to be your hymen, or I don't know... Fuck."

133

Was Xavier rambling? "Oh," I said uncertainly. "That's a lot of pain for so little progress."

Xavier let out a laugh. He pressed a kiss against my temple. "God, Evie, still joking in a situation like this."

He pushed himself up on his arms, and began pulling out. I dug my fingers into his shoulders. "What are you doing?" I asked incredulously. I hadn't come this far to have him backpedal.

He gave me a look like I'd lost my freaking mind. "I'm not going to go any farther. I'm not the guy that should pop your cherry."

I hated that wording. I tightened my hold. "Don't you dare stop now," I said fiercely. He frowned at me.

"You're already inside of me. What does a couple more inches matter?"

"More than a couple inches. You saw me naked," he said cockily.

I snorted.

Then he became serious again, his voice low and compelling. "Evie, you can't want this."

Anger surged through me. "You mean you don't want this now that you've turned on the light and can see all of me." My lower lip began to tremble. *To tremble.* I wanted to slap myself.

Xavier looked like he had no clue what the fuck I was talking about. "Don't be ridiculous."

I tried to roll away, but with him over me and his erection still in me, that was impossible. "Of course. Why would anyone want to bang the poor fat little virgin, especially Xavier, the Beast, Stevens?"

His mouth came down on my lips hard, silencing me. His tongue thrust into my mouth, shutting me up in the best way possible. After a moment of surprise, I kissed him back fiercely. And then he lowered himself, his muscled chest pressing against my breasts. He cupped my head with his palms, caging me in with his forearms. He kissed my ear, murmuring. "I hope you won't come to regret this, Evie, like I will."

I didn't get the chance to consider his words because he pressed his hips forward. The pressure inside of me became close to unbearable. He looked down at my face, an intense look on his own. My gaze locked on his, on the gentler, concerned note in his gray eyes.

I dug my fingernails deeper into his shoulders, but he didn't even wince. He kept slowly pushing deeper into me until I could feel my body yielding to his pressure, and then he slid all the way in. The air left my lungs in a whoosh. It hurt like hell.

He kissed my temple, then my forehead. My heart fluttered at the gentle gesture, so unlike the Xavier of the tabloids. Our bodies were flush together. He was so strong and powerful, for once making me feel small and delicate, and not like the dumpling that I was. I wanted to tell him that I'd fallen for him many movie nights ago. "I really wish your Maserati were a compensation for your penis size," I said, out of breath.

He chuckled. "Sorry, Evie. I don't need to compensate for anything."

As if I didn't know it. I winced again. His thumb stroked my cheek, lightly, almost lovingly. "Tell me when it's okay for me to move."

I wasn't sure if that would ever be the case. My body definitely wasn't in favor of movement.

"You're making a face as if you're trying to solve a complicated equation. This is sex, not Sudoku."

I huffed. "You are not being split in two."

His expression softened. "That bad, hmm?"

That look on his face—it was worth the pain.

"I've had better experiences."

"With whom?" he asked harshly.

I frowned. "Not like that. You were the first guy to get to second base. And the few kisses I've had, had been more disturbing than memorable."

"You Americans and your bases," he said with a grin, then lowered his voice. "No guy ever touched your wonderful tits?"

"That's the thing that caught your attention?" I asked indignantly.

His eyes travelled over my upper body in apparent awe. Heat rose into my cheeks.

"They are marvelous," he said reverently.

I started laughing, and slowly the tension in my core loosened. I fell silent. Again, stunned by the man above me—*inside me*. "You can move," I said quietly.

And he did. He was slow and gentle, as if we had all the time in the world. He never took his eyes off my face even when his own became more and more strained. I could have watched him forever, if there hadn't been the little issue of pain. Xavier didn't falter in his thrusts, and when he reached between us and his fingers found my sweet spot, some of the pain disappeared. I wasn't sure how long he could continue, but his stamina was admirable. Eventually, I dared to whisper, "Can you come?"

Xavier's brows snapped together. "I want you to come first."

Admirable but unrealistic. "I don't think I can come," I got out, flushing.

Xavier faltered in his thrusts. "That bad? Should I stop?"

"I want to see you come," I admitted.

"I don't want to hurt you worse."

"Please, Xavier."

Something in his eyes shifted, something that filled my chest with warmth.

He kissed me lightly. "I'll be quick. I'm not going to last much longer if I let loose. You're too fucking tight." He sped up a bit, his thrusts hitting deeper than before.

I clung to his neck. "Come."

By now, he was moving faster and harder than my body was happy about, but I wanted to see him come. I didn't think I'd ever wanted anything more.

And then he finally tensed, his head falling forward as he jerked inside of me. Sweat trickled down his chest. I slid my fingers through the fine dark hairs there, over the steel of his muscles. He breathed out, his stomach flexing. He stayed like that for a while, and I couldn't help but feel a stupid sense of triumph that a man like him wanted me.

He pulled out and let himself fall to the bed beside me before he slid his hand under my waist and pulled me toward him like I weighed nothing. I pressed my face into his chest, marveling at the hammering of his heart, at his musky scent.

I was utterly and completely in love.

And the throbbing between my legs was joined by another pain, a hollow sensation in my chest, because Xavier didn't do love. He didn't even date. He fucked and rucked. Everyone knew it.

"Are you all right?" Xavier asked in a deep after-sex rumble I'd never heard before, a voice like warm honey and crisp autumn leaves.

My throat tightened.

Xavier tensed. "Evie?"

"I'm fine," I said quietly but firmly.

Xavier drew back, probably to look at my face, but I pressed my cheek harder against his chest, scared my feelings for him would be plain as day.

"I want to see your face," he murmured. His voice had a quality to it I didn't recognize. My curiosity won out and I finally lifted my head.

Xavier's dark brows were drawn together, his short hair mussed up, and guilt shone in his eyes. He had no reason to feel guilty. Everything between us had been my choice. He didn't say anything, only searched my face, and I let him. I took my time admiring him, the dark stubble ghosting his strong jaw and sharp cheekbones, the piercing gray of his eyes like a summer sky before an impending storm, those kissable lips capable of the most infuriating smirk in the history of humankind. Love hadn't been part of the plan.

"Did I hurt you?" he asked quietly. His worry upped my emotions, and it took considerable effort to keep it from showing on my face.

"It's getting better." I had a feeling the real hurt was yet to come, in the morning, when the harsh reality smacked me in the face. "Can we go to sleep now?"

He nodded but the look of regret and guilt remained, and I knew why: he, too, was thinking of the next morning.

I kissed Xavier once, lightly, sweetly, then rested my cheek against his firm chest. He shifted and the lights went out. It took me a while to feel tired, and even longer to fall asleep.

CHAPTER FOURTEEN

EVIE

Sunshine tickled my face. I opened my eyes, staring out at a familiar skyline, at the blue late-summer sky over the harbor bridge. I knew at once where I was and the soreness reminded me what had happened. I'd been here too many mornings picking up the pieces after Xavier was done with his latest conquest.

And now I was that conquest, only nobody would tell me beautiful lies. The bed shifted under someone's weight. He was still here?

Hope flooded me. Slowly, I rolled over until I faced his direction.

His back was turned toward me, ripped and broad. Glorious muscles. I fought the urge to run my fingertips over them. I licked my lips, wondering what to say. Too many thoughts whirled in my head.

I was glad that I didn't find words before Xavier turned around to me. His expression silenced any romantic nonsense I'd wanted to utter.

I was one of *those* girls.

The girls I'd pitied for being stupid enough to think they could finally be the one for Xavier. The one to change his Casanova ways. Hadn't Xavier himself ridiculed their idiotic hopes?

Good lord, I was a stupid cow.

Xavier's eyes were guarded, and worse: guilty. He didn't say anything, didn't have to. I knew how this usually went, had been there to usher the girls out or see Xavier practically push them out. I wouldn't let it come to that. I wanted to salvage the little bit of dignity I still had. I slid out of bed, pulling the blankets with me. I couldn't bear the idea of Xavier seeing my imperfectness in the bright morning light.

Wrapping the blanket around my body, I began picking up my clothes from the floor, then quickly left the bedroom and headed for the guest bathroom downstairs. My first walk of shame.

I didn't bother with a shower. I needed to get out of Xavier's apartment as fast as possible. My composure was hanging on a thread.

I stepped into my skirt, dragging it up over my too wide hips. Then my nylons ripped as I tried to pull them up. I dropped them in the garbage bin, and tugged my tank top and sweater over my head. I slid into my pumps before I hurried out of the bathroom. Xavier was standing in his open kitchen, two cups of coffee in front of him, his eyes following me with that horrible guilty look in them.

If he thought I was having awkward post-coitus coffee with him, he had lost his mind. It was obvious that he wasn't sure how to let me down easily. I was his assistant after all, and not some stranger he could give a fake phone number to. I considered saying something like "thanks for the night" or "good lay," but I knew I wouldn't be able to pull it off.

Instead I snatched my purse from the sofa and practically fled the apartment without another word. I wasn't sure if I could ever face him again.

XAVIER

Evie escaped from my apartment as if the devil was after her. There really was no other way to describe it. I couldn't deny it: I was relieved. I rubbed my temple. Last night was a huge fucking mistake. Not my first and definitely not my last, but perhaps the one I'd come to regret the most.

I got up and went upstairs into the bedroom. I needed to grab a shower. My eyes landed on the white sheets. I stopped. "Fuck," I said at the not-so-white sheets. Evie was the funniest woman I knew. She was the best assistant I'd ever had. The first female friend. And I had listened to my fucking dick and popped her cherry.

She knew me. She knew I didn't date. Then why was I feeling like the biggest asshole in the world?

She *knew* me. Maybe this was just sex for her, an easy way to get rid of her V-card. Fuck. Evie was a friend. She was...more than that: my conscience and ass saver. And even that still felt too inadequate a description for what Evie meant to me.

The sound of a key being turned gave me a burst of hope as I hurried to the landing, but it disappeared when I saw Nancy come in to clean the apartment.

It was my day off, nothing scheduled for the day except for training with Connor in the afternoon, but I felt restless.

Nancy came upstairs and gave me a curt nod in greeting. She was one of the least talkative women I knew. As usual she moved toward the bed first to strip it and do laundry. She paused, eyes going from the red spot to me.

"Evie is a good woman," was all she said. I wasn't sure how she knew. "She came out of your apartment looking like she'd seen a ghost. What have you done now, Xavier?"

That was a guilt trip I didn't need. I moved into the bathroom and got into the shower, needing to clear my mind. If Nancy didn't want to see my meat she'd just have to clean with closed eyes, damn it.

———— ◆◆◆ ————

I hauled my ass over to the gym. Connor and I wanted to do weights. Of course, I spotted Fiona with him, sitting on his lap in the waiting area of the gym. She was already dressed in street clothes, so she wouldn't bother us during our session.

"Hey," I said.

"Hey, dickhead," Fiona said with a roll of her eyes. Connor smiled as if she'd told the joke of a lifetime.

"Can I ask you something about your sister Evie?" I asked as I put my gym bag down on the floor, stopping a few steps from them—safety distance.

Fiona gave me a questioning look. "You're not her type."

"You don't even know what I was going to ask," I muttered. "And I am her type. I'm every woman's type."

Fiona shook her head. "You aren't my type, Xavier."

Ignoring her usual bitchiness, I said, "Is your sister the no-strings-attached kind of girl?"

She chortled with laughter. "Get that idea out of your head quickly, Xavier," she said. "Evie is the waiting-for-the-love-of-her-life kind of girl. She won't spread her legs for anyone but a guy she's in love with."

Where was a bottle of whisky when you needed it? I had feared it might be the case. Deep down I had maybe even known it.

She froze, eyes going wide, then she rose slowly.

Connor gave me an are-you-raving-mad look as he glanced between his girlfriend and me.

Shit was about to hit the fan.

"Oh no," Fiona said, laughing uncertainly. "Don't tell me..." She fell silent, scanning my face. She shook her head. "You *didn't.*"

"You make it sound like I had to force her. She was more than willing, believe me."

Stupid mouth.

Fiona lost her shit. She threw her purse at me, which I dodged. It hit a guy behind me but Fiona didn't care. She staggered toward me. I didn't bother trying to get away. I probably deserved whatever ass kicking she had prepared.

"You can have every girl, but couldn't you have kept it in your pants in that one case? This isn't some joke, Xavier. Evie deserves better. I hope your horniness was worth hurting the nicest person you'll ever meet."

I stayed silent. There was no cool comment on my lips. Evie *was* the nicest girl I knew, and the only one whose snarky comments had almost made beer shoot out of my nose.

She shook her head again, in disgust this time. "I'm going to pick up the pieces of your selfishness, you bastard, because for once, Evie can't do it."

Fiona pushed past me, snatched her purse from the floor and rushed out of the gym without another backwards glance.

When she was gone, I looked at Connor. "She makes it sound like I'm the only one who's messed up. Evie is my assistant. She knows me."

"Everyone knows," Connor agreed as he stood. "The press reports about it every day."

I slung my gym bag over my shoulder. "See. She knew what she got herself into."

Connor shrugged. I wished he wasn't giving me that disappointed look, as if I'd broken his stupid little heart.

It's not his heart you've broken.

"What?" I asked angrily.

"She knew you threw away the attention groupies and the it-girls. But you spent almost every day with her. You introduced her to your family. You had movie nights with her."

"I introduced her as my assistant!"

"You never have before with other assistants." Connor sighed and gripped his gym bag. "Know what, mate, I don't care. I only know that I'll have to live with a fucking mad Fiona for the next few days while you're probably going to fuck the next girl tonight."

"Nobody forces you to be with Fiona."

He gave me a condescending smile. "See, that's what you don't understand. While Fiona drives me up the walls half the time, the other half she makes me the happiest I've ever been."

I rolled my eyes. I'd liked him better before Fiona. "Did you know that Evie was a virgin?"

Connor grimaced. "Fiona mentioned it to me."

"And you didn't tell me?"

"Mate, why would I talk about Evie's virginity to you, or anyone for that matter?"

I nodded.

"To be honest, I didn't think you'd make a move on her."

"Yeah, well, you were wrong."

"Obviously." He shook his head. "Trust you to fuck anything as long as it has a pussy."

"Careful," I growled.

A slow grin spread on Connor's face. "Are you being protective of Evie?"

"We're here to do weights, not gossip," I said, tightening my hold on my bag and moving past Connor before his annoying expression made me want to punch him.

EVIE

A key turned in the lock.

I didn't move from my spot on the sofa, nor did I look up from the empty bucket of ice cream in my lap, chocolate chip with cookie dough. I was about to start the second bucket, even though I was already feeling pretty sick. Heels clicked on the hardwood floor as Fiona walked over to me and sank down beside me, carrying a bag with another bucket of ice cream and a bag of chips. She knew me too well.

She regarded me and I knew she knew. "How did you find out?" I croaked.

"Came across the ass hat in the gym."

I cringed. "And he told you?"

"He asked if you were the no-strings-attached kind of girl. I threw my purse at him."

She stroked my head, then she reached over, grabbing the ice cream bucket and stealing my spoon before shoving a spoonful into her mouth. My eyebrows shot up. She took another spoon before offering a spoonful to me.

"I must be a pitiful sight if you'll forget about carbs and risk your size zero," I said jokingly. My voice was scratchy from crying for hours.

Fiona shoved another spoonful into her mouth, almost defiantly, then spoke with ice cream in her mouth. I couldn't remember the last time Fiona had displayed such an unladylike behavior. "Who cares about carbs?"

And then the tears came again. "I'm such a stupid cow, Fiona."

"I know," Fiona said quietly, putting the bucket aside and wrapping her arm around my shoulder.

I gave her a look.

"You are," she said affectionately. "How could you let that dickhead get so close, and worse, his dick?"

"I don't know. It just happened. He can be so funny and caring and gentle."

"But he can also be the biggest womanizing egocentric asshole in the world, Evie. And you know it. Hell, you've seen him do all kind of assholey things. You complained to me about all of them."

"I know." But he'd never been like that to me. Until now. For some reason I'd thought things could be different between us.

"It's my fault. I shouldn't have asked you to become his assistant. But I didn't think he'd make a move toward you."

I pulled back, realizing something. "You thought he wouldn't make a move because he didn't do fat girls, right?"

Guilt flashed across Fiona's face. "You aren't fat," she said.

"Don't sugarcoat it. I'm nowhere near a size zero."

Not for lack of trying, by God. Deep down I wondered why Xavier had slept with me at all. I couldn't blame it on an alcohol-induced slip in judgment because we had only drunk non-alcoholic beer. Maybe he'd wanted to find out how it was to bang a curvy girl.

"I'm sorry, Evie. I'm a bitch."

I nodded. She hugged me. "Do me a favor: forget him. Move on. There are so many decent men out there that will treat you right."

As if it was that easy. "I don't think I can," I said miserably. "And I'm his personal assistant. I have to face him every day. I don't think I can bear seeing him with another girl again."

"Then quit. You'll find a new job. Give him your three-week notice and let him continue his shitty life. With a little luck, he'll get a bad case of syphilis and his dick falls off."

"There's a clause in my contract that I can't leave until I've found him a suitable assistant or six months have passed."

"It can't be that hard to find a new assistant for him."

"Last time you had to get me from the States because all the respectable assistants wanted nothing to do with him."

"Well, then he'll have to settle for a lousy assistant. That's not your problem."

I sighed. If this had been only sex, maybe then it could have worked but for me at least, emotions had been involved.

"Come on, let's watch one of the horrible splatter movies you're into," she said, turning on the TV. "Just let me put the ice cream in the freezer since you already have two buckets."

I nodded and leaned back. Fiona returned, wrapping an arm around me. Turning on the TV, we watched in silence for a long time until I got tired of the itchiness of my skin that reminded me too much of last night. "I should grab a shower. I didn't want to do it in Xavier's penthouse this morning."

Fiona wrinkled her nose. "You should have told me that you still have Xavier all over you, then I would have put on gloves hugging you," she said teasingly. I shoved her and she fell back with a smile.

My own lips pulled into a small grin. Trust Fiona to make me feel better. She'd always been good at consoling me. When people had teased me for my weight in school, she'd let me cry on her shoulder, and later kicked their asses.

I got up and winced. God, it hurt like a bitch. Fiona gave me an understanding look. "Sore?"

"Yeah," I said, embarrassed.

Fiona got up. "I can't believe you lost your V-card to that asshole."

"I'm already in pain, do you need to add fuel to the fire?"

"That bad?" she asked, then shrugged. "I mean you kind of deserve it."

I rolled my eyes.

Her eyes hardened, turning protective. "Was he being an inconsiderate asshole?"

"He didn't know."

"Yeah well, doesn't mean he has to act like a caveman."

"Fiona, I really don't want to talk about it, but he was really careful after he figured it out."

"Then why are you so sore?"

I cocked an eyebrow in Xavier's manner. "I don't have to compensate for anything." Even just imitating him sent a stab into my heart.

"Oh man, I'm going to announce my entrance next time," Connor muttered.

Our heads whirled around. He was leaning against the doorway with a disturbed expression on his face and his gym bag in his hand.

Heat shot into my cheeks. That was the icing on my embarrassment cake.

"How long have you been eavesdropping?" Fiona asked accusingly.

"I'm not eavesdropping. This is my home and you were talking loudly in the middle of the living room."

Fiona gave him a look that could have lighted a drenched piece of wood on fire.

"Great," I muttered. "Now I can't face Xavier *and* you."

Connor gave me an understanding look, but I didn't want his pity. It was my own fault for forgetting what kind of man Xavier was.

"Do you need painkillers?" Fiona asked quietly.

Connor shook his head, grimacing, and went upstairs. "Do me a favor and lower your voices when you discuss your female needs."

I gave her an exasperated look. "This day needs to be over quick."

CHAPTER FIFTEEN

XAVIER

The next day I didn't wake to Evie's snarky comments or the warning hiss of my espresso unit. When I checked my phone, the first thing I registered was Evie's short message, telling me she was sick and couldn't come to work. After that my eyes found the time: I had exactly five minutes to get to training. Damn it!

I jumped out of bed. So close to the start of the season I really couldn't risk the coach putting me on the bench.

I got ready and reached the training grounds in record time, but still too late.

Connor jogged up to me after the coach was done screaming at me for being twenty minutes late. "One day without Evie and you are already late."

"She was supposed to wake me. She didn't show up with some half-ass apology about being sick." She wasn't sick. We both knew it. Guilt hit me like a fucking wrecking ball again.

Connor narrowed his eyes. "Can you really blame her? She probably didn't want to see you."

"She's my assistant." The possibility she was still my friend was highly unlikely, and the stab that sent through me almost knocked my damn breath out of me.

"And she was still asleep when I left. The painkillers knocked her out."

I stopped mid-run. "Painkillers?"

Connor kept jogging in place beside me, the corners of his eyes crinkling in that annoying way. "Apparently you acted like a caveman with your enormous stick."

"Did I hurt her?"

Connor began to laugh softly, eyes full of mirth as he jogged in front of me.

I shoved his shoulder, pushing him out of my way. "You know what, Connor, fuck you."

I started running again. I wouldn't get another lecture from the coach because Connor was messing with my mind. Connor fell into step beside me again, still with that fucking air of self-righteousness.

"I don't know why *you* are pissed. You didn't have to listen to Fiona and Evie talk about being sore all night. That's not my idea of a relaxing evening, trust me."

"Is she all right?" I asked.

"Ask her yourself if you really want to know. I'm not getting involved in this. I'm already the bad guy because you're my best friend, so thanks."

"I assume that means I'm no longer invited to barbecue tomorrow?"

Connor groaned. "Fuck, I forgot about that." He glanced my way. "I'm not sure if it's in your best interest to be around Fiona at the moment. I can't guarantee your safety. Fiona is royally pissed at you."

"More pissed than her usual pissed self?"

"Trust me, Xavier, you haven't seen Fiona this pissed yet."

I would have loved to see Fiona that pissed. Pissing her off was my favorite pastime, but I was wary about being around Evie after what happened. "Don't worry, Connor. I can keep myself entertained. Enjoy your barbecue while I find somewhere I can put my enormous stick."

Connor shot me a glare. "Really? You're just going back to fucking the next random girl?"

I returned his glare. "What else am I supposed to be doing?"

He sneered. "I don't know, but maybe you should start thinking about it." With that, he sped up even more. What the hell was that supposed to mean? Since when was he the authority on women? I still remembered our bachelor days too well, before Fiona.

After training, I picked up my phone and tried calling Evie but she didn't pick up. She also ignored my messages. Evie wasn't the petty or vindictive type, so if she acted this way, she was really hurt.

I wasn't sure what to do, and that was the worst.

EVIE

I sent Xavier a message that I was sick and ignored his messages and calls. When I didn't show up the next day either, Connor cornered me in the kitchen where I was preparing an afternoon snack for myself. Fiona was gone recording a workout with another Instagram fitness star, or he probably wouldn't have dared to say the banned "X-word."

"Xavier needs you. You need to return to work, really," he said imploringly as he stepped into the kitchen.

I raised my eyebrows over my cup of coffee, then took a bite of the chocolate mug cake I'd made in the microwave. "I'm sick."

"No, you're not," he said. "Xavier is an asshole, I'm giving you that, but he's my best friend, and the best player on our team. I can't have him messing up this season because you don't kick his ass. I know you're hurt because he did what he always does, and never stops talking about."

I flushed at the realization that Xavier probably shared everything with his best friend. Had they had a good laugh about me? I didn't want to know how badly I'd embarrassed myself, having no experience and not looking the model-type. "I hope you enjoyed his stories about me," I muttered.

Connor's eyes widened. "He didn't say anything about you, Evie, I swear. And if he'd tried, I would have shut him up with a fist to his fucking mouth."

I cuffed his shoulder lightly. "You're a good guy. Fiona is lucky to have you."

Connor smiled briefly, then he sighed. "He's driving us up the walls. The team and me in particular. He was late to a press conference and two trainings so far. The coach is going to lose his shit soon."

"That's not my problem," I said, but it was. Connor was right, and despite what Xavier had done, or rather what *he and I* had done, I didn't want to hurt Xavier's career. He lived for his sport.

"It is. You are his assistant. Act like a grown-up about it, okay? Just save his sorry ass until you've found him a new babysitter." He left without another word, and I stared at his back. Broad and muscled like Xavier's. I should have never gotten anywhere near a rugby player to begin with.

But Connor had a point. I was a grown woman. I had been raised to be responsible for my actions and accept the consequences they brought. And I would do just that. Tomorrow morning I'd wake up Xavier like I had done every day these last few months. I'd act like his assistant and babysitter like before. I'd do my job until I found someone else to do it for me.

Xavier—The Beast—Stevens wouldn't stop me. Not because of one regrettable night. So many women had lost their V-card in a worse way; so what if I didn't get my happily ever after?

I unlocked Xavier's apartment and stepped in, my stomach in knots. I was a bit later than usual. It had taken more time than I'd thought to give myself a pep talk. I put the mail down on the bar counter and my purse on the stool, then hesitated briefly, taking a deep breath. I went toward the winding staircase to call up for him to get his ass down here when Xavier's voice rang out.

"Fuck, yes!" Xavier groaned.

I took a step back as silence followed.

Then a female voice rang out. "I knew you'd love to wake up like that."

"Sucking my dick was a nice touch, yes."

I whirled around and hurried back into the kitchen area. I snatched up my purse and rushed toward the front door, then paused with my purse clutched against my chest. I wouldn't run. This was my job.

Evie, you are going to get through this.

I had known what I was getting myself into when I'd started this job. I had read the tabloids, had listened to Fiona's stories. I took a deep breath and put my purse down on the counter, turned on the espresso unit to announce my entry loud and clear, then climbed onto the barstool.

I sorted through the mail and set it out on the bar ordered by importance. I put two cute fan letters from school classes to the top because they made me smile. Then I checked my phone for appointments for the day. Xavier had training at nine a.m. and an interview at three p.m. I glanced at the clock. It was 8:15. If he managed to finish his business with his conquest quickly, we should be on time for training today.

There had been silence upstairs for a while now. I hoped that meant they were done and not that their mouths were occupied. And as if on cue, a blonde head appeared on the upstairs landing. Everything I was not. Lean, fit, perfect. My stomach squeezed so tightly, I was surprised I didn't eject my breakfast.

She slowly made her way down, dressed in a micro-skirt I wouldn't even fit my thigh into and a glittery top. Xavier followed close behind her, his get-the-heck-out face already on, and as usual dressed in nothing but briefs, black this time. But unlike every other morning before today, I knew now how it felt to run my fingers over the ridges of his stomach, how his mouth felt on my skin, how it felt to have him inside me, and I couldn't unremember it.

He paused briefly when he spotted me, and his expression slipped: guilt.

I lowered my eyes to my mobile, pretending to be busy with business, which wasn't even a lie. I still had about twenty-five emails I needed to read and respond to.

"Is this your assistant?" the girl asked.

Xavier didn't say anything, and I didn't bother to look up or confirm her assumption. His strong legs appeared in my peripheral vision. "Evie," he said simply.

That deep voice. I was a glutton for punishment. I masked my emotions, and I peered up at him. "We have forty minutes to get you to training," I said in a professional voice. Sophisticated and in control, both qualities I longed for at the moment.

"You haven't answered any of my messages."

"You can't be late again. Your coach will put you on the bench next game."

"I was worried about you."

"You also have an interview with *Women's Health* at three p.m."

The blonde followed our conversation like a tennis match.

"Spare yourself the embarrassment and just leave," I told her. "He won't meet you again. He never does."

She blanched, then pursed her lips. "Only because you don't get laid, fatty, doesn't mean you have to let it out on me."

I didn't even feel offended. I was already too broken up to care about an insult from her, and I had heard worse in school. Nothing was as cruel as teenagers.

Xavier whirled on her, making her take a step back. "I liked you better when your mouth was busy swallowing my cum."

She sucked in a shocked breath. And I stifled my own gasp. That was low, even for Xavier. I'd never heard him talk to a woman like that.

"Leave—you heard what Evie said."

She shot me the nastiest glower possible before she strode out, her head held high. I wished I'd managed that kind of departure three days ago and found myself relieved that nobody had recorded my walk of shame. That would have been the headline of the year.

"That was unnecessarily cruel," I told him.

He turned back to me, with a look that made me more than a little nervous. "She got what she deserved. I don't know why it's always the same."

"Oh, you know, women can be foolish sometimes," I said lightly.

Xavier grimaced. He rubbed the back of his head. "Listen, Evie, I'm—"

"Late, I know," I interrupted him. "We need to leave now. Get dressed." I hopped down from the barstool, grabbed my purse and headed toward the door. "I will be waiting for you. You've got five minutes."

I threw a glance over my shoulder at a pained-looking Xavier. "I'll leave in exactly five minutes with or without you," I warned as I stepped outside, closed the door and leaned against the wall in the hallway.

Four minutes and fifty-five seconds later Xavier stepped out of his apartment, dressed in his usual training gear. I turned and quickly called the elevator, my back to him.

He stopped close beside me. "How are you?"

Oh my God, was he being serious? "This conversation isn't happening."

"Evie—"

The elevator stopped on the floor and I moved in, then leaned against the wall. Xavier hesitated a moment before he joined me inside and pressed the button for the ground floor.

I had a hard time not checking him out in the mirrors. "I quit," I said.

His head snapped around to me. "We have a contract."

"I know. And I'm going to find you a good replacement for me, don't worry."

"I don't want a replacement. I want you."

Not in the way I want you.

"Six months. That's the maximum you get. After that I can leave without a replacement."

He glared. "If that's what you want."

I nodded. It was far from what I wanted, but it was the best outcome I could hope for. The moment the elevator arrived downstairs, I rushed out. We didn't talk again during the drive.

We arrived on the training grounds at five to nine. Xavier jogged toward the field as I took my usual seat on the bleachers.

"That girl of yours saves your ass again," the coach said with a wave at me.

I smiled in return. Soon someone else would have to save Xavier's ass, even if it was the sexiest ass I'd ever had the misfortune of knowing.

CHAPTER SIXTEEN

EVIE

Xavier and I barely talked in the following days. Mainly because my answers consisted of one-word replies and Xavier wasn't used to women giving him a hard time, so he just gave up.

I entered his apartment as I did every morning, loudly, to prevent more embarrassing incidents from occurring.

I was busy preparing a cappuccino for myself when the sound of steps drew my eyes up, and I froze when the same girl as yesterday morning came down the staircase. Xavier didn't do a girl twice. Ever.

I was still staring when Xavier followed after the woman. Then finally I focused on the milk foam, but I listened.

"So tonight?" the girl said in a flirty tone.

"Sure. You'll pick me up at my place at eight?"

I couldn't stop myself from looking up. A third date? When he'd moved from one girl to the other it had been bearable, but seeing him with someone for real, the way I wanted to be with him, broke my heart into tiny pieces.

"I can't wait," she crooned.

My chest constricted painfully. Xavier led the girl to the door, let her out, then turned and our eyes met. He frowned. "So what's on today?"

He sounded all businesslike. Like my boss. He had never sounded like that before. So that was how it was going to be?

Good. That would make things easier for me as well.

"Not much. Training. In the afternoon, I was going to answer your fan mail and update your social media, but I'm doing it from home."

"Sure," Xavier said casually.

XAVIER

Connor came over in the afternoon to pick me up for a beach run. He was still giving me that badly disguised disappointed look, and it was making me furious.

We'd been jogging for less than five minutes when I lost my shit on him. "Can you stop the annoying self-righteous bullshit? You weren't a saint before Fiona either."

Connor stopped. "That's right, but I wasn't too big of a dickhead to realize when I found someone good."

"I slept with Evie once, that's it."

Connor scowled. "So you're just going to let her walk away? For what? For that Dakota girl whose guts you're probably hating already? What's that all about anyway?"

It took me a second to remember who the fuck Dakota was. "Fuck if I know. And Evie decided to quit. There's nothing I can do to stop her."

"You know what you'd have to do to make her stay."

"I don't date, Connor, and you fucking well know it, and especially not someone like Evie."

Connor got in my face. "What's that supposed to mean? You had no trouble fucking her despite her looks, but she's not dating material because of it or what?"

"That's not it, you stupid asshole," I growled.

"Then what is?"

"Evie's not interested in media attention, and she's a good girl. She's not the girl for me. She needs someone straight-laced, some decent bloke who makes her happy."

"You are such an idiot."

"I know," I said regretfully. "But if it makes you happy I'll dump Dakota tonight. We're meeting in that new trendy club everyone's raving about. She probably hopes someone from the press is there as usual."

EVIE

I scanned my emails on my tablet. The recruitment firm I'd contacted to help me find a new assistant for Xavier had asked me for a meeting next week. "Blake asked again if Evie was available," Connor said from inside the kitchen where I was heading.

My eyes widened. I didn't know Blake had asked about me in the first place, but he had always been nice when I saw him. Had he been flirting with me? I'd always been so focused on Xavier that I hadn't paid much attention to any of his teammates.

"What did you say?" I asked, barging in before Fiona could say anything. I didn't like them discussing my love life, or the lack thereof, without me.

Connor and Fiona turned around as if I'd caught them in the act. Connor rubbed the back of his head, then glanced at my sister like he needed her to stage-whisper the answer.

"I told him I wasn't sure."

Fiona scowled. "I told you to tell him she was available."

"Yeah, well. I wasn't sure because of…Xavier."

"There's nothing between Xavier and Evie."

"Excuse me, I'm here," I said. "When did Blake ask before?"

"A couple of weeks ago, around the time when you drove out to Xavier's family farm with him. I thought…"

"Thought what?" I asked.

"I thought it meant Xavier might be interested in you as more than his assistant."

"He was interested in more of her and he got it," Fiona muttered.

She was right, but so was Connor. I'd also believed it meant something that Xavier had taken me to his family. I hadn't exactly thought he wanted me as a girlfriend, but I was sure we were friends. But friends didn't sleep with each other, and they definitely didn't move on to the next conquest right after.

"Do you have Blake's number?" Fiona asked Connor.

I narrowed my eyes at her. She was meddling again.

"Sure," Connor said slowly.

"Then send him a message that you asked Evie and she's available."

"I never said I was available."

"You had your heart broken by a womanizer who's already out chasing the next skirt. You are available," Fiona said firmly.

I bit my lip. Blake was kind of cute. He was nice, pleasant to talk to and he was a sexy rugby player. There was just the little problem that he wasn't Xavier. "I'm not sure that's a good idea."

"Why?" Fiona asked almost angrily. "He's flaunting his latest conquest in your face, and you sit back and cry your eyes out because he snatched your V-card and tossed it into the dirt like an expired coupon."

"Wow, ouch," I muttered.

Fiona looked apologetic. "Sorry, but it's true. Don't feel sorry for yourself. Do something to feel good about yourself. And Blake is the right guy for it."

Connor glanced between us, his mobile in his hand.

"Okay, tell him I'm available," I said finally.

Fiona grinned and kissed Connor's cheek as if he'd just won a match. I rolled my eyes. Fiona was a bit too invested in my love life.

Connor typed a short message, then nodded. "All done."

"Maybe he isn't interested in me anymore. Or maybe he just asked to be polite. Who says he's even interested in me?" I tugged at my blouse.

Connor snorted. "Men don't ask about a girl's dating status if they're not interested in getting hot and heavy with her."

"Hot and heavy, huh?" I said with a laugh. "The last hot and heavy experience had me sore for two days, so thank you, but no."

Connor grimaced. But they had started poking their noses in my business. Now they had to deal with the consequences.

Fiona leaned beside me against the counter. "Your second time will be better, trust me."

"I'll take that as my clue to leave," Connor muttered, and slipped out.

Fiona shook her head with a small smile. "Wimp."

My phone beeped with a message. Fiona's eyes widened. "That's him."

"You don't know that," I said, but when I stared down at my cell, I saw that it was indeed from Blake and he was asking me for a date.

"And what's he saying?" Fiona asked, twisting her neck to catch a glance at my phone.

"He's asking if I would like to go out with him tonight."

"Wow, he's eager. That's good."

It seemed like a good thing, and it was flattering, though I still wasn't sure if Blake was really interested in me like that. "What do I say?"

"You say yes, for God's sake. Go out with him."

"I don't know. I'm not sure I'm ready to have my heart broken again."

"Then keep your heart out of it."

As if it was as easy as that.

"Evie, do me a favor, and go on a date with Blake. He's a decent guy despite being a rugby player. He's never been one for whoring around."

I hesitated, but Fiona was begging me with her eyes, and then I remembered that Xavier was supposed to meet Dakota again tonight. Why should I be home alone when he was out having fun?

I messaged Blake back and agreed to meet him the same evening. He wrote back within a couple of minutes, saying he would pick me up at eight for dinner and a club afterward if I was up for it. I was.

Fiona clapped her hands. "Okay. Now we need to get ready."

"We?"

"You will look spectacular. Blake will fall over backwards when he sees you."

I didn't protest. Fiona was a woman on a mission, and the last few times she'd helped me get ready had worked out well. Too well in Xavier's case… But I definitely wasn't going to sleep with Blake or anyone any time soon.

Blake picked me up at eight, dressed in slacks and a white dress shirt, the sleeves pushed up to his elbows. His blue eyes slid over my body. I was still insecure in outfits like this. Tight dark red leather skirt reaching up to my waist to accentuate it, and glittery silk top stuffed into the hem. The outfit accentuated my waist, hips and breasts. Everything it was supposed to, as Fiona put it. With my heels, I was almost eye level with Blake, which was new, since Xavier was almost a head taller than me even with these shoes. Blake was still tall and incredibly muscled.

"You look beautiful," Blake said with an easygoing smile, and I quickly pushed Xavier out of my mind. It would have been unfair of me to compare Blake to Xavier.

"Thank you," I said with an earnest smile.

"Ready to go?" he asked.

I nodded. "Where are we going?"

"It's a nice fish restaurant close to the harbor. I've been there a few times. They serve delicious oysters."

Oysters and I didn't go well together, but I didn't say anything. "That sounds great."

Luckily, they had more than oysters and I ordered a nice tuna steak. Talking to Blake was easy. He was interested in my life in the States and never mentioned my current job. A big plus. When we left the restaurant around eleven, I was relaxed and glad that I'd accepted Blake's invitation. He was a gentleman like Fiona had said. "Still up for some dancing?" he asked with an inviting grin as we settled in his car.

"Definitely," I said. His eyes darted to my lips, and my stomach flopped. I quickly lowered my gaze to my hands resting in my lap, trying to dissuade him from a possible kissing attempt. Blake looked kissable, no question, but I wasn't ready for that kind of leap yet.

Dancing seemed like the right kind of distraction. Of course, kissing would still be an option then as well. I'd cross that bridge when I came to it.

Blake started the car and turned on the radio. "What kind of music do you like?"

"To be honest, I'm a lazy listener. I always listen to the current charts."

"Then this radio station should do the trick."

It did, but the lack of conversation also allowed my mind to drift, and as usual it drifted to the one man I shouldn't be thinking about, the man who was probably banging Dakota right this second.

There was a long queue in front of the dance club when we walked toward it. Blake had his hand resting on the small of my back as he led me past the queue with self-assured steps.

He waved at a few fans screaming his name before he shook hands with the bouncers, who nodded at me. They let us through without hesitation. "Do rugby players ever have to stand in line for anything?" I asked with a laugh, remembering how Xavier had gotten into every club or restaurant without waiting.

Blake chuckled. "Not around here, no."

The club was already crowded despite the early hour but most people were still in the bar area, warming up for the dancing part.

"Drinks?"

"Yes, please." We moved toward a free table close to the bar. The tables near the windows with a view of the harbor were already occupied.

Two mojitos later, I was ready to hit the dance floor. I usually didn't get tipsy around people I barely knew but I needed to get Xavier out of my head. I wasn't completely trashed, but a nice buzz had loosened my limbs. Blake took my hand as he led me through the crowd. The bass throbbed through my body and I began moving to the rhythm, swinging my hips like I'd never done before. Blake smiled, a slower, more intimate smile and touched my hips lightly, his eyebrows rising in silent question.

I put one hand on his shoulder to show him the touch was okay. I wasn't even worried what he'd think of my softness. Was that because I wasn't interested in him? Or was it just the alcohol in my system?

He was a good dancer, and I enjoyed myself tremendously. Blake moved a bit closer and his face moved even nearer. He was going to kiss me. His blue eyes were soft. Would it be so bad to kiss him? He was nice and sexy. Not arrogant, infuriating, self-assured, and an impossible manwhore, and yet it wasn't his lips I wanted on mine.

Blake's mouth was only an inch from mine, and my eyes were about to flutter shut when suddenly Xavier was there, shoving Blake away from me. Blake stumbled a couple of steps back, but caught his balance quickly.

"Have you lost your mind?" I hissed.

Xavier glared at Blake, ignoring me. "Hands off."

"What's your problem?" Blake shouted over the bass, stepping up to Xavier.

"My problem is that you have your fucking hands all over Evie."

"Evie is single. She can go out with whoever she wants," Blake said.

Xavier took a step toward him and Blake did the same. They looked like two bulls about to lock horns. *Men.* I noticed a couple of familiar faces watching with rapt attention and taking pictures with their mobiles: the bloodhounds from the tabloids. They weren't allowed to take their cameras inside the club but of course they found a way to take photos. Damn it. That was the last thing I needed. And if the coach found pics of Blake and Xavier beating each other up in public, they both would sit on the bench in the upcoming game.

"Let me have a word with Xavier," I told Blake with an apologetic smile. "I'll be back in a minute."

I gripped Xavier's forearm and began dragging him through the crowd, cringing when I saw more cell cameras turning our way. He followed without protest. I didn't stop until we were outside in a side alley, away from the blaring beats and curious eyes. I released him and he bent down to kiss me, his lips brushing mine lightly before I shoved him back.

"What are you doing?" I muttered. I couldn't believe his nerve.

He let himself fall backwards against the wall. "I thought this was the beginning of hot make-up sex."

"You are impossible," I said, trying hard not to look at how tightly his shirt hugged his chest, how disheveled his hair looked, how sexy his dark stubble was. God, have mercy. Why did this man have to be so gorgeous? It wasn't fair. "There won't be any kind of sex between us."

A slow smile spread on Xavier's face. "I hate unfinished business."

"What are you talking about?"

"You didn't come last time."

"Stop it," I said sharply. I didn't like the way he talked about it. "Where is Dakota?"

He grimaced. "Inside somewhere. I don't know. I don't care."

"Maybe you should return to her."

He straightened, sighing. "Listen, Evie, I can't stop thinking about you. I don't date—"

"What about Dakota? This is your third date. Don't you call that dating?"

He laughed. "No. I'm definitely not dating her. This is a three-night stand and it ends today."

"You sure?" I said.

"Yes, I'm sure. What about you and Blake?" he said almost angrily. He was *angry*?

"Blake and I aren't your business, but if you must know, this is our first date."

Xavier stepped closer. "So you haven't...?"

"Haven't what?" I asked.

"Haven't slept with him?"

My eyes widened. "Of course not! I haven't even kissed him, or anyone else for that matter. I don't move on as quickly as you do, Xavier." And I shouldn't even have agreed to the date with Blake, I realized now. My emotions were too all over the place to drag someone else into the mess.

Xavier ran a hand through his hair, sighing. "That's what I was trying to tell you before. I don't date, you know that, but we could be..."

"Could be what?" I challenged.

He didn't say anything but his eyes moved to my chest, and the look in them sent a sweet tingle through my body.

I took a step back. "I could be your assistant with benefits? Is that what you have in mind?"

He frowned as if my vehemence surprised him. Did he really think I would agree to something like that?

"Right. That would work out well for you. I'd still organize your life and you could sleep with me whenever you felt like it, and as an added bonus you wouldn't even have to be faithful and could keep up the one-night stands."

He raised one cocky eyebrow. "You'd get mind-blowing sex out of the arrangement. It could be worse."

"You just don't get it. All that matters to you is the next high, the next conquest. For you it's all about having fun. But I'm not like that. For me sex is about intimacy, about allowing closeness and about trust. It's about caring and loving."

"If that were true, you wouldn't have slept with me."

Tears gathered in my eyes. My nails dug into my palms in an attempt to hold on to my composure. I had never really cried in front of Xavier, and I never would.

Xavier's expression froze. His gray eyes flickered with guilt. "Evie, I don't..."

"Date, I know, Xavier," I snapped, tired of hearing him say it.

"People expect certain things from me. I have a reputation to uphold.

Dating you would—"

"Ruin your reputation? Heaven forbid Xavier—The Beast—Stevens would be seen with a dumpling."

"Dumpling? What the fuck are you talking about?"

"Don't pretend you don't know. I'm too fat to date someone like you." For the first time tonight I wished I had chosen a different outfit, not one that accentuated my curves like this.

Xavier stepped closer, engulfing me with his tantalizing scent, making me wish for something that wasn't going to happen. "You are fucking gorgeous, Evie. Your tits are marvelous and so is your butt and your hips. You are soft in all the right places."

I peered up at him, my heart filling with hopeless emotions. He cupped my cheeks and kissed me, soft and passionate. I wanted more, wanted all of him, and that was the problem. I pulled back before I could lose myself. "I can't. Not like this. Not without commitment. I don't want to be like all the other girls again."

"You are nothing like them," he murmured, his hands still against my cheeks, warm and gentle.

I could feel myself falling into his eyes again. "But you treated me like them."

"I didn't know how to act around you. I...I was confused."

"Confused? You?"

He smirked. "Because it was you. And because you were my first virgin. I never wanted the burden of having that kind of important place in a woman's memory. And then that virgin was *you*."

Ouch. I stepped out of his grasp. "Sorry about having burdened you like that," I said with a roll of my eyes.

"No," he said in a low voice that sent a sweet tingling down my spine again. I was utterly screwed. "I have to say I like being the only one."

"The only one would imply that there will be no others, but as we're not even dating, there will eventually be someone else."

Xavier's face darkened. He gripped my hips. "I don't want there to be someone else. Not Blake, and not anyone else either."

I shook my head. "Then we're at an impasse."

"Evie," Xavier said in a pained voice.

I drew back from him and he dropped his hands from my hips. "No. Xavier, there's only one way you can have me, and that's in a real relationship and not as an affair."

He didn't stop me when I turned on my heel and walked off. My heart was thudding wildly in my chest, and I felt hot and flustered. When I found Blake at the bar, nursing a drink, trying to ignore the crowd of females who were attempting to catch his gaze, a wave of guilt washed over me. "I'm sorry," I told him.

He smiled but it was less bright than before. "Are you okay?"

"Yeah, I'm fine. I'm sorry for what Xavier did."

He stood, frowning. "It's not your apology to hand out. Do you want to leave?"

"Yes, I'm not in the mood for partying anymore. Please don't be mad."

He shook his head. "I'm not. It was a lovely evening up until Xavier barged in."

"It was," I said with a small laugh. My eyes were drawn to a scene behind Blake where Dakota threw her drink into Xavier's face, whirled around and rushed off.

Blake followed my eyes. "You and him?" There was no judgment in his voice, only a hint of resignation.

"No, it's not like that," I said quickly.

"Okay," Blake said, but I could tell that he didn't believe me. We headed out of the club and on our way back to my home, he engaged me in polite conversation but I could tell that he was more cautious than before.

When he stopped in front of the house, I turned to him. "It was a lovely evening and you are a wonderful guy."

He grimaced. "I've heard those words before," he said bitterly. "Women always fall for the asshole type. Xavier is living proof."

I wanted to protest but snapped my lips shut. "I'm sorry," I said eventually. "It wouldn't be fair to you to keep seeing you. Right now, it isn't the right time for me to look for someone."

Blake nodded. "It's okay. Thank for the evening."

With a last smile, I got out.

Fiona was expecting me in the entryway like an eager puppy. One look at my face and she frowned. "Don't tell me he turned out to be an asshole too."

"No, he was a gentleman."

"Then what?"

"Xavier shoved Blake when he tried to kiss me."

"He did what? Has he lost his mind? You are his assistant, not his girlfriend. I'm going to kick his ass tomorrow."

I touched her arm. "Don't. Just let it drop. I don't want any more drama. I've had enough for a lifetime."

CHAPTER SEVENTEEN

XAVIER

I met my brother in our favorite pub, where they had a new selection of craft beers on tap every week and the best fish and chips in town. Marc was already in our usual booth when I stepped in. I waved at the owner of the pub, who never made a big deal when I came over. This was a place where I didn't have to worry about paparazzi taking a photo of me. They had done enough of that last night. I didn't buy the tabloids but I'd caught glimpses of their headlines, and all of them included me. Most of them with Blake and Evie, some with Dakota when she threw her drink in my face. The latter I didn't mind. The former made me raving mad because I knew the pictures would bother Evie.

"Fifteen minutes late," Marc commented as I slid into the chair across from him. "For before Evie-Xavier that would have been good, but now I expect better." He had already ordered two glasses of a dark amber beer. I raised the glass to my lips and took a generous gulp.

Marc scanned my face. "What's going on?"

"I fucked up," I said.

Marc gave me a look. "Tell me something I don't know," he joked, then sobered. "It's not about Evie, is it?"

He sounded like this would crush him. What was it with Evie and winning over everyone she ever met? The coach, my teammates, my family...Blake. I still wanted to punch his face for dancing with Evie, for having his hands on her hips, for trying to kiss her. He wanted her, wanted what I wanted for myself. What if Evie decided to go out with him again? Or someone else?

"I slept with her," I muttered, setting the glass down and waiting for the tongue-lashing to begin.

Marc shook his head once, disapproving, then took a long sip from his beer, all the while assessing me like I had admitted to committing murder, and not sex.

"Can you stop that disappointed older brother look? I'm feeling shitty enough."

"Why?" he asked. "You slept with almost every single one of your assistants and you never felt shitty about it, or about any of the other women you slept with and disposed of like a dirty rag."

"Evie isn't just any woman. She's..."

Marc leaned forward, curious. "She's what?"

I frowned. Evie was important. Important to me. "Never mind."

Marc pulled away with a sigh and sank back in his seat. "Okay, so you slept with her...but I assume you didn't throw her out of your apartment right after?"

He was starting to piss me off. "I didn't throw her out. She left the next morning before I could say anything."

"Which was probably for the best because you probably wouldn't have made things better with words."

"Probably," I conceded, taking another sip. I wasn't sure what I would have said, but not what Evie wanted to hear, that was clear.

"If she left, maybe things aren't that bad. Maybe she'll at least agree to keep working as your assistant."

"I was her first, Marc."

His brows drew together. "First what?"

"You're awfully slow for a lawyer," I muttered. Then sighed. "Evie was a virgin."

Marc put his glass down and stared. Suddenly anger took over his face. "You slept with her knowing she'd never been with a guy? That's low, even for you, Xavier. Fuck. Even your dumb ass must have realized she's got feelings for you and that's why she wanted you to be her first."

For Marc to say fuck, he must be really pissed on Evie's behalf, and he reached his goal. I felt even worse, which had seemed hardly possible. Every woman I'd been with since I'd slept with Evie had made me feel more guilty. They hadn't been the distraction I'd hoped for. All they'd done was show me that Evie was one of a kind.

"I didn't know…at first. And when I figured it out, it was too late."

Marc shook his head again. He grabbed the empty glasses and rose. "I'm getting us another round. I've got a feeling we'll both need it."

He returned with two glasses filled with an almost black concoction. "Dark Ale. Chocolate and malt notes," he said as he put a glass down in front of me and sat down.

"I assume she quit her job."

I nodded.

"That leaves her six months to find you a replacement."

I nodded again.

Marc sighed. "Mom will be really sad, and Willow, too. And Milena and the kids as well."

173

I scowled. "I get it. I ruined this for everyone. We all love Evie and I fucking lost her."

Marc tilted his head in that annoying attorney way, like I had just revealed a crucial hint. "We all love her?"

"It's a figure of speech, Marc. Get off my back," I said, getting angry.

Marc sat back and was quiet for a long time. "Maybe it's not too late. Go to her, tell her how you feel. Evie seems like a woman who doesn't hold grudges. Maybe she'll give you another chance."

"For what? A relationship? You know I don't date, Marc. Have never, will never."

"I love Milena," Marc said quietly, and I braced myself because that voice rang all my alarm bells. I knew he was going to address a topic I hated. "There was a time when I thought like you, when I thought the world was better off with me not dipping my toes in the dating pool, but with her I could not let her get away. I'm not like him. Sometimes I get angry and I yell, and Milena yells back, but not once did I call her names, threaten her or consider raising my hand to her. And not only because I don't want to lose her—because I would lose her if I treated her like that—but because I don't want to treat her that way."

"Good for you, because I'd run you over with my fucking car if you ever treated Milena and the kids like shit."

Marc smiled. "I know." He sighed. "You and Evie seemed perfect for each other. I've never seen you laugh so much around a woman."

"Evie is the funniest and smartest woman I know."

"What's the problem then? Is it because she doesn't look like the supermodels you usually parade around?"

I narrowed my eyes. "Evie's hot, and I don't give a damn if she's supermodel material or not." The press was a different matter. They would descend on her like vultures if word got out that we were dating.

"Then what?"

I sighed. He didn't get it. "There's always that one messed-up puppy in the litter that'll chew your face off when you're sleeping. We both know you and Willow aren't that kind of pup."

Marc shook his head. "You won't chew anyone's face off, Xavier."

"You never know. I don't want to fuck up Evie's life."

Marc snorted into his beer. "You're doing an awful job so far."

Nothing like an older brother who made you feel like the biggest asshole in the world. He and Fiona would get along well if they ever met.

———— ◆ ◆ ◆ ————

Evie still did everything she was supposed to do. She was responsible and took her job seriously, but now she made sure to keep her distance. Our banter was gone, and she never got close enough so we could accidentally touch.

"Xavier, are you listening to a word I'm saying? Can't you at least pretend to give a shit?" Evie said. My eyes were drawn to her where she was perched on the barstool, tablet in front of her, scowling at me.

I hadn't listened. I was still working up my courage to say what needed to be said.

She sighed. "I'm done with the first draft of the job announcement. You don't have to worry about anything going public. I contacted a recruitment firm who will discretely look for possible candidates. If you like I can go over the announcement with Marc."

"I don't want another assistant, Evie," I said firmly.

Her green eyes met mine, and the look in them was a punch in the balls. Fuck. I'd never meant to hurt Evie. "I told you I won't keep working for you. It's not going to work. After what happened..." She swallowed. "It just won't work."

I straightened from where I'd leaned against the fridge and moved closer to her but stopped when she tensed. "Evie, listen, I know I acted like a major asshole."

"You did, but I can't blame you for it. I knew how you treat women."

Ouch. Another blow. "You aren't like other women."

"For sure," she muttered, scanning the length of herself, then frowning down at her iPad.

Screw it. I closed in on her and she jerked her head up in confusion. "I don't want to lose you."

She pursed her lips. "I'm not going to become your assistant with benefits."

"I don't want you to be an assistant with benefits..." Fuck, was I really going to say it? "I want you, all of you. I want to give this dating thing a chance. I want to give us a chance, if you'll let me."

Her eyes widened then narrowed. "You don't date. You said it yourself."

"I know," I said quietly, leaning closer to Evie until I could have counted the freckles on her nose and cheekbones. "But I want to date you."

There it was. I'd said it, and despite the burst of panic, *fucking panic*, I didn't want to take the words back. If dating Evie was what it would take to keep her, I'd give it a try. I was pretty sure I would have done anything right then, just to keep her.

EVIE

These words were too good to be true. "What exactly do you consider dating?"

Xavier was still close, so close I had a hard time focusing on more than the curve of his mouth and manly scent.

"Go on dates, spend time together, sleep together. I'm not an expert when it comes to dating, Evie."

"Me neither," I said. I regarded Xavier. He looked earnest, and I knew he wouldn't lie about something like that, certainly not to get me into his bed again. My heart wanted to jump at his suggestion, but my brain pulled the brakes. "Last time we talked about it, you said people expect certain things from you. That didn't change. The press will be all over us once word gets out that we're dating."

A flicker of worry passed Xavier's face, and my stomach tightened. "See, that look tells me all I need to know. You're worried about being seen in public with me." I tried pulling away, but Xavier braced himself against the counter to both sides of me.

"That's bullshit, Evie. We're seen together all the time."

"Not as a couple, and you know it."

"I don't give a fuck what the press writes about us, but last time they threw shit at you, you were upset and I don't want that, and it'll only get worse. The Blake incident was already a wet dream come true for the tabloids."

"You're worried about me?"

"Fuck, yes. Of course I'm worried about you. I know the nasty shit the press likes to throw at me, and they won't go any softer on you once they find out you're my girlfriend."

I swallowed. "You said the g-word."

Xavier chuckled. "I'd rather find your G-spot."

I shoved Xavier's shoulder lightly. "You're impossible." But I wasn't angry or annoyed. I was confused and happy and scared, though. "Xavier, this is a big deal, for me, for us. If you're doing this because you feel guilty or want to settle unfinished business or don't want to lose a good assistant, then I'd rather you say it now."

Xavier pulled back slightly, looking like I'd slapped him. "I wouldn't mess with you like that just to settle unfinished business. I thought you'd be happy."

"I'm happy, but I'm also worried. You were always so adamant about not dating and now you change your mind. A few days ago you were still screwing Dakota, and now it's me you want. That doesn't add up."

Xavier sighed. "I never wanted Dakota. She was meant to distract me from you. I felt guilty after I slept with you, and when I realized I was going to lose you forever that just scared the shit out of me, but I was being a stubborn fucker and thought I couldn't date anyone, least of all you."

"Least of all me," I repeated. "Yeah, I can see how dating the chubby redhead would be a blow to your image."

Xavier grabbed my hips and stepped between my legs, bringing our faces close. "Don't twist my words in my mouth, and don't let your insecurities over your body be mine."

I snapped my mouth shut. Xavier had never been truly angry at me, but now he looked mad. He leaned down slowly and brushed his lips across mine. I held my breath but he didn't deepen the kiss; instead he pulled back a couple of inches. "What I meant is," he said firmly, "I never wanted to date because I didn't think I would be good at it."

I huffed. "If you've never tried it, then you can't know."

"My father was a major asshole, Evie," Xavier said suddenly, and I became still. Except for that brief mention after the women's shelter, he had never talked about his father, nor had anybody else from his family. His gray eyes held apprehension and pain at a memory from his past. I touched his chest, trying to encourage him without words to go on. "An abusive asshole, physically and mentally. He beat my mother and later Marc and me. He was a horrible human being, but Mom stayed with him for a long time. He could be charming if he tried, and he always managed to convince her that he would change, that he wouldn't beat her again. She tried protecting us and got beaten up for it all the time. He punched her and kicked her, tore at her hair, called her horrible names..."

He fell silent.

"So," I began. "You're worried you'll be like him?" It was a ridiculous notion. Xavier wasn't violent or cruel. He was a womanizer, and while he had certainly broken a few hearts, that was a far cry from being an abusive asshole. Most women knew exactly what they were getting into when they slept with Xavier. He was all over the news with his sexual endeavors. Even I had known.

"I look like him," Xavier said. "And I have his charm. Women want to believe whatever I say. I can be convincing."

"Let me stop you right there," I said. I jabbed my finger into his hard chest. "I don't know your father but I know you, and you aren't abusive, Xavier. You are funny and cocky and caring. You take care of your family, you protect them, you love them. You would never hurt someone you love or care about. You are not your father, trust me."

He still didn't look convinced.

I took his hand, strong and rough. I curled his fingers until they formed a fist, then I raised it between us. "Can you imagine punching me?" I asked, bringing his fist to my cheek.

He tensed, his eyes wide and horrified. "No."

A small smile tugged at my lips. I brought his fist to my lips and kissed his knuckles. "Not even when I annoy you?" I teased.

"No, never, and least of all when you annoy me."

I unfolded his hand and pressed his palm against my cheek. "What about a slap? Ever thought about slapping me?"

"No," Xavier said in a low voice. He was still tense, his eyes intense as if I was telling a story that had him on the edge of his seat.

"Hurting me?"

"No."

"Insulting me?"

"No, fuck no," he almost growled.

I released his hand and smiled. "See. You have nothing to worry about."

Xavier sighed. "I never wanted to risk anything. Love turned my mother into a fool. She let him hurt her. And he almost destroyed our entire family."

"But he didn't. You have a wonderful family. What about him? Where is he?"

"I don't know and I don't care. Last time I saw him was when he was sent to jail thirteen years ago."

My eyes widened. "Oh. Why?"

"My mother left him. She tried to get into a women's shelter but they were all crowded, so she went to a friend instead. My father found her, beat her up and threw Willow down a staircase."

Tears sprang into my eyes. "That's why she's in a wheelchair?"

"Yeah," Xavier said quietly. He looked away and swallowed. I slipped off the stool and wrapped my arm around his middle, then pressed my cheek against his chest, holding on to him tightly. Xavier wrapped me into a tight embrace in turn and rested his chin on top of my head. We stood like that for a long time and I wondered if anything would ever feel as wonderful as being in Xavier's embrace, hearing his heartbeat, feeling his warmth and strength.

When we finally pulled back, I wasn't sure what to say. I doubted Xavier had ever talked to anyone outside of his family about what happened, and that he entrusted such a horrific memory to me felt like an incredible gift.

"Taking a depressing trip down memory lane wasn't how I imagined this conversation would go. I thought there would be hot make-up sex."

I rolled my eyes, allowing Xavier to lighten the mood. "There won't be any kind of sex today." Then added when Xavier gave me a cocky grin, "Or tomorrow. Or the day after tomorrow."

Xavier nodded once, resigned. "I guess that means that's no to dating me. I get it. After that depressing story I wouldn't want to date me either," he said jokingly, but I caught the hint of vulnerability behind his words.

"Don't be ridiculous," I said. "I didn't say no to dating. I said no to sex."

"Isn't that the same?"

I snorted. "For you maybe." Then I turned serious. "If you're serious about giving dating a try, about us, then we should start our relationship from scratch. And that means go on dates, and no sex. For you it's always only been about sex when you were with a woman, but I need this to be about more than that. I can only give us a chance if you agree to a no-sex rule for the time being."

"You mean no sex with other women, right?" he said, grinning, then sobered at a glare from me. "If that's what it takes, then I can deal with the no-sex rule."

"You sure? You're making a face as if you got banned from playing rugby for life."

Xavier leaned down. "It feels like it."

I raised my eyebrows. "If you don't think you can do it, then we should just forget it. I don't want to get hurt, Xavier. More than I'm already hurt, that is."

"I don't want to hurt you, Evie. I want to try dating, but I can't promise I'll be good at it. Maybe I'll mess up, but I will do everything I can to make this work. Even endure blue balls."

"Okay," I said, feeling my pulse speed up at what I was going to say. "Then let's try this."

Xavier smiled. "So you're agreeing to date me?"

"To 'try dating' is how you put it, but yes."

"Does that mean I'm allowed to kiss you now?" Xavier murmured, his lips already so close his breath ghosted over my mouth.

My next words cost me incredible effort and even more restraint. "Not yet. Maybe after our first official date, if it goes well."

Xavier cocked one eyebrow in that annoyingly cocky and sexy way. "First date? What are we going to do?"

"Surprise me. Your calendar tells me that you're free tonight."

He chuckled. "Maybe dating my assistant isn't the best idea after all."

I bit my lip. "Do you think it'll be a problem? I already have that announcement written."

"No," he said quickly. "I don't want anyone else. I want you to be my assistant. And it is kind of hot."

I was secretly relieved. The idea of Xavier working closely with another woman didn't sit well with me. Xavier wanted to try dating, but he was used to chasing after every skirt. I didn't trust him enough yet to be comfortable with another assistant in his life, and I needed the job. "Then I'll stay your assistant for now." I glanced down at my watch. "And that means that we've got exactly twenty minutes to get you to training. Oh shit!"

I pushed past Xavier. "Get dressed. We need to leave. Your coach will blow a gasket if you're late."

"Bossy as usual," Xavier said, but he jogged toward the stairs and then up. My eyes followed his perfectly shaped butt in those tight briefs. Dating Xavier was going to be tough.

I quickly scanned my calendar, then cursed. I needed to pick up Xavier's tuxedo and my dress from the dry cleaner, talk to the caterer regarding Xavier's birthday party, which was going down in only two weeks, and I had a lunch date with Fiona. When Xavier came down the stairs in his training clothes, I ushered him out. "You'll have to drive on your own. I have a few things I need to do. You don't have anything scheduled in the afternoon except for surfing with Connor, so you don't need me for that either. I guess that means we won't see each other until tonight. Let me know when you'll pick me up for our date and if I need to get dressed up. On second thought, something where we don't need to dress up would be good. I don't want us to go somewhere we'll be the center of attention. Somewhere private would be better."

I paused.

Xavier was watching me in amusement.

"What?" I asked, flushing. I had been rambling.

"It's cute when you're nervous. Does dating me make you nervous, Evie?" Xavier asked in a low voice, leaning close, that wolfish grin on his face.

Not one to let him get the best of me, I touched his hip and pressed my breasts up against his chest. "Of course not. Does dating me make you nervous?"

Xavier's eyes darted to my neckline and his chest heaved against mine. Before I lost my own game, I stepped back, patted his chest and said, "I can't wait to see what you have planned for our first date."

Then I quickly walked off and toward Fiona's scooter, which I had borrowed frequently in the last few days since I'd avoided being in a car with Xavier. I raced off before my body overruled my mind and I dragged Xavier back up into his apartment and let him have his way with me.

CHAPTER EIGHTEEN

EVIE

I was completely distracted during my lunch with Fiona, and of course she noticed it. Even a couple of years of separation didn't change the fact that as twins we picked up on each other's moods.

"Okay. What is this about? You're nervous and distracted."

"I'm not," I tried to salvage the situation.

She cocked one blonde eyebrow in a very Xavier-like fashion, which increased my nervousness. "You just put salt into your cappuccino."

I stared down at my cup, then brought it to my lips, took a hesitant sip and grimaced. "Okay, fine. I have a lot on my mind right now."

"Is it still because of that asshat? Is he giving you a hard time?"

For less than a second I considered telling Fiona about Xavier and me, but then my fear won out. Xavier and I weren't really Xavier and I yet. We had agreed to try dating, but that was all. I knew what Fiona would say if I told her about it. She'd declare me insane, and maybe I was for giving Xavier a chance after everything. Though really, he hadn't done anything wrong if you looked at it closely. He had never lied to me, never pretended our night together would be more than sex, and yet I had slept with him. I was the one who hadn't been one-hundred percent honest, who had kept my virginity a secret. Given Xavier's reaction, he probably wouldn't have taken things that far between us if I had told him in a less precarious situation. I was as much to blame for that night as he was. That he moved on to another woman so quickly, that was all him—but again, nothing I couldn't have foreseen.

"Evie?" Fiona asked.

I blinked. I'd drifted off again. "Sorry. He didn't do anything. He's being his usual cocky self." Which wasn't a lie.

"Have you made progress finding a new assistant?"

"I still need to go over the job announcement with Xavier's brother."

Fiona frowned. "It's taking too long. And it'll take even longer finding someone who's willing to become his assistant."

"There are enough women out there who would do anything to be close to him," I said with a hint of bitterness.

Fiona scrutinized me. "You sound jealous."

"I'm not."

"You're not still hung up on him, are you? He's already moved on with several women, and you should move on too. He's not worth wasting another thought over. Just because he was your first doesn't mean he has to mean anything."

It wasn't that easy, and Fiona knew it. She had left the States because she had caught her first love cheating. Admittedly that was worse than what had happened to me. She and Aiden had been dating for three years, and he'd screwed her best friend. I was lucky in comparison. "Let's not talk about Xavier, all right?" I'd only end up letting something slip, and then our lunch date would take a turn for the worse.

"Then let's talk about Blake," Fiona said.

I sighed. "I told you it didn't work out between us."

"You went out with him once and your date was rudely interrupted by Xavier. You can't count that. Give him another chance."

My mobile beeped in my purse. Glad for the distraction, I took it out and glanced at the screen. The message was from Xavier.

I'll pick you up at seven at the corner of your street.
Don't want to cross your evil twin sister's path.
Dress code: casual. Make sure you're hungry and thirsty.

Grinning, I quickly keyed in my reply.

Good thinking e.g. Fiona. P.S. Don't call her evil.

I returned my phone to my purse, then looked up and caught Fiona watching me with narrowed eyes. The smile dropped from my face and a treacherous blush crawled up my throat.

"Who was that?"

"Uh, nobody."

"That infatuated smile didn't look like nobody."

Damn it. Why did Fiona have to be such a bloodhound when it came to sniffing out my emotions? "I...I met someone." There it was, the lie I didn't want to rely on.

"A guy?" Fiona asked, stunned.

"No, a llama," I muttered. "Of course a guy."

"Where did you meet him? And why didn't you tell me you were looking for someone? Is that why you don't want to see Blake again?"

"It's pretty fresh…and I met him online."

"Are you sure he's not some crazy serial killer?"

"I'm a grown-up, Fiona. I can handle my own love life. I promise I will tell you more once there's more to tell, okay?" *And once I'm sure dating Xavier isn't the worst idea of my life.*

"Okay," Fiona said slowly, but I knew she'd keep me on my toes. I had to make sure she didn't meddle. This thing, whatever it was, between Xavier and me was still too fresh to have her messing with it.

Xavier picked me up at the corner as we'd discussed. I had made sure to check the street for Fiona's nosy face several times but didn't spot her. I slid into the passenger seat. "You are on time," I said, surprised.

Xavier flashed me a grin. "You're welcome."

I shook my head with a laugh but quieted when Xavier's eyes slowly wandered over me. I wasn't dressed in an overly sexy way, but the pencil skirt accentuated my hips and my blouse gave a nice view of my neckline. The appreciative flicker in Xavier's eyes sent a pleasant shiver down my spine. "You look gorgeous, Evie," he said in a low voice that I could feel all the way between my legs. It didn't hurt that Xavier looked good enough to devour himself with the dark blue dress shirt and beige pants.

"So where are we going?" I asked to distract myself from the dangerous sensations I was feeling.

"A microbrewery and pub I often visit with my brother. They have a nice selection and fantastic tasting options with delicious food to pair."

I grinned. Xavier was spot-on with his choice. Then another thought crossed my mind. "So in public? Aren't you worried about us being seen?" It was still too soon. I knew the press would ruin it for both of us if they found out this early in our...date trial.

Xavier pulled out of the street and sped up. "Like I said, I've been there before. It's off the beaten path. I know the owner well. He always gives me a secluded booth."

"Okay, that sounds good," I said slowly. Xavier had more experience dealing with the press and them trailing him, so I had to trust he knew what he was doing.

Xavier glanced my way. "So I did good?"

"Very good so far. We'll see how you keep faring."

"And if I fare well, I get that kiss you promised?"

I swallowed. "Maybe."

I didn't miss the surprised look the owner of the brewery gave us when we stepped in, and of course felt self-conscious because of it. Xavier probably had never brought someone like me here. Xavier's hand rested lightly on my lower back, and his biceps grazed my shoulder blade as he led me inside.

As if he could read my mind, Xavier said quietly, "I've never brought anyone but Marc here."

That made me smile, and Xavier's expression softened in a way it seldom did. We settled in a cozy booth in a corner with comfortable vintage leather benches and a table, which seemed to be made from old wine barrels. When the owner came over with the menu, Xavier shook his head. "The beer tasting with the matching bites."

"You will love their food," Xavier said when he turned back to me. If the spicy, warm scent was any indication, Xavier would be proven right.

I bit my lip, suddenly unsure what to say, how to act around Xavier. Luckily, the owner came our way with two wooden slabs that each held four small glasses of beer.

"You know the drill," the owner said with a wink.

Xavier nodded.

I stared down at the four beers. The glasses were the size of bigger shots, not more. "I hope the food isn't as tiny as well or we will have to hit a fast-food joint afterward."

Xavier laughed. "Oh Evie, you are perfect."

I flushed. "So what's the matter with these tiny beer glasses?"

"The tasting consists of twelve beers in total. If they all were regular sized, I'd have to carry you out afterward."

"First of all, I can hold my liquor pretty well, and second there's no way you can carry me. I'm too heavy."

"Wanna bet on it?"

"I'm not sure I want to bet with you."

The wolfish smile. "Why not?"

"Because you don't play fair."

"Come on."

I pointed at the beers. "Tell me a bit about them."

Xavier gave me a knowing look, but he let me distract him. "The first one you should taste is the one on the right—it's the lightest and won't ruin your taste buds for the others."

"You sound like a sommelier. Is there something like that for beer?"

He grinned, and raised his glass. "To us."

I clanked my glass against his and emptied it in one swallow.

Xavier's grin widened. "Just because they're shot glasses doesn't mean you have to ex them."

I raised my eyebrows in challenge. "Don't tell me it's too much for you to swallow." The moment the words left my mouth, I knew I'd given Xavier the perfect opening.

"I'd rather watch you swallow," he growled, then downed the beer.

My cheeks blasted with heat, eyes widening.

Xavier shook his head, regret passing his face. "I shouldn't have said that. Fuck. I'm already making a mess of this."

I gave a shrug and pointed at the next glass. "What's up next?"

Xavier leaned forward, lightly brushed my heated cheek with his thumb then kissed the hot skin. My eyes flew up to his. "I don't know how to treat you," he admitted in a low voice. "One moment I want to have my way with you, the next I want to protect you from me."

I frowned. "You don't need to protect me. I can protect myself. Just treat me like you treated me before sex was an issue. Like a friend, a human being. Not a vagina with limbs."

Xavier choked out a laugh. "Okay. That image definitely ensures that your sex ban will be successful tonight."

I smiled. "It would have been successful either way."

Xavier didn't get the chance for a comeback because the owner came with the food. A tray with plates of finger food. Everything looked delicious, and the moment I slipped a small fried ball of what proved to be slow-cooked pulled pork into my mouth, I knew I loved this place. I groaned as the decadent taste spread in my mouth.

Xavier watched me in rapt attention, and I wondered for whom the sex ban would be harder, me or him.

"Did you tell anyone about this?" I asked curiously when I'd finished my eighth shot of beer.

"Only Willow, and that was by accident. She called me this afternoon and

I let something slip. And you?"

"If I tell Fiona she'll go berserk on us, and I don't know that many people around here yet. I don't want to jinx this."

He nodded. "My family will probably be happier about this than yours."

I shrugged. "Fiona doesn't have to like you as long as I do."

"And you do?" Xavier asked in a low voice.

"You have to ask? I wouldn't be sitting here if I didn't find you quite tolerable."

"Ah, Evie, your romantic declarations warm my heart," he murmured with a soft laugh.

I grinned. "You know what you're getting. The snark will stay."

"I hope so."

We smiled at each other, and Xavier's eyes moved down to my lips once more. If he kept it up, I'd have to ask for ice to put in my panties.

"So how did Willow react to the news?"

"What do you think? She was over the moon. She's been wanting me to find someone forever."

"That's lovely," I said.

Xavier's expression darkened. "It's because she doesn't have a life herself. She's always at home with Mom. She should be doing what other teenage girls do. Sneak out, get drunk and flirt with guys so I can kick their sorry asses." He emptied his last beer. "But she won't because she can't, because she's stuck in that wheelchair."

I touched Xavier's hand and he turned his over and linked our fingers, his gray eyes sad and dark. "That wheelchair doesn't have to stop her from living her life. She can date, she can flirt and get drunk. A disability doesn't have to stop her, it doesn't have to define who she wants to be," I told him.

"That won't happen on that farm."

"She could move to Sydney after school. She wouldn't be alone. You and I could help her."

Xavier squeezed my hand, then brought it to his lips and kissed it. "Evie, I don't deserve you, I hope you realize it, but I should tell you I have every intention of keeping you, deserving or not."

A pleased flush spread in my body, and I leaned forward and gave Xavier a soft, light kiss, then leaned back before it turned into something more heated.

It was the only kiss we shared that night, though I could tell Xavier wanted to kiss me when he dropped me off on my street. "Thanks for the lovely date," I told him, turning around to him in my seat.

"Does that mean you'll agree to another date tomorrow?" Xavier asked with that annoying sexy twitch of his mouth.

"Yes. What did you have in mind?"

"We could go to the beach, sunbathe and take a dip."

Parading my flaws around in front of Xavier in a bathing suit? No, thanks. I frowned. "I don't think that's a good idea. The last time paparazzi got us on the beach."

"That's because I'd announced on my Instagram that I was filming a workout there, but it's a weekday."

I looked away. "I'd prefer if we did something else."

"Evie," Xavier began, but I held up my hand. "How about we go to the Royal Botanic Garden? I've wanted to visit it for a while."

"Okay, but the risk of people recognizing me there is pretty high too."

"Put on a cap," I said with a grin.

He chuckled. "I doubt that will fool anyone. But if that's what you want?"

"I do," I said. I knew we probably wouldn't have much time to go on dates in the days afterwards, since the start of the season was less than a week away.

I left the car with a last smile and closed the door, then practically floated home because the date had gone so much better than I'd hoped. Xavier had been as much of a gentleman as he was capable of, and we hadn't had a moment of boredom or awkward silence. I risked another glance over my shoulder. Xavier hadn't driven off yet, and a small shiver passed through my spine again. I'd wanted to kiss him so badly in the car just now.

I could only hope Xavier had enough restraint for the both of us because if the sex ban depended only on my control, it was doomed.

CHAPTER NINETEEN

EVIE

Xavier did indeed show up wearing a cap for our date in the Royal Botanic Garden, which to be honest didn't make him any less striking. A man of his size and muscle mass had a hard time blending into the background, even if he covered his head. I had chosen a cute summer dress with a narrow waist, low neckline, and ballerina flats. Xavier took his time admiring me as I strode toward him. We'd agreed to meet in front of the entrance and not have Xavier pick me up, so Connor and Fiona didn't get suspicious, though me dressing up like that had definitely raised Fiona's attention. She would find out eventually, and probably be butt-hurt I hadn't confided in her from the start.

When I arrived in front of him, I stood on my tiptoes and kissed his cheek. His arm came around my waist at once and his head dipped, his eyes locking with mine. "This outfit is meant to kill me, right?"

I tried to hide my smugness but failed when Xavier let out a low growl.

"You are a vixen."

His lips lightly brushed across mine, but I gently pushed back. Xavier held out his hand. "Can we risk holding hands?" Amusement tinged his deep voice.

We took our chances and strolled through the botanic garden hand in hand. It wasn't overly crowded, and many people around looked like tourists who weren't aware who Xavier was. The views of the opera house were spectacular, and so were the rose garden and fountains. "You didn't strike me as the flower girl," Xavier said after a while. "You like beer, ribs and action movies. But roses get you?"

"They are pretty. I'm allowed to enjoy pretty things too, right?"

Xavier pulled me to a stop and stepped close. "Sure. You enjoy the pretty flowers, I enjoy you."

I rolled my eyes. "Nice try to charm your way into my panties again. It won't work today."

Xavier let out that deep rumble of a laugh. "So the ban's still in place?"

"It is," I confirmed.

"Am I allowed a kiss at least?"

Considering we were in a public place, I deemed a kiss a safe option. "Okay—" The words had barely left my mouth when Xavier claimed my lips and kissed me. Kissed me like he really meant it, and my toes curled in my ballerina flats as his tongue tasted me, teased me, and his warm palm pressed against my back.

I drew back after a moment, a little dazed. We were still close and Xavier was looking at me as if he wanted to eat me.

"I think that's enough kissing for now," I murmured.

Xavier exhaled, but he stepped back as if he didn't trust himself so close to me. To be honest, I trusted myself far less than him.

In the days after our second date, Xavier and I didn't find time for another one. His first match of the season had him busy, body and mind, and I was actually glad for the small break since it allowed me to get a better grip on my feelings and my desires—or that's what I was trying to tell myself, at least. We'd only seen each other for work-related reasons, and I hadn't allowed any physical closeness during that time, but now that the first match was over and Xavier's team had won in a spectacular fashion, we'd agreed on a third, more intimate date. I wasn't sure why I had agreed to a date at his penthouse, maybe because he'd asked me right after the match, when I'd still been high with the euphoria of watching Xavier play a breathtaking game. But it was too late to back out now. I didn't want Xavier to realize how strong of an effect his closeness had on my body.

Yet, I couldn't get a grip on my nerves about my third date with Xavier. Which was ridiculous. I'd spent so many evenings with him in his penthouse, and many more work hours, but this felt different. This was the first time that I came over to his apartment not as his assistant but as his date, as his girlfriend.

I had considered wearing something sexy, but instead I'd opted for a soft coral cashmere sweater that hugged my chest, and jeans. I wanted to feel comfortable, and not give Xavier any ideas, though knowing him, he'd get them anyway.

The moment Xavier opened the door, I reminded him. "There won't be any sex tonight."

Then I took him in. The tight shirt, the low-cut jeans, the light scruff, and those eyes. Suddenly I felt like I needed reminding more than he did.

He grinned. "You said that already."

I'd said it more than once, had sent him two texts today alone with the same message. I nodded once, suddenly feeling shy. I had never felt shy around

Xavier. Maybe this was a bad idea.

Xavier opened the door a bit wider. "Won't you come in? I promise I won't bite unless you want me to."

"Xavier," I said in warning, but my stomach did a stupid little flip.

This man would definitely be my undoing.

I took a resolute step into his penthouse and walked toward the kitchen island, where I dropped my purse on one of the stools before I headed toward the fridge and opened it. Smiling to myself at his consideration, I grabbed a craft beer for myself and one for Xavier. No low-carb beer tonight. I put them down on the counter and was about to check Xavier's snack drawer when his warm breath ghosted over my ear. "I'd say 'make yourself comfortable,' but you're already doing just that."

I whirled around, startled, and swatted his chest. "You scared me!" I didn't take my hand off his chest. Why wasn't I pulling away? He was even closer than I'd expected. One arm propped up on the kitchen island, leaning half over me. Breathing became difficult with him so close, with his manly scent, with the way his tall body made me feel delicate for once, with the way his eyes undressed me like I was actually sexy.

His face came closer. Hell, he was going to kiss me again. I knew where it had led last time we were alone in his apartment.

I quickly turned back around to the counter, and Xavier let out a chuckle against the back of my head. Even that low rumble sent a sweet shiver down my spine.

This was such a bad idea. The worst idea of a long string of bad ideas.

I should leave before I made an even bigger mistake.

I grabbed both beer bottles and used one to open the other, then handed it to Xavier before I took a spoon from the drawer and opened my beer with it.

"You are the only woman I know who can do that, and it's fucking sexy," he said with a strange smile. "From the moment I first saw you do that, I knew you were perfect."

I took a swig from my bottle. "Not perfect. Deep down I'm lazy. I was tired of searching for the opener all the time and since I never had a boyfriend who could do it for me, I had to teach myself how to do it."

Xavier watched me strangely over his bottle, then took a deep swig as well. "Why did you never have a boyfriend?"

I sighed, flushing. That wasn't a topic I wanted to go into detail over, but at least it distracted me from more dangerous thoughts, like how much I wanted to grab Xavier by his jeans pockets and jerk him toward me. I leaned back against the counter to bring more space between Xavier and me. "As long as my sister still lived with us, boys always only saw her, not me. She was the athletic cheerleader and I was the chubby bookworm."

Xavier made a disgusted face. "I don't get the appeal."

"Come on," I said. "Fiona is your type, don't pretend it isn't so. I've seen the women you took into your bed in the last few months."

I glanced down at myself. I wasn't anything like them. Shoving that unpleasant thought aside, I took another gulp of my beer.

"She's good-looking all right, but she's annoying as fuck."

"But you made a move on her before she was with Connor."

Xavier grimaced. "She told you?"

I snorted. "We're sisters. Of course she told me. I'm really glad she turned you down. That would have been too weird."

"I've done weirder things."

"Don't remind me," I muttered.

Xavier became serious again. "Come on, Evie. I can't believe there weren't any guys making a move on you. I'm sure one of them would have gladly helped you with your V-card."

"There were a couple, but I didn't want to do the deed just to get it over with. I wanted it to happen with someone I cared deeply about and who cared deeply about me." My insides pulled tight. Why couldn't I keep my stupid mouth shut? This was the second time I'd as good as admitted to Xavier that I was in love with him. I was such a stupid cow.

I downed the rest of my beer, avoiding Xavier's gaze. Damn it. I could feel the waterworks beginning. I fought it and when that didn't work I quickly pushed past Xavier, opening the fridge to grab another beer for myself. If I kept up the tempo, I'd be drunk before we even started the movie.

When I turned back around with the bottle, one traitorous tear slid down my cheek. Xavier brushed it away with his thumb and I wanted to die on the spot.

"Evie—"

"Don't say something only because you feel guilty," I interrupted him.

Anger flashed on Xavier's face and he backed me into the counter, then supported himself to both sides of me and glared down at me. "Don't assume you know everything about me, Evie, only because you know me better than anyone else. You are important to me and I care about you. And I fucking cared about you when I popped your cherry."

I swallowed. "I know you better than anyone else?"

Xavier chuckled and pulled back. He took my beer, opened it with the spoon and nodded toward the living area. "Let's watch a movie."

"That was my beer. Give it back," I said.

Xavier smirked. "Make me." He took a provocative swig as he walked backwards toward the sofa. Something snapped in me, and I stormed toward him and tackled him. *Tackled Xavier—The Beast—Stevens.* God help me, Xavier must have fucked my brains out.

Xavier's eyes widened in surprise when I collided with him, but he had no chance of bracing himself. The air was knocked out of me from the impact against his hard muscles, and then we were falling. I released a very embarrassing screech, clenching my eyes shut, as we tumbled over the backrest of the sofa. I landed hard on top of Xavier, straddling him.

When I finally opened my eyes, Xavier was watching me incredulously. Somehow he'd managed to land with the beer bottle still in his hand and miraculously full. "What was that?" he asked.

I stared down at him, realizing I was sitting on him, and I flushed, couldn't help it because I could feel him growing hard against me. He set the beer down slowly, and I should have moved off him. Instead I kept staring at him as he grew even harder against me.

Evie, haul your ass off of Xavier.

And then Xavier's lips curled in that cocky way, and I lost it. I crushed my mouth against his and he responded immediately. Grabbing my ass with one hand and claiming my mouth with his tongue, he rolled over until he was wedged between my legs and I could feel him right where I was aching.

He ground himself against me, hard, eager for more, and kissed me even harder. I ran my hands over his back, gripped the hem of his shirt and pulled it over his head.

My God, that body.

His hand tangled in my hair as he angled my head the way he wanted it and his tongue delved even deeper. My toes curled. Before Xavier I didn't know they could do that. But Xavier could kiss. Boy, could that man kiss.

His other hand slid down my side then he sat up and tugged at my sweater, and then that was gone as well. He let out a low growl. "Another layer?"

I glanced down at myself, at the thin tank top I had put on under the sweater, and finally sanity set in. I put a hand against Xavier's naked chest, and shook my head. "We should stop."

Xavier leaned forward. "Do you really want to stop?"

His voice was pure sex, seduction put into words, and my core responded with a wave of heat. What I wanted was to keep kissing Xavier, to rip every last piece of clothing off him and taste every inch of his perfect body, discover all the places I hadn't paid attention to last time.

I closed my eyes, trying to sort through my emotions.

"Evie?" Xavier asked, voice softer than before.

"Stop," I got out.

Xavier's weight lifted off me, and I had to bite my tongue not to reach for him and pull him back. When I opened my eyes again, Xavier sat on the end of the couch, nipping at his beer, his body tense and his shirt back on.

I straightened as well and smoothed my hair away from my face. Was he angry? "Don't tell me you are pissed because I told you to stop. I told you no sex."

Xavier raised his eyebrows. "What makes you think I'm pissed?"

"You are all tense and sitting on the other end of the couch."

He smirked. "I'm tense because my cock threatens to burst through my pants, and you have no intention of helping me with it. And I'm sitting over here because you are even worse at this no-sex rule than I am."

I flushed and sat back against the couch. Xavier wasn't the only one who had a problem in his pants. My privates felt like they had turned into a puddle of lava. I was actually worried it would look as if I'd wet my pants if I got up. I shifted to alleviate some of the tension.

Xavier's keen eyes watched me. "Evie, why do you insist on that stupid no-sex rule? You want this as much as I do."

I didn't deny it. "Because I want this to be more than sex. I'm not one of your conquests. Well, I don't want to be."

"You aren't. You know you mean a lot to me. That's why we are here. That's why I agreed to give this dating thing a chance."

"This dating thing," I muttered.

He sighed, and moved closer. I eyed him cautiously. "This isn't easy for me, Evie. I've never dated anyone. But I'm here, willing to give this a chance, because I don't want to lose you."

I held my breath, my heart swelling with emotions. He cupped my cheek and I got lost in his eyes. I wasn't sure if I would be strong enough to stop him again, even if I knew I needed to, if I wanted to protect my heart. His lips brushed mine, but with my last resolve I drew back an inch. "Please Xavier, don't..." I swallowed. "I know you're aware of your effect on women and you use it, but don't...I can't do this yet."

CHAPTER TWENTY

XAVIER

The look in Evie's eyes and her broken whisper were a bucket of ice water. Fuck. She begged me not to take things further because she knew she wouldn't be able to resist. She wanted me as much as I wanted her. She was fucking wet. I knew it, and she'd be tight and hot around my cock, but her expression was almost desperate and I couldn't be that kind of asshole with her. Not with Evie.

"What about kissing? Because I really want to fucking kiss you, Evie," I rasped, and she gave a small resigned nod, and I dove in, my lips taking her soft mouth. Evie opened up as she always did, letting me in, meeting my tongue with eagerness and with the hint of innocence that drove me completely insane. I'd have never thought it would turn me on, but with Evie it fucking did. Maybe it was because everything about Evie did.

I tangled my hand in her soft curls, pulling her even closer and her palms pressed up against my chest, fingernails grazing my skin, and my dick actually leaked pre-cum. Fuck it. Her hand slid lower over my ribs, my abs, and I almost lost my shit and threw her over my shoulder all caveman style and carried her upstairs to fuck her in every which way I could imagine.

I wrenched my mouth away, heaved a breath and grabbed my beer for a huge gulp. Evie's lips were red and swollen and she was panting, which made her impressive tits swell with every intake of breath, and that skimpy top wasn't hiding all that much. Fuck, I almost asked her to put her sweater back on. It would have made the no-sex endeavor so much easier. "You mentioned a movie," Evie said in a dazed voice.

"Yeah," I croaked, then cleared my throat. "Got the new *Mission Impossible* for us."

"Great," Evie said. "I'll get myself another beer since you took mine and some snacks."

"Let me," I said, but Evie was faster. "Stay. I need to splash some water on my face anyway."

That sounded like a good plan. I needed some cold water in my pants. I watched Evie's ass as she headed for the fridge, and my mind had her undressed, bent over the couch and my cock wedged between those amazing globes within a second.

Groaning, I leaned back and rubbed my temple. This was going to be fucking hard.

"Are you in pain, Xavier?" Evie asked teasingly from her spot at the open fridge door.

"Do you need a dry pair of panties?" I shot back, and Evie's eyes widened, cheeks turning pink. Bull's-eye.

She grabbed the beer before she took a bag of chips out of my snacks drawer. Before Evie it had been mostly empty but I knew she had a sweet and savory tooth, so I always kept a few snacks handy.

"Beer and chips, you really went all out for our date night," she said.

I tensed. "You said you didn't want anything special. We can still order something to eat. The Indian place you love so much."

Pressing the cold bottle against her cheek, she came toward me, dropped the bag in my lap, and touched my shoulder. "I'm actually not that hungry. Chips, beer and a movie where Tom Cruise kicks ass are my kind of date."

I grinned because this was Evie. I opened the chips bag and Evie settled beside me. I put my arm over the backrest, not sure if it was a good idea to wrap it around her, to bring her closer. Evie eyed me with those fucking gorgeous green eyes, and worried her lower lip. "How do we do this?"

I chuckled. "We turn on the TV and watch."

She gave me a look. "That's not what I meant."

"What do you want?"

She made a funny face, which made me groan inwardly because I could imagine what she wanted but was too stubborn to ask for. "I think it would be nice to be in your arms." Her cheeks flushed and she snatched the bag from my lap and took a chip out. "But we can sit on either side of the couch. That's fine with me as well." It wasn't. Her expression and voice made that pretty clear, and to be honest, I wanted Evie in my arms.

Deciding to cut this nonsense short, I wrapped my arm around her waist and hauled her against my side. After a cry of surprise, she put her head down on my shoulder, one hand on my stomach and her soft body curved into me. A few stubborn wayward hairs tickled my nose so I smoothed them down. Evie released a soft sigh and relaxed all the way into me. I took the remote and started the movie, then put the bag of chips back into my lap.

"If this is some trick so I touch you by accident, it won't work," she said teasingly.

"I don't want you to touch my cock by accident, I want you to do it on purpose because you want it," I said in a low voice, and Evie gave a small shudder.

Smiling to myself, I turned back to the screen. Soon we were both immersed in the movie, which as usual was so much more entertaining thanks to Evie's snarky commentary. My hand on her waist began to travel up and down her side, enjoying her soft curves. It wasn't something I had ever considered liking. Evie's breathing deepened when my fingers brushed her ribcage.

By now, I was glad for the bag of chips in my lap because it hid my fucking boner.

When the movie was finally over, Evie lifted her head, looking slightly disheveled. She stifled a yawn. "I should probably get home."

"You've had a few beers. Why don't you spend the night?"

"Xavier," she began, but I quickly interrupted her. "Just sleep. I don't want you to go home now and it's not like you've never slept here before, and I'm not speaking of last time."

"But things are different now," she said softly, then sighed. Seeing Evie this hesitant and wary around me made me realize just how badly I'd messed up. I'd never intended to take things that far with Evie. In the beginning I hadn't even been interested in her in that regard, but that changed pretty quickly, and now here I was, horny like a teenage boy.

"I can't speak for you, but I'll keep my hands to myself."

She rolled her eyes in that fucking adorable way. "Your virtue is safe with me."

"That ship has sailed a long time ago."

"How long?" she asked, curiosity taking over.

I chuckled, leaning closer. "A long time ago." Evie didn't need to know that I'd lost it in a car when I was fifteen with a woman five years older who was also my brother's ex. She'd done it to spite him, and I had been too desperate for pussy to say no.

Her brows furrowed. "Maybe I'll just ask your brother next time I see him."

"He might just tell you. My family is fawning over you."

"They are, aren't they?" she said with a hint of smugness.

I could have kicked myself. It wasn't something I wanted to share with Evie. They all had been on my back, asking about Evie since I'd brought her over. They would order fireworks the moment I told them we were actually dating.

"Stay tonight, Evie," I said quietly, cupping her cheek.

Her lashes fluttered and she nodded. "Okay."

For a moment, her agreement almost immobilized me. Me. Xavier—The Beast—Stevens. I could shove a boulder off me, but that breathy whisper got to me.

I snatched the chips bag off my lap and put it away. Evie had drawn back, and her eyes were doing the quick scan of my body that sent a clear message straight to my dick. I stood, knowing I was giving her a show of what exactly her appraisal did to me.

Evie averted her eyes, tucked a strand of hair behind her ear, swallowed. I held out my hand for her. She tilted her head up, eyes narrowing ever so slightly as she considered my expression. Then she put her hand in mine so I could pull her up. "Where will I sleep?"

"My bed," the words practically shot out of my mouth.

"I really don't think that's a good idea."

It wasn't. Not with the way Evie kept undressing me with her eyes, not with the way my cock was straining against my pants, not with Evie's sweet scent flooding my nose. "I will behave if you do," I murmured.

Her lashes fluttered and she didn't say anything, which was all the answer I needed, and it gave my dick more encouragement than it required.

Evie followed me upstairs into my bedroom. Her fingers stiffened in mine.

"Only sleep," she said in warning, but there was still that hint of insecurity in her expression.

"Evie, I would never do anything you don't want."

She gave me a resolute look. "Only sleep." I really wasn't sure if she was reminding me or herself.

I released her and went over to my drawer to rummage for one of my shirts she could put on for sleep. I pulled one of my favorite shirts out and handed it to her. After a moment of hesitation, she disappeared in my bathroom. Running a hand through my hair, my eyes found my bed. Sleep was the last thing I wanted to do, but I didn't want to mess this up with Evie again.

When Evie emerged five minutes later wearing only my too-large shirt, my heart skipped a fucking beat at the sight of her in my clothes. My shirt reached her thighs, and my eyes were drawn to her soft flesh, imagining how it would feel to be wedged between her legs and taste her. No man had ever done that to Evie, no man had ever been between those luscious thighs. I could have kicked my horny past-self for not eating Evie out. Why had I pounced on her like a fucking stag in rutting season? And my shirt did nothing to hide Evie's marvelous tits. I'd never considered myself a breast man. But with Evie...

"Xavier," Evie said quietly, warningly. My eyes snapped up to her face. Her cheeks were flushed, her pupils dilated. She'd be wet and warm if I reached beneath the hem of my shirt. Her gaze darted down to my briefs and the boner they had no chance of hiding.

I snapped out of it and moved toward the bathroom, but briefly stopped beside Evie to rasp in her ear. "You look gorgeous." She shivered and I quickly continued into the bathroom to get ready for bed, and splash some water in my face, not that it would do anything for my dick.

Evie lay on her side in my bed, the covers pulled up to her shoulders when I returned into the bedroom. Her eyes followed me as I made my way over to her. I'd been with enough women to know desire, but damn it, I wasn't sure what to do with the other emotion in her eyes.

I slipped under the covers and Evie's warmth and scent hit me like a wrecking ball. Moving closer without a second thought, I put my hand on Evie's waist. She sucked in her breath, those stunning green eyes locking on mine and making my stomach flutter as it had never done in all my life. I needed a taste. I leaned forward and Evie's palms came up to my chest, but she didn't push, and our lips connected.

Her taste, her soft lips, her scent and the desperate breathy sighs she made, they all wreaked havoc with my resolve. My hand slid down over her hips, and lower, until I reached bare skin, Evie's soft thigh, and she moaned into my mouth and pressed closer. She was warm and smooth, and I hooked my palm under her thigh and slung her leg over my hip, then hauled her even closer. Her hot center pressed against my cock, and the thin fabric of our clothes did nothing to hide the proof of Evie's arousal from me.

She paused in our kiss, her eyes opening, staring straight at me, and I knew she would abolish the no-sex rule. If I slid my fingers between her thighs, she'd let me, and she wouldn't stop me from burying myself in her tight heat either.

But Evie's earlier words flashed in my mind then, about my effect on women, and how I used it, and her plea not to take things further than she was ready for—mentally, because her body was ready for the full program, no doubt there.

I closed my eyes and took a deep breath. "You are not good at this no-sex rule, Evie," I groaned.

"Sorry," she said. "But it's really difficult to think straight if you keep kissing me like that. It makes me wonder how it would feel to come with your hands on me. I've only ever come with my own hands."

That reminder wasn't helping matters. I was the only man who had ever touched Evie's lovely pussy. And I was also the asshole who didn't make her come during her first time. I'd thought she'd come during intercourse. I'd thought we'd fuck more than once that night. If I had known Evie was a virgin, I would have made her come a few times before shoving my dick into her. If I'd known she was a virgin, I probably wouldn't have slept with her at all.

I cupped her ass and said in a low voice, "Let me show you how it feels to come, Evie."

"That defies the no-sex rule," she whispered.

"I promise no sex, only a mind-blowing orgasm for you." I traced my lips down her throat and nibbled on her soft skin.

"You...you are so full of yourself. It's annoying."

I smiled against her skin. "I love annoying you."

She huffed but quieted when I kissed the spot below her ear. "So mind-blowing orgasm, yay or nay?"

There was a pause, then a soft word left her lips. "Yay."

The word was breathless and throaty, and fuck if it didn't make me even harder. "Fuck, Evie. I've never been this hard in my life. Even adamantium can't compare."

"If you keep up the X-Men references I might reconsider the no-sex rule," she said with that dirty laugh I loved.

"Don't give me ideas," I warned as I propped myself up on my elbows and gently pushed Evie on her back before I moved down her body, then brushed my hands over her calves and thighs. I nudged them apart and was about to move between them when Evie closed her legs.

"What are you doing?" Evie asked, wide-eyed.

I hovered above her legs. "Putting my tongue to good use."

She blushed a beautiful shade of pink. "You don't have to."

I grinned. "I want to."

"Really?"

She looked incredulous and her blush deepened further. Evie was going to be my undoing. I shook my head. "Fuck, I keep forgetting how little you've done so far."

She pursed those kissable lips. "Do you have to make me sound like a medical case?"

"I'm a very good doctor." I flashed her my dirtiest smile.

She closed her eyes. "My God, Xavier, you look like a wolf about to pounce."

"I'm a hungry wolf about to eat you," I said in a low voice.

Her eyes peeled open. I stroked her legs and hooked my fingers in her panties and dragged them down slowly. Evie shivered, biting her lip.

Her cheeks were still a lovely shade of pink. I didn't know how I could have missed all the telltale signs of her inexperience during our first night together. I'd been too wrapped up in my own fucking need.

My eyes trailed over her legs, up to the dark blonde triangle at the apex of her thighs. A stunning sight.

Evie was still tense under me as my fingers stroked her thighs.

I lowered my head to the trimmed curls and pressed a kiss against her mound, my lower lip lightly brushing her soft folds that hid her clit.

"Oh," she breathed out, eyes flying open. Her legs were still clamped together. Her eyes flitted down to me. I kissed her again, but this time I used my lower lip to part her folds and brush her clit.

"Oh!" she gasped.

"Oh?" I asked quietly. Her leg muscles softened. I hooked my palm under her knee and guided her leg to the side, baring her to me.

Her eyes flickered with insecurity and nerves. I lightly bit into the soft flesh of her inner thigh, feeling unexpectedly possessive. My gaze returned to her inviting pussy. No one had ever seen Evie like this. I blew out a harsh breath and licked the soft inside of her thigh.

She quivered, her legs parting a bit more. I smiled against her skin as I lowered myself between Evie's thighs, slid my palms under her butt and pulled her toward my mouth. She tensed again but I knew it wouldn't last long.

I gave her clit a light lick and she jerked. "Oh hell!"

"Does this feel like Hell?" I slid the tip of my tongue along her slit, up to her clit.

She moaned.

"Tell me how it feels, Evie," I whispered as I took another long lick over her folds, giving her clit a gentle nudge at the end.

"Good," she gasped as I gave her clit a little loving with my lips.

"Only good?"

"Stop talking, Xavier," she muttered, and I chuckled and really dove in. Parting her folds, I tasted her sweetness, making sure to let Evie hear just how delicious she was to me.

The sounds falling from Evie's lips as I worshipped her with my tongue were music to my ears. Her body was beautifully responsive and sensitive to my ministrations, and I couldn't get enough of it. She rewarded me with her first orgasm almost too easily, but I kept up the light suction on her clit, which drove her completely wild and pushed a finger into her, curling it upwards, trying to see if I could find Evie's G-spot. She arched up when my pad pressed against her inner wall. Bull's-eye.

This time I took my time bringing her close to the brink, only to retreat and focus my attention on less sensitive spots like her inner thigh. Soon Evie was wriggling and moaning without holding back, desperate for another release. "Xavier," she gasped. "Please—"

"Please what?" I asked as trailed the tip of my tongue over the valley between her thigh and pussy before giving her clit the lightest push, making Evie gasp again.

"Please stop being a dickhead."

I chuckled and sucked her clit a bit harder while I thrust my finger inside of her until Evie cried out again as she came. She trembled under me. I kissed her stomach, pretending I didn't notice her tensing. She was still self-conscious about her body but I hoped we could work on that.

Her strawberry-blonde hair spilled around her as she tried to catch her breath. She was a goddess.

For a moment, I considered taking this further and burying myself in her, but she smiled in that cute embarrassed way that let my protectiveness overrule my desire.

Ignoring my cock, I stretched out beside Evie and pulled her closer. Her gaze searched mine as if she waited for me to make a move.

EVIE

My heart was galloping in my chest like a herd of mustangs. I couldn't believe how amazing this had felt, how utterly breathtaking. Xavier regarded me with a hint of smugness and I really wanted to take him down a notch, but damn it, he had reason to be smug. I wanted to push him back down between my legs for another round, but that would definitely have ended my no-sex ruling. Could it even still be considered in effect? Going down on someone definitely counted as a form of sex. It did in our stupid non-disclosure clause, that much was certain.

Xavier made a low sound in his throat, cupped the back of my head and pulled me in for a languid kiss. Tasting myself on his lips was strangely erotic.

"I had to shut you up," he murmured after he drew back a few inches.

"I didn't say anything."

"Your mind was working on overdrive. I could see it from that pinched expression you always get. Don't overthink this, Evie."

"I don't get a pinched look," I said indignantly.

Xavier flashed me the grin that melted every pair of panties in a radius of at least one mile. "You do, and it's never a good thing. Just enjoy the moment."

"You know me too well," I said with a sigh. "It's a bit unsettling."

He regarded me. "It is."

I bit my lip, surprised by the serious note in Xavier's voice. He was still hard against my thigh, and yet he didn't make a move. He must have known that I would have abolished that no-sex rule in a heartbeat if he'd tried. Yet he didn't. "Why did you agree to give this a try?" I whispered.

"I told you: because I don't want to lose you."

"As an assistant?"

Xavier nodded, then cupped my cheek. "As an assistant, as my friend, as the woman who gets me hard without even trying. I don't want to lose your snarky comments when we watch movies, or that eye roll you give me when I do something that annoys you. You don't take my bullshit. You don't blow candy up my ass. You stand up to me, but you are never mean or petty about it. You don't play games. You are fucking amazing."

I swallowed. "This isn't your attempt to get me to sleep with you again."

Xavier smiled cockily. "Evie, you and I both know you changed your mind about the no-sex rule the moment I started eating you out."

Maybe he thought I'd contradict him, but Xavier had been honest, had said words I'd never thought possible, and I would be honest as well. "You're right," I admitted softly.

Xavier's expression turned intent. I leaned toward him and after a deep breath, I whispered, "I don't care about the no-sex rule anymore. I've already lost my heart to you, and sex won't change it. I can't resist your charms, and you know it. I want you."

Xavier buried his face in my neck, his breath hot against my skin. "Fuck, Evie, why are you doing this to me?" he rasped. "Don't leave it up to me to do the honorable thing. I've never done anything honorable in my life."

It wasn't true. He only never made honorable acts public. He was cocky about everything, showed off his women and wealth for everyone to see, but his good deeds, those he kept to himself. He'd saved his grandparents' farm, played with those kids in the women's shelter, and gave money to good causes that meant a lot to him, especially facilities that fought against domestic violence. "I don't want you to do the honorable thing now."

He rolled onto his back, closing his eyes as if in pain. "I promised you I would respect your no-sex rule," he said regretfully. "And I fucking will, even if it kills me."

I smiled, despite my body's cry of protest.

"See, that look tells me you wanted me to do the honorable thing after all," he murmured, watching me through half-closed eyes.

I kissed him. Then I sat up, and, banishing my nerves, I scooted down until I was on eye level with the tent in Xavier's boxers.

"Evie," he said in a low voice.

"Shh," I said. "I need to remember what the instructions said."

Xavier chuckled. "What?"

I peered up at him. "I read up on this. There are very helpful articles on the internet."

He smiled but it was tense with desire. "I'd love to read those articles."

"I didn't know you'd want to learn how to give a blow job." I reached for his waistband and dragged down his briefs, turning Xavier's undoubtedly cocky reply into a groan as his erection bounced free.

I shook my head. "You are so freaking big, it's ridiculous."

The look on his face set fireworks off in my body. I curled my fingers around his base, then lowered my head. Xavier grew even tighter under my touch. I stopped inches from his tip, my gaze going to his face.

He watched me eagerly. I had to stifle a smile. It was hard to believe that I did this to him, to Xavier.

"I won't be any good at this," I said quietly. "Nowhere near as good as the women you've been with." I felt like I needed to make this clear lest his expectations rose too high.

Xavier shook his head and touched my cheek before slowly sliding his fingers into my hair. "I don't give a fuck about any of them, but I do about you, Evie."

I returned my gaze to his erection before I got emotional and closed my lips around his tip. Xavier released a low groan. I took my time exploring him until I figured out what made Xavier moan. Surprisingly I found myself enjoying this more than I'd ever thought possible, and not only because it made me feel desirable and in control. Soon he was panting and making small upwards thrusts into my mouth.

"Evie, you need to pull back if you don't want to swallow," Xavier groaned as he rocked his hips upwards with more force.

My brows pulled together in consideration. I hadn't made up my mind yet if it was something I wanted. Xavier took the choice off my hands and pulled me back. Seconds later he released on his stomach, shuddering and groaning.

I could feel a grin tugging at my mouth, and Xavier shook his head with a low curse. He gripped my arm and pulled me against his side, claiming my mouth. "You're good at everything you do, aren't you, Little Miss Perfect."

I was many things, but little or perfect definitely weren't among them. "I'm sure there's still room for improvement. Any tips?"

Xavier chuckled against my mouth, and the look in his eyes was like a hot chocolate after a day in the cold. "The tip is always a good tip."

I shoved him lightly. "The truth. I can only improve with honest criticism."

Xavier cleaned his stomach with a tissue before he pulled me half on top of him. His eyes moved down to my breasts that were pushed up against his firm chest then they returned to my face. "This isn't school, Evie. You don't have to prove anything. Just be yourself."

"Am I not always?"

He regarded me quietly for a moment. "Yeah. You are. Nothing fake with you."

I swallowed, deciding it was time to lighten the mood. "Not even my breasts."

Of course, it had the desired effect. My breasts were always a good icebreaker with Xavier. His eyes took their time taking in the way my breasts were pushed up, and he grinned. "Your breasts are perfection."

I wondered what he thought of the rest of my body. Instead of asking I rolled my eyes at him. His expression lit up, and he leaned forward and kissed me. Just kissing. Slow and gentle. There was no urgency in the kiss, no underlying tension. We just kissed, our mouths lightly brushing, tongues exploring, for a long time.

Xavier's fingers lightly stroked my scalp and I traced my fingertips through his soft chest hair. Eventually, Xavier extinguished the lights, and I drifted off to sleep with my cheek against his chest.

CHAPTER TWENTY-ONE

EVIE

I woke before sunrise, still pressed up against Xavier. It felt like perfection, but how often did perfection really last?

Suddenly I was worried about waking beside him in the morning, about having him wake beside me and not want me here. We hadn't done the deed but we hadn't exactly done nothing either.

I wanted to be the one to determine the morning after this time. Untangling myself from Xavier, who rolled over with a soft groan but kept sleeping, I slipped out of the bed and fumbled my way toward the bathroom. I picked up my discarded clothes, quickly got dressed and walked downstairs. My phone showed I'd missed five calls from Fiona and about twenty of her messages.

I should have told her I would stay the night somewhere else, but it had never been the plan, and she would have asked questions I didn't want to answer yet. Fiona would kill me if she found out I'd returned to Xavier's bed.

I grabbed my purse, then decided to leave Xavier a note. Problem was I had no clue what to write.

Eventually I settled for:

Thanks for the chips and the beer. It was a perfect date.

I decided against signing. For one, Xavier knew who had written the note, and even my name, and second I wasn't sure how to end the note. "Love, Evie" was out of the question. If I mentioned the word love around Xavier, he'd be running for the woods.

"Kisses" or "XOXO" might just have the same effect.

I still wasn't sure how to classify this thing between us. A dating trial run? That option didn't exist on Facebook.

Checking the calendar, I realized Xavier only had an afternoon workout today, so I'd have enough time to head home, get a couple hours of additional sleep and shower before I had to be back in his apartment to wake him.

Grabbing my purse, I left the note in front of the coffee maker and left.

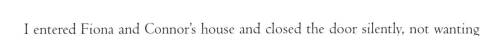

I entered Fiona and Connor's house and closed the door silently, not wanting to wake them.

"Where have you been?" came a voice out of the dark.

I cried out, clutching my purse against my chest. "Jesus, Connor, being six foot four and built like a wall, you shouldn't stalk women in the dark. That might give someone a heart attack one day, or get you thrown into jail."

The lights in the living room came on, revealing Connor leaning in the doorway, hair all over the place and only in low sweatpants. I wasn't sure what it was with rugby players and their aversion to walking around fully dressed.

"I promised Fiona to wait for you so she could finally get some sleep." He took in my rumpled state. I hadn't bothered straightening my hair and my clothes had seen better days. "You were with Xavier."

I flushed. "What makes you think that? I could have been with someone else."

Connor shook his head. "You aren't the type to move from one guy to the next so quickly."

I wasn't sure if I should be annoyed or pleased that he pegged me down as the steady type.

"Don't tell Fiona," I whispered.

Connor moved closer, looking worried. "Listen, Evie, you are a grown woman, and perfectly capable of making your own decisions, even if Fiona disagrees, but this one is really fucking bad. I love Xavier like a brother, but he's not boyfriend material. He doesn't want to be. He's content being the asshole child of the press."

"I'm a grown-up, you said it yourself. I'm perfectly capable of digging my own grave," I said teasingly, even if his words hit a bit too close to home.

Connor looked doubtful.

"I'm going to sleep a few more hours. I'm pretty tired," I said. My cheeks heated when Connor grimaced. I quickly rushed upstairs into my room, hoping that Connor would keep his mouth shut. Fiona would kill me if she found out I was giving Xavier another chance. I knew she was worried about me, and my cowardly escape from Xavier's apartment this morning proved she had reason to be. Connor's warning replayed in my brain over and over again as I crept under the covers.

Xavier was trying to be a boyfriend…sort of, for me. Wasn't he? We were giving dating a chance. We hadn't put a name on exactly what we were yet, but so early on in this trial that was to be expected. He didn't want to lose me, and I didn't want to lose him. My heart was already irrevocably lost anyway.

Even the hot chocolate and banana bread I'd had for the sole purpose of their sugary contents calming my nerves didn't work. I was ridiculously nervous as I arrived in front of Xavier's door to wake him. How was I supposed to act around him after last night? Kiss him good morning? Or would that presume too much? I stepped inside Xavier's apartment, half worried about finding him in a compromising situation, worried that he'd changed his mind about the dating thing after last night.

I froze when I spotted Xavier standing close to the window, looking out toward the harbor bridge.

He turned, a cup of cappuccino in one hand, and my note in the other. I cringed inwardly. Maybe that note hadn't been a good idea. Xavier looked... disappointed...or sad. I wasn't sure.

"You're up," I said dumbly as I made my way toward the kitchen island, where I perched on a stool and set the mail down on the counter.

For a moment, Xavier didn't do anything; then he walked toward me. My eyes were drawn to the flexing muscles of his stomach as they always were. Xavier was utter male perfection. Why would he ever consider changing his ways for me? For poor chubby Evie?

When he stopped close enough that the scent of fresh espresso and his own manly scent wafted into my nose, I finally looked back up into his face. His frowning face. No smirk or grin or cockiness for once. "I woke to an empty bed and when I came down expecting to find you here, I got this instead." He held up the crinkled note.

"I'm always good for a surprise. You said it yourself," I joked half-heartedly, but with the way Xavier's gray eyes were boring into me, humor was difficult to pull off.

221

He moved close. "Why did you leave, Evie?"

"I didn't want to impose on you or overextend my welcome," I said lightly.

His strong hands came down on my thighs and he kissed me briefly. "You are always welcome, and you know it."

I regarded him. "After our first night together, it didn't feel that way."

"Fuck," he groaned. He cupped my cheek, his face so close it was becoming increasingly difficult not to end this conversation by kissing him. "I feel like an asshole because of it. I told you I'm sorry. I can't change what happened but I'm trying to make up for it, and for the record, I don't want you to leave. I want to wake up beside you."

I swallowed. "Noted. Next time I'll stay."

Xavier grinned. "How about tonight? Let's have another movie night and this time you'll stay for breakfast."

I snorted. "That's a line most guys crash and burn with, you realize that, right? It's in the player's handbook of bad pick-up lines. Didn't you get the memo?"

Xavier laughed, and my insides began their usual fluttering. "Will you let me crash and burn with my line?"

His lips found mine again, and I allowed myself to enjoy his kiss for a moment longer before I pulled back. "It's a yes to the date. If I'll spend the night, that depends on your behavior."

Though really, it was a bit hypocritical of me to put all the blame on Xavier. I had failed at keeping to my own rule last night, and I had a feeling tonight wouldn't be much easier.

The wolfish grin. "I'll be a good boy, Evie."

I chuckled. "We'll see." Maybe Xavier wasn't the bad boy the press made him out to be, but he definitely wasn't a good boy. Not that I wanted him to be.

This time I entered Xavier's apartment without last night's warning. We had sushi and watched an old James Bond movie with Sean Connery, even if I usually preferred the newer versions. The no-sex ban was firmly in place. We were being good, even if Xavier's arm around me was distracting, albeit not as much as his hand which cupped my ass the entire time. My fingers kept drawing lazy circles on Xavier's chest and stomach, but our eyes were firmly focused on the screen until about halfway through the movie, which was when Xavier gave my ass a firm squeeze and my fingers accidentally brushed the bulge in his pants. It all went downhill from there pretty quickly, as far as the ban was concerned, at least.

Two hours into the date, I was sprawled out on my back on the sofa, my legs draped over Xavier's broad shoulders and his face wedged between my thighs as he did unspeakable things with his tongue and mouth. I clutched the headrest with one hand as my other held Xavier's head in place. Not that he needed any encouragement. He was eating me like a starving man would a plate of burritos.

"You taste like heaven, Evie," Xavier growled against my center before he closed his mouth over my folds again and sucked. He pulled me even closer, his shoulders pressing up against the backs of my thighs. I cried out, getting closer and closer. It felt so dirty having him do this to me on the sofa. I felt his finger against me before he slipped it in. Exhaling, I still marveled at the sensation of having something inside me. Xavier groaned against my heated flesh, the vibrations sending another spike in pleasure through my nether regions. "Fuck, you are so tight."

He moved his finger in and out slowly before his lips found my clit again, sucking almost roughly, and I came apart. Clinging to the sofa, I shook desperately as a breathtaking wave of pleasure raced through me and small dots burst in my vision. Xavier kept up his magic, making sounds of approval as he sent me into blissful oblivion.

As I tried to catch my breath, my fingers slipped off the headrest and dropped down beside my body. Xavier pressed kisses to my center and inner thighs before he lowered my legs, which were pretty useless at this point, and climbed back up to hover over me. His hair was all over the place from my tugging and his chin glistened with my arousal. My cheeks blasted with heat at the sight, but at the same time a new wave of desire took hold of me.

Xavier's expression darkened with desire, too, as he watched my heaving chest, but he made no move to take things further. He leaned down and kissed me, exhaling a low breath. Even still in his jeans the heat of his erection seemed to scorch my inner thigh. He wanted me, and I wanted him. I had to be insane to insist on the stupid ban at this point. I couldn't even resist a piece of candy the first day into the New Year after another weight-loss resolution; how was I supposed to resist Xavier? That man was pure male eye candy.

"Can we go upstairs?" I asked, out of breath, my skin heating more at what I was suggesting.

Xavier groaned against my mouth, then kissed me with my taste still on his lips. He clambered off the sofa and held out his hand. Taking it, I allowed him to pull me to my feet. My dress fell down my legs, covering my ass and privates. Xavier let me toward the winding staircase. It was impossible to miss the huge bulge in his pants, and a hint of nerves filled me. Last time had been very painful, but I wanted to feel Xavier inside of me again. I wanted nothing more.

CHAPTER TWENTY-TWO

XAVIER

I was about to burst straight through my pants. Trying to stifle my eagerness, I led Evie toward my bed at a measured pace, even if I'd wanted to throw her over my shoulder and sprint toward my bedroom the moment she'd asked me to take her upstairs. I had sworn to hold back, but Evie was so fucking eager, so responsive, it wreaked havoc with my resolve. Arriving at the bed, I turned to her. Her cheeks were flushed, her hair disheveled, and her eyes shone with desire.

Cupping her cheeks, I pulled her in for another kiss, wanting her to taste her sweetness. She moaned into my mouth, pressing those amazing tits against my chest. Good Lord. I turned with her in my arms and tugged at her dress. She stilled but allowed me to pull the piece of clothing over her head. Only the light from below allowed me to see Evie, but she was mostly in shadows, a fucking shame. I reached behind her back and unhooked her bra, allowing her breasts to spring free, and I exhaled. Even in the half-dark, they were a sight to behold.

"Xavier," Evie whispered, insecurity in her voice.

"Lie down," I rasped, and for once she didn't give me a comeback, which showed me how nervous she was about her nakedness. I wanted to see her, all of her, but turning the light on would have only upped Evie's nerves. Deciding to distract her, I started to strip for her slowly, despite my cock's urgency to find a warm home. Evie's eyes followed my hands as I unbuckled my belt and inched my pants down, followed by my briefs.

She released a soft breath, so close to a moan that it sent a jolt straight into my balls. I grinned, satisfied that my body had that effect on Evie.

"That self-satisfied grin lights up the dark in the most annoying way," Evie muttered. Sarcasm was always a good indicator that Evie was starting to relax. I turned the switch that turned on the lights in the bathroom. The soft glow spilled onto the bed and Evie, allowing me to see her gorgeous face.

I climbed on the bed before she could get self-conscious again and claimed her mouth for a kiss, but I had to have a taste of her breasts. Evie squirmed under my body, moaning and gasping as I stroked and kissed her tits.

"Xavier," she whispered, needy and throaty.

My hand trailed down her side, along her soft flesh, over her round hips as my mouth around her nipple kept Evie too distracted to worry about all the things she tended to worry about. My fingers brushed her soft hair, then lower, feeling her wetness. I pushed a finger into her, then added a second, and Evie came with a violent shudder, her muscles squeezing me tightly. I groaned around her nipple. My cock was trying to dig for mineral oil in the mattress. But there was still the no-sex ban in place.

I didn't want to presume her request to go upstairs meant she wanted sex. With any other woman, yes, but with Evie I didn't want to fuck up again. She was too important to let my dick run and ruin the show again.

As if Evie could read my mind, she said, "I want you."

"What about the ban?" I teased as I kissed my way up her throat.

"Shut up," she murmured, then gasped when I swiped my thumb over her slick clit.

Grinning, I reached over her for the packet of condoms in my drawer. I ripped it open with my teeth and rolled the condom down my cock. I squeezed myself once. Hard as it could be. When I looked up, my smirk fell. Evie looked anxious.

I climbed up until my body covered hers, my weight resting on my forearms. She raised her head and met me with a kiss. Her arms came around my back, then slid down to my lower back, where they came to a halt as if she didn't dare move lower. "All yours," I said with a grin.

She squeezed my butt and I flexed my muscles in response, causing her to laugh that unrestrained, full-body laugh I couldn't get enough of.

I moved my hips until my cock was pressed up against her opening. Warm and wet and welcoming.

She held her breath, her fingers against my ass tensing, her body bracing for pain.

"Breathe, Evie. I don't want you to pass out. You'll miss a life-changing performance," I rasped, because I was so very close to losing every shred of my sanity.

She smiled, but it was shaky. Fuck. Pain was the fucking last thing I wanted her to feel. I wanted this to be good for her.

"It'll be less painful this time," I told her. I really hoped it was true. The idea of hurting her again didn't sit well with me.

"How would you know?"

"I read a few articles in preparation for tonight."

Her body shook with laughter under me, eyes bright and playful. "You *didn't*."

"I can't have you laughing at me," I murmured in a low voice, grinning. I shifted forward, my tip entering her, and I almost breathed a sigh of relief when I slipped in easier this time. She was still incredibly tight, deliciously so, but there wasn't that firm resistance like last time.

She fell silent. I watched her face as I pressed forward. The occasional wince made me slow even further until I was finally buried completely inside her. For a moment I was sure I'd come on the spot because she was so tight and the sensations threatened to overwhelm me but I could exert control if I wanted to.

Evie drew in a deep breath. "You are too big. I don't get why women sing praises to well-endowed men."

I chuckled as I stroked her cheek. "You'll sing the same praises very soon, Evie, trust me."

She squirmed slightly under me, as if she was trying to find a comfortable position and failing. Her movement sent jolts of pleasure through my cock and I released a low groan. Evie watched me curiously, then repeated the move. I hissed. Of course, she moved again.

"You vixen," I muttered. "If you keep it up, this will be a short ride." I went through my mental list of off-putting images and quickly got a grip on my over-eager cock. I couldn't remember the last time I'd been at risk of shooting my ammunition so soon.

Evie finally lay still under me, and her muscles didn't squeeze me quite as tightly anymore. "Okay?" I asked, not wanting to hurt her.

She smiled, eyes trusting and tender. "Okay," she whispered. I had to kiss her again. Her lips were pure perfection. I slid out of her a few inches then pushed back in. I kept a slow rhythm until her winces turned into small sounds of pleasure. With every moan from her lips, I pushed a bit deeper. I didn't increase my speed. I got the impression that her body wasn't ready for it yet.

There would be time for it later—and there would be a later, because I had no intention of letting Evie slip out of my hands and my bed ever again.

I captured her lips with mine. I didn't stop kissing Evie as I drove her closer and closer to the edge. Her eyes held mine the entire time, and for once I had no trouble returning a gaze because I didn't have to pretend to care for the woman under me. I wasn't sure when my feelings had changed, when I'd started caring for Evie like this. I'd liked her from the start, her snark and sharp comebacks, her earnest laughter and amusing temper, but this was more than like...

I pushed the thoughts aside and kissed Evie harder, then lowered my mouth to her nipple.

She moaned, then pressed her lips together as if she was embarrassed by the sound. "Let me hear you," I murmured, and the lovely pink on her cheeks spread all the way down to her breasts. Fuck. They were absolutely marvelous. Full, round and big. Even I couldn't fit them in my palms. I returned my gaze to her face when my balls tightened. No way was I going to come before Evie this time.

I propped myself up on one arm, reached between us, and Evie tensed when my fingers grazed her stomach. I froze, groaning as her walls fisted me even tighter. "Evie, relax," I got out and imagined the hairy asses of Connor and the other ruggers.

Thankfully, Evie loosened up and my cock slid in and out more easily. I finally reached my goal, her clit, and began rubbing it. Evie released a long moan, and again she tightened.

Hairy asses. Saggy old women tits.

Fuck.

I kissed Evie hard, my fingers moving faster against her nub as I slowed my thrusts to be safe. And then Evie's eyes widened and she shuddered under me. I quickly pulled back to hear her moans and watch her face as it twisted with pleasure. I pushed up on my palms and slammed harder into her, but it didn't take long before my own orgasm hit me like a wrecking ball.

EVIE

Xavier pulled out of me slowly, then slid off me and wrapped me in a gentle embrace. He smelled spicier, warmer, like sex and sandalwood maybe. I tried to catch my breath in Xavier's arms. Closing my eyes briefly, I pressed my cheek against his chest. Xavier's fingers found their way into my hair, lightly stroking my scalp. His lips brushed my temple like he had done before. It was such a caring, gentle gesture that butterflies fluttered in the pit of my stomach.

He drew his head back. "Are you okay, Evie?"

I looked up at him. "Better than okay."

A slow smile spread on his face. "Good."

I could tell he was trying and failing to keep the cockiness from showing.

I rolled my eyes. "Don't be so smug about it."

"I can't help it. I'm feeling all cavemanly knowing I'm the only guy who's been inside of you."

"This is the second time you've been inside of me. No reason to be smug about it."

"Last time I couldn't appreciate the situation like it deserved. I felt too bad for hurting you."

I propped myself up on his chest. "You really felt bad?"

His brows drew together. "Of course I did. I wanted to make you come, not bleed. When I saw the blood on my sheets, I felt like the biggest asshole on the planet."

Horror widened my eyes. "There was blood?"

Xavier nodded.

"Oh God, please tell me, Nancy didn't clean the sheets."

"That's what you're worried about?"

"She did clean them, didn't she?"

"She cleans everything."

I dropped my forehead down on his chest. "Please tell me at least she didn't know it was mine."

"She saw you leaving my apartment."

I groaned. Xavier chuckled. "Now come, there are worse things than being a virgin. Or are you ashamed that you gave it away to me?"

I lifted my head, trying to figure out if Xavier was joking. He wasn't. "There's no one else whose sheets I'd rather have ruined," I teased.

Xavier shook his head with a grin, then he kissed me again. Soon the soft brush of mouth against mouth turned into something more heated.

Xavier drew back to look at me. "Are you tired? I'm up for another round if you want." The wolfish grin.

My core tightened but I shook my head. "Too sore, you brute," I said.

His grin faltered.

"I was joking," I told him, and he growled and rolled himself on top of me. "I was joking about the brute part, not the sore part."

He kissed me and I could feel him harden against my thigh, but before I could change my mind about the sore part, Xavier rolled off of me and wrapped me in his arms. "Staying on top of you gives me ideas that won't work while you're sore," he murmured.

I smiled against his skin.

"Sleep tight, Evie," Xavier said eventually, kissing my temple.

It took a long time for me to fall asleep. I was too scared of the next morning and Xavier's reaction, which didn't even make sense because he had told me he wanted me to wake up beside him.

———————— ✦◆✦ ————————

I woke facing the windows again, looking out toward the ocean. I tensed, remembering my walk of shame the last time I'd slept with Xavier. I listened for Xavier and when I heard his even breathing, I relaxed slightly. He was probably still asleep. After all, I was usually the one waking him. I considered getting up and leaving again, suddenly worried to face him. Mentally putting on my big-girl panties, I turned around and sucked in a breath when I met gray eyes. Xavier was propped up on his elbow, supporting his head with his palm, covers bunching around his hips, revealing inch after inch of perfectly sculpted chest, and he was watching me with a look I couldn't read. What was he thinking? Was he regretting his decision to give dating a try? Definitely not the sex part, but everything else?

"Good morning," he said in his early morning rasp. Goose bumps rose on my skin hearing that voice, and Xavier's gaze dipped lower. Heat rose into my cheeks when I realized that the covers had bunched around my hips as well, laying my breasts bare to Xavier. I quickly pulled them higher, but Xavier snatched the fabric from my fingers and moved closer. His smell, all man and sex and something warmer, filled my nose. "Still sore?" he asked in a low voice, and his erection dug into my thigh.

More heat shot into my face. He brushed his thumb over my cheekbone. "Oh, Evie." His hand slid down my back to my ass. I had hardly any time to worry about its size or jiggle before Xavier squeezed one cheek, his fingers grazing my sensitive flesh in the process.

I gasped, curled my palm over Xavier's neck and pulled him in for a kiss. He complied with unbridled eagerness and before I had time to process what was happening, he was over me, his strong thighs spreading my legs, and I forgot all about my soreness, kissed him harder and rubbed myself against his erection, wanting friction. His tip slid over my wetness, and I gasped as Xavier groaned. I arched up again, needing more, but Xavier resisted and pushed himself up on his arms.

I frowned, suddenly self-conscious. Had I done something wrong? Been too eager? "What?" I asked hesitantly.

Xavier grimaced. "Condom."

"Oh," I said. "I forgot. I thought I did something wrong. This is new for me." I snapped my lips shut at the amused curl of Xavier's lips.

He slid his mouth over mine, then up to my ear. "I know. But you can't do anything wrong. I'm here to teach you."

I snorted and hit his shoulder. "You are so full of yourself!"

He raised his eyes. "Am I?" The challenging gleam made me nervous and excited at the same time. He straightened so he was kneeling between my legs, his naked body on display and his erection impressively hard.

I couldn't take my eyes off him even as my face burnt. Everything about him was perfect, every muscle, every hair, even his erection. "You keep looking at me like that and I'm not responsible for my actions, Evie. Even my control has its limits."

I gave him a teasing smile. "When have you ever displayed control? And who says I want you to be controlled?"

"Fuck." Xavier snatched up a condom, ripped open the package and rolled the condom down his cock. Then his lips claimed mine and he pushed into me almost all the way.

I drew back from his mouth, wincing. "Control would be good after all."

Xavier stilled at once, gray eyes flashing with concern. "I didn't want to hurt you."

"It's my fault. I was a bit premature in my evaluation of my level of soreness."

Xavier chuckled. "I love it when you talk dirty."

I poked my tongue out at him.

He shook his head, and kissed me again. "I'm sorry if I went too rough again. This is new to me too. I've never been with a woman who didn't have a lot of experience."

As if I didn't know that. I had seen his last fifty conquests. "We can figure this out together," I said softly.

His eyes became impossibly warm. "You have loosened around me."

"I'm good."

He pulled out and pushed back in, then settled into a slow, gentle rhythm.

"You can go harder," I said when the soreness between my legs turned into a pleasant throbbing.

Xavier curled his hand over my leg, lifted it so my foot pressed into his backside, and slid even deeper into me.

"Oh," I gasped, digging into his shoulders. "Yes, like that."

"Even during sex you boss me around," he murmured against my throat before he bit down lightly. I didn't bother with a comeback, too wrapped up in the sensations.

His pants became louder as he thrust into me with practiced precision, never faltering, never taking his eyes off me even as his expression turned more strained. He moved his hand between our slick bodies and pressed down on my clit, and I came apart. "Xavier!" I cried out as my body convulsed with bolts of pleasure.

Xavier slammed harder into me and despite the twinge it brought, the ripples of my orgasm spiked and then he jerked hard, his movements becoming uncoordinated as he spent himself inside me.

I ran my hands over his pecs, my breathing fast, but for once not as fast as his as he panted, his firm muscles flexing and twitching under my fingertips. He grabbed the base of his cock as he pulled out and discarded the condom with a careless flick of his wrist before he lowered himself on top of me and buried his nose in my hair. I closed my eyes, wanting this moment to last forever. But then I remembered something. Today was Friday. My eyes shot open. "Xavier. I need to look at my mobile."

"Hmm?"

I tried to shove him off, but moving a mountain would have been easier. When it became clear that he had no intention of budging, I brushed my fingers up his ribs to his armpit. He choked and shoved off me. "You are lucky your opponents don't know there's an easy way to take down Xavier—The Beast—Stevens," I said with a smile.

"You are a vixen," Xavier said as he stretched out on his back.

I sat up, searching the nightstand, but both Xavier's and my cell phone were downstairs where we'd left them last night. Of course, there wasn't any other clock in his bedroom since I was his alarm. Gripping the blanket, I tried to take it with me and cover myself with it as I made a move to stand, but Xavier lay half on top of it.

I tugged. "Xavier. I really need to check the time."

"I'm not stopping you," he said in amusement.

I narrowed my eyes at him. "I need the blanket to cover myself."

"Nobody can look inside the apartment. You know it's mirrored glass."

"Give me the blanket," I muttered, yanking with more force. I had seen the girls he'd been with. Fitness and bikini models, actresses who didn't play the character roles, athletes. Nothing was jiggling on their bodies. Everything was firm and smooth. And Xavier... he was a model athlete. His body fat percentage was in the single digits. Not even my dress size was single digits.

I couldn't be naked in front of him in bright daylight.

Xavier sat up, but he didn't release the blankets, and he was too heavy for me to free them without his cooperation.

"Don't hide yourself from me, Evie."

I swallowed, and said as firmly as my emotions allowed, "Give me that blanket, Xavier." Then added softly, "Please."

He swung out of bed and I wrenched the blankets toward myself, wrapping them around myself before I stood. I made sure everything was covered in a satisfying way before I dared to move, but Xavier was in my way. He had absolutely no trouble strutting around in his birthday suit. "We need to work on this," he said quietly, cupping my cheek.

My brows pulled together. "On what?"

"On your confidence."

Easy for him to say. I had seen the photos of him as a kid and teenager. He had always been an athlete, and now he was pure male gorgeousness. "Not today," I said lightly and quickly maneuvered past Xavier and down the stairs, barely avoiding breaking my neck as my foot tangled in the blanket. I caught my fall with a tight grip on the handle. Xavier shot me a look.

Ignoring him, I rushed toward my purse and fumbled for my phone. My heart halted when I saw the time. It was almost 9:40, and the team had a press conference on the pit at ten.

"Oh shit, we're late!" I hissed. "Xavier, get dressed! And stop the staring!"

He chuckled. "Bossy." But he moved into his bedroom. I collected my own clothes from the floor in the living room and bedroom, then hurried into the bathroom. There was no time for excessive grooming. If Xavier was late for this press conference, his coach would kill him, and me.

My jeans blouse and chino pants weren't really the outfit I'd have chosen for a press conference. To make matters worse, my blouse was wrinkled and I couldn't find my panties. I tried my best to smooth out the wrinkles and brush my hair with my fingers as I headed out of the bathroom. Xavier was dressed in his white training shorts and a red sweatshirt. He didn't look like he'd had a rough night. Of course, he had years of practice cleaning up after sex, and he had fresh clothes at his disposal.

Xavier chuckled. "You look a bit worse for wear."

I glanced down at myself. "I don't have time to go home and change."

Xavier kissed me. "You're fine."

We headed downstairs, where I grabbed my purse before we hurried toward Xavier's car and raced off. We were lucky we didn't get pulled over considering all the traffic rules we broke on our way.

We arrived at the training ground five minutes too late. Xavier parked his car smack in the middle of the parking lot, so none of his teammates would be able to get out, and shoved the door open. I followed after him as he stalked toward the gathered team and the press, all the while trying to brief him on the attending journalists. Most of them were sports journalists but there were a few prone to asking compromising questions, and Xavier was prone to compromising answers.

Heads turned our way, eyes latching on to Xavier before they moved on to me, and I almost cringed when I caught Connor's raised eyebrows and Fiona's shocked expression. The journalists didn't look too impressed with me either, and a few seemed amused.

Was it that obvious what had happened between Xavier and me?

I tried to stop myself from blushing, which was a losing battle. The coach narrowed his eyes at Xavier, before he frowned at me.

I moved to the back of the journalists as Xavier joined his team in the front.

"Now that we're finally complete, we can begin," Coach said in annoyance.

Fiona tried to catch my eyes from her spot beside the team. As a cheerleader her place was in the front. She would kick my ass the moment we were alone. I had promised her to stay away from Xavier, and now I had slept with him two more times. But things had changed.

Suddenly something dawned on me. Xavier hadn't held my hand or given any kind of indication that we were together. For everyone around us, it looked like I was one of his playthings.

My stomach tightened. I barely listened to the questions of the sport journalists, but then Maya Nowak spoke up, directing her question at Xavier. She was a journalist Xavier had banged a few weeks back, and who had written a few less favorable articles about him after that. "Some people wonder how you manage to focus on sports considering the nights you spend partying and your other escapades."

Xavier smirked. "I have an assistant who keeps me in line." My stomach began to plummet. Then he added, "Who also happens to be my girlfriend, who will stop future escapades." He looked at me and so did everyone else. The journalists actually twisted their heads around to stare straight at me, and a few of the photographers took photos.

Connor and Fiona looked at Xavier as if he'd grown a second head.

It took me a moment to gather my wits about me and smile.

"That's all very interesting," Coach Brennan drawled. "But we are here for rugby, not gossip."

Xavier winked, and a tiny part of me rejoiced at him making us public, but the other part worried about everyone's reactions. Maya regarded me like I was a bug she wanted to squash, and she probably wasn't the only one who wouldn't be happy that Xavier had chosen someone like me.

A witch hunt was about to begin.

CHAPTER
TWENTY-THREE

EVIE

Maya wasn't the one I should have been worried about. Fiona was the one who looked like she wanted to chase me with a pitchfork, and maybe poke Xavier's privates with it repeatedly. I perched on the bench, watching their public training and bearing her silent anger. Maybe I deserved it. Blake gave me a quick smile when our eyes met, but there was nothing flirty about it anymore. He was a good sport about the whole thing and I had to admit, he was a guy I might have fallen for if Xavier hadn't gotten in the way.

The second the cheerleading training was over Fiona made a beeline for me. I knew running was futile. Fiona was fitter than me and fueled by anger. She'd catch me.

She stopped right in front of me and put her hands on her hips. "I hope this is a joke."

"Good morning to you too," I chirped.

She didn't crack a smile. "I spent an entire day and night drying your tears after that asshat popped your cherry, and now you're his girlfriend?"

"Shhh," I hissed, looking around. "Can you please lower your voice? I don't think everyone needs to know about my private affairs."

"That's the right word. Affair. Do you really think Xavier's being serious? He's lazy. He doesn't want to lose an assistant and thinks why not sweeten the deal by getting nasty with you as well."

"Sit," I ordered and pointed at the spot beside me, tired of her treating me like a child. If I wanted to get nasty with Xavier, in or outside of a relationship, that was my decision.

Fiona sank down.

"Listen, Fiona, I know you mean well, but you left me alone for over two years when I needed you the most, and in that time I learned to take care of myself. I don't need your protection."

Hurt flashed on her face and I felt bad instantly. I took her hand. "That came out harsher than I meant it to. I appreciate how protective you are, but I need you to trust me. I know what I'm doing. Xavier and I discussed this."

She still looked doubtful but nodded. "I'm giving him the benefit of the doubt for now, even if he doesn't deserve it."

"You are?" This seemed too understanding for the Fiona I knew. She didn't give in that easily.

"I really hope this works out. I don't want you to get hurt. If he cheats on you, I'll shove one of my stiletto heels up his arrogant ass."

"I don't think he'll cheat on me," I said, and it was true. Xavier would end it before that happened.

"That's what I always thought," she muttered.

"You never really talked to me about what happened with Aiden."

Her face closed off, but then she sighed. "Maybe tonight. Make sure to get me drunk. It'll make things easier."

"Red or white?"

"A chardonnay."

I rolled my eyes. "Less carbs?"

"No, tasty," she said with a grin.

Coach Brennan walked toward us. "Can I have a quick word with you?"

"Sure," I said hesitantly.

Fiona got up. "I won't disturb you."

"I was very concerned when I heard that Xavier was looking for a new assistant."

Where had he heard that? My God, rugby players were the worst gossips.

"I hope his statement today means I won't have to worry about it anymore. That boy needs you."

He was the only one who called Xavier "boy." Built like a bull himself and twice Xavier's age, he was probably the only one who could pull it off.

"I'll stay where I am. Kicking Xavier's ass into gear is too much fun."

He laughed.

My smile died on my lips when I noticed Fiona slipping into the changing rooms, and a moment later Connor leaving. I couldn't believe her!

XAVIER

Connor shook his head. "Are you sure about this, Xavier? I really like Evie, and I don't want her to get hurt. She's a nice girl."

She wasn't just a nice girl. She was an amazing girl. "I really like Evie, too, and hurting her is the last thing I want," I said, for once not cracking a joke.

Connor nodded. "Fiona won't take your word for it. She's furious."

"I saw her face. She looks like she wants to play ping pong with my balls."

"Probably."

"She'll have to deal. Evie is a grown-up and can make her own decisions," I said as I headed for the shower. As usual I took my sweet-ass time, until I heard a high-pitched voice.

"I need a word with Xavier," Fiona said.

"Maybe you should take some time to cool off."

I could imagine how Connor was trying to placate his girlfriend, and I also knew it wouldn't work.

"I don't need time to cool off. I need to talk to the asshat. Give us a moment."

I didn't hear the next few words, but I turned off the shower and stepped out. Fiona stood with her arms crossed against the wall, glaring at me.

She didn't seem to care a flying fuck about my nakedness, and if she thought I had trouble having a conversation in my birthday suit, then she didn't know me at all.

"Fiona, what a pleasant surprise," I said, mirroring her stance against the shower wall.

Her lips curled and she threw the towel she was holding at my head. "You have no shame."

I caught it before it could slap me in the mouth and wrapped it around my waist. "You pranced into our changing room and disturbed my shower."

"What was that?"

"What was what?"

"You know what I mean! Why did you tell the press that you were dating my sister?"

"Because it's the truth. Evie and I have been going out for a few days now."

Fiona frowned. "Is this some kind of game to you? A new form of entertainment to keep the press busy? Evie isn't your toy."

Anger surged through me. I straightened. "Maybe you think you are the only one who cares about Evie, but you are fucking wrong. Your sister isn't a game or toy to me or whatever else you think, and you underestimate her greatly if you think she'd let me treat her like that. Evie can take care of herself. Fuck, she even managed to take care of me."

Fiona's face seemed a tad less hostile, but that might have been the flickering light. "So you really mean it?"

"I mean it," I said with a sigh. "Your sister is the funniest, kindest, snarkiest woman I know."

"She is," Fiona agreed softly.

"I'm going to do anything I can to treat her right, Fiona."

Fiona nodded, and I was pretty sure her eyes watered a little. Of course she had to ruin our moment. "Make it up to her for that shitty first time you gave her, that's all I ask. Your mouth has to be good for more than bullshit talk."

I cocked one eyebrow and smiled arrogantly. "Evie finds my mouth very entertaining, trust me."

Fiona surprised me even more by grinning. She came closer and patted my shoulder. "Good for you, and good for her."

She turned on her heel, her long hair slapping me in the face, and stalked toward the door. "And I will castrate you with my fake nails if you hurt her, just so you know."

"Duly noted," I muttered before she sauntered outside.

Someone knocked, then Evie's voice rang out. "Xavier, are you okay?"

I began laughing.

She poked her head in. "What's so funny? I was worried Fiona might have strangled you with a towel, and here you are all merry."

"I'd be even merrier if you'd come in and shower with me," I said as I dropped the towel to give her a good view at my already growing cock. Evie flushed and dragged her gaze back up to mine as I stopped in front of her. I touched her cheek and kissed her slowly. "Come on, Evie. Help a guy out here."

She pulled back, sighing, then shook her head. "I don't want people to get the wrong impression."

"What impression? You are my girlfriend, and trust me, if they want to get the wrong impression they'll make sure to get it even if you don't give them reason for it."

"Still. This is still fresh. I don't want to give the press more ammunition than absolutely necessary."

"Okay," I said, then heaved a monumental sigh. "I might take a bit longer so I can wank myself off."

Evie groaned. "Now I won't be able to get that image out of my head."

I flashed her a grin. "Ask your sister for a spare pair of panties. I'm sure she's got plenty of them lying around in her locker for all the eye-fucking happening between her and Connor."

"Another image that will haunt me. Have fun," she said with a laugh, then closed the door in my face. I leaned my forehead against the cool surface, smiling like a fucking imbecile. That woman was too good to be true.

CHAPTER TWENTY-FOUR

EVIE

Xavier's twenty-fifth birthday party was scheduled for tonight. I'd spent weeks inviting guests and the press, testing catering services (completely selfless on my part), and searching for the perfect location, only to have Xavier tell me this morning that he wished we could spend it somewhere alone, but sadly that wasn't going to happen.

I wasn't too eager for the party either because the guest list included about two dozen women who had their eyes set on Xavier, and whom he had chosen as guests specifically as potential conquests before we had started dating. Now we were a couple, and all these women would probably still descend on him like a locust swarm.

Fiona had groomed me to perfection. She had smoothed my naturally curly hair with a hair iron, only to curl it with a curling iron afterwards. It didn't even make sense, but she insisted it was crucial to give my curls the necessary sheen.

The shininess of my hair was the least of my worries.

"This is the first time you and Xavier will appear at a public event as a couple," Fiona said gently as she applied my lipstick, then perched on the corner of the vanity.

"Yeah," I admitted. "When I sent out the guest lists, we weren't a couple yet, and there will be many single females making an appearance."

Fiona gave a shrug. "He's with you now, so it shouldn't matter."

"Do you really think I can hold someone like Xavier? He could have any girl he wants."

Fiona gripped my shoulders. "The question is if he can hold you, because I'm still not convinced he deserves you. He can thank his lucky stars that you gave him another chance after he popped your cherry so rudely."

"He didn't pop it rudely. What came afterward was rude, but nothing I hadn't expected."

"Yeah, well. I haven't forgiven him for that stunt yet. I'm angry for the both of us since you don't have the necessary bitchiness to hold on to grudges."

I laughed. "Did you just insult or compliment me?"

"Both," Fiona said with a grin.

"Only you," I muttered.

She sobered. "He's good to you?"

I had lost count of the times she'd asked me that question since the press conference a few days ago. "He is. He is patient and gentle and loving and funny."

Fiona sighed. "Good Lord." Then she smirked. "And how's the sex? I mean with all the practice he's had he should be a grenade in bed. Or is he one of those who only ever cared about themselves, so they don't know how to please a woman?"

I stood. "I'm not sure I want to have that kind of conversation."

"Come on, give me something."

I could feel my cheeks heating. "He's very considerate." Then because I couldn't hold it in, "And I just can't keep my hands off him. Everything he does feels amazing."

Fiona smirked. "That's what I wanted to hear."

I couldn't remember the last time I'd been this nervous.

The bell rang and Fiona jumped up from the vanity. "It's Xavier. Oh, his chin is going to hit the floor."

I stood and allowed myself one more look in the mirror. The tight black leather skirt reached from my waist to my knees with a slit on the left up to my thigh, and the wrap-around top in a shimmery green material had a low V neckline. The black sling-back heels made my legs appear much longer than they were.

"Come now," Fiona urged. "You look fabulous."

My eyes slid over Fiona's tight dress, but for once I didn't try to compare us. With a nervous smile, I walked past her and toward the stairs. I wasn't even halfway down when Xavier spotted me, and Fiona had been right: his lips parted and his eyes widened, and he looked at me as if I was the sexiest woman to have ever walked on earth. Xavier in his dark suit with the white shirt, no tie, looked perfectly handsome as well.

Xavier shook his head as he kissed me hard. "Evie, how can I let you go out like this?"

I tensed until he rasped his next words into my ear. "You look so fucking sexy, I won't be able to keep my hands off you. Do you really want me to ruin my suit by coming in my pants?"

I laughed. "You're a big boy with lots of restraint."

"No, I'm not, and we both know it."

I had already wished him a happy birthday this morning, twice, but right now I felt like another congratulation was due.

"Hey, keep it PG-13, will you?" Fiona muttered as she drifted into Connor's arms, who regarded her with open adoration.

"We will if you do," I countered.

"I can't guarantee anything," Connor said, wrapping an arm around my sister.

Xavier exchanged a grin with his best friend. "Me neither."

We arrived at the party with the first guests since I had insisted Xavier be on time for his own birthday party, and because I wanted to give a few last-minute instructions to the service personnel. They worked for the hippest hotel in town so I knew they could handle a birthday party, but I wanted to be sure. After all, we expected about four hundred exclusive guests.

The hotel bar that I'd rented for the occasion offered a spectacular view over the opera and Sydney's nightly city lights.

Xavier accepted the congratulations with his usual charm and cockiness, but his arm remained firmly wrapped around my waist, not allowing me to blend into the background as I'd done in the past.

I noticed people's curious glances, especially from the women who'd been invited as potential conquests, but I tried to ignore them. We mostly hung around with Xavier's teammates—even his coach had come—since Xavier didn't seem to care much about pretty much anyone else. His family wasn't invited since they stayed out of the public eye. We'd visit them for a late birthday celebration later that week.

The moment I untangled myself from Xavier to visit the ladies' room, I noticed one of the women make their way toward him, but his eyes were on me and when he finally did look at her, his expression couldn't have been more hostile. Smiling to myself, I disappeared in the restroom and moved into the only free stall.

The toilets next to me flushed and high heels clicked before water started running. "I can't believe he chose that girl to be his girlfriend."

"I know," said another female voice. "Have you seen her hips and ass? I mean, I know the media is all over plus-sized models at the moment, but he's an athlete."

I peered through the gap between the door and the stall, spotting two tall, skinny women with dark hair.

"Everyone needs a fatty treat now and then," the one with the darker, almost black hair said, then they both laughed. They applied lipstick as I leaned against the stall, feeling heat rush into my head and tears sting my eyes.

"I guess that's it, but still. I actually wanted to give him a go tonight. He's an asshole but he's supposed to be so good in bed."

"I know. Just do it. I mean, come on. If he's got the choice between you and that girl, he'll forget all about her."

More giggling, and finally they left.

I drew in a deep breath, trying not to let their words get to me, but it was a losing battle. They had voiced all of my concerns. How could I hold Xavier when girls like that kept throwing themselves at him? I couldn't compete with their bodies. Everyone with eyes in their head could see it.

I pushed out of the stall. Even if their words hit too close to home, I wouldn't hide like my fourteen-year-old self from the mean girls in school.

Checking my reflection to make sure my eyes were satisfyingly dry—my flushed skin was a losing battle—I returned to the party.

Xavier was talking to the two bimbos from the ladies' room, who worshipped him with their eyes as if he was the second coming of Christ. His body was Greek god worthy, no argument, but I'd gouge my eyes out with my stiletto heels before I'd ever give him that kind of simpering look.

I squared my shoulders and walked over to the bar to grab a beer. Fuck looking sophisticated with a fine glass of white wine, I wanted my liquid carbs.

The bartender handed me the bottle and a glass. I took the former, not the latter, and took a large gulp as I tried to look completely unfazed. Fiona and Connor were doing something that could be considered dancing but was probably classified as a public misdemeanor in certain countries. I didn't know Fiona could twerk. With a tiny butt like hers, that shouldn't have worked, but she pulled it off magnificently and Connor looked more than a little impressed.

"Are you going to twerk for me too?" Xavier growled in my ear, making me jump and almost drop my bottle. "With your wicked ass that would make me come in my pants for the first time since my teenage days."

"I don't twerk," I said quickly.

Xavier wrapped his arms around me from behind, pulling me against his body. "That's a shame."

I could see several heads turning our way, including the two bimbos from the restroom. "We've got an audience."

Xavier followed my gaze to the two girls whispering among themselves.

"I don't give a flying fuck," he muttered, then kissed my throat before he took my hand and tugged me toward the dance floor. "Dance with me."

I quickly left the beer bottle on the bar and followed him. "Xavier, I can't dance."

"We've already established that you're a fast learner," he said with his wolfish grin. "And I'm a good teacher."

Holy mother of too sexy ruggers.

Xavier gripped my hips and began to move to the beat. Soon we were grating and twisting and shaking and rubbing, and the room faded to the background. Xavier's arm snaked around my waist as he jerked me closer to his body, his mouth coming down to my ear. "The moment we're out of here, I'm going to eat your pussy and fuck you senseless if you let me."

I choked back a laugh. If I let him? If I wasn't worried about it making headlines tomorrow, I'd have jumped Xavier right here on the dance floor. My eyes must have answered his question because he groaned. "This might be the first time I won't be the last to leave my birthday party."

We stayed two more hours because, like Xavier had pointed out, it was his birthday party and it would have been rude if the guest of honor had left first. We didn't make it home for the naughty business. We didn't even make it out of the parking garage of the hotel before Xavier's fingers slipped beneath my skirt and brought me the first high of the night. We did, however, make it into the elevator of his apartment building before his pants hit the floor and I showed him what I'd learned—while Teniel's voice blared out of the speakers asking why the elevator had been stopped. Eventually he gave up.

Xavier didn't let me finish him, though. Instead we stumbled into his penthouse, where we dropped to the floor and Xavier made good on his promise to devour me. After that he took me right there on the floor with my clothes still on. Rug burn had never been more appreciated.

CHAPTER
TWENTY-FIVE

EVIE

I woke before Xavier and slipped out of bed to check my phone out of habit, knowing that last night's party would have made headlines somewhere. I grabbed my bathrobe and put it on over Xavier's shirt, desperate to cover as much of me as possible. Moving toward the panorama window in the bedroom, I scrolled through the emails when I caught sight of a message from Maya Nowak. It contained only a link. I clicked on it even as dread settled in my stomach.

She must have worked on it all night to have it up this early. Maya's article was even nastier than I'd feared. I should have expected it. When we'd invited the press originally, Xavier and I hadn't been an item yet, and he'd wanted her there for the very reason that her articles always got the most attention.

She commented on every single one of my imperfections: the cellulite on my upper thighs, which apparently was unmistakable through the cheap leather of my skirt, my wide hips, my soft stomach, my big butt. She made it sound like Xavier had only chosen me to pay all of his past conquests back by being with someone this disgusting.

Heat rushed into my head as I read her words. I knew I wasn't Instagram fitness model material, but I definitely wasn't the visual trainwreck she described. My emotions wavered between anger and embarrassment. The latter made me mad at myself for allowing someone I didn't even like to make me feel that way with a few words. The covers rustled as Xavier sat up in bed.

"Evie? What's wrong?" Xavier asked as he pushed out of bed completely naked, completely perfect. I was about to close the article when Xavier took my phone from me and scanned it. His expression turned furious, then he threw my mobile on the bed and cupped my face.

"She is a spiteful creature, Evie. Don't waste a single thought on the bitch."

"She is right in one point though. Look at you," I said, motioning at his body, at the perfect muscles. Not a gram of fat, no jiggle, nothing but pure male gorgeousness. Everyone who looked at us would always wonder why a man like Xavier would settle for a woman like me. I had seen those surprised looks, and the whispers that followed. I finally motioned down at myself, safely covered by a bathrobe, hiding all my unfavorable places, which according to Maya was my entire body. "And look at me, Xavier. We don't match. You belong with someone like Dakota. Someone who doesn't look like she enjoys beer and burgers with bread. Someone who fits a size zero."

I swallowed hard, because this feeling of never being enough, of lacking because I wasn't thin enough, cut deep. It had been a part of me for so long, it was difficult to shake off.

"This is the biggest pile of bullshit I've ever heard," Xavier muttered.

I gave him a look. "I know what kind of girls you've had before me, and they were all fit and thin."

He stroked my cheek with his thumb. "Yes, they were."

My stomach plummeted at his admittance, which was ridiculous considering that he was stating facts everyone knew.

"I chose those women for a night. I didn't give a damn about their personality, or anything really, except for their bodies. But you, I don't want for only a few nights. I want you for forever."

My eyes grew wide, and Xavier too looked a little stunned. "You... I can't believe you said that."

Xavier kissed my mouth, a gentle, slow kiss. "Fuck. Me neither. But it's true, Evie. I've never enjoyed someone's company more than I do yours. I trust you. I love your brand of humor, your loyalty, your snarkiness and your smile. I love every last piece of you, Evie."

I blinked. "And I love you."

"Fuck," he breathed, then kissed me again.

Xavier slid his palms under my bathrobe and slowly pushed it off my shoulders. It fell to the ground. I was still in Xavier's shirt, but he grabbed the hem and began pulling it up. I touched his arms, stopping him. "Xavier—" I began, terrified of being exposed to him in bright daylight, when my flaws had always been hidden in the half-light so far.

"Evie," Xavier said firmly. "I just laid my feelings bare to you. Let me see you." He softened his voice. "I've touched every inch of your body. I know where you are soft. My hands know every inch of you. There's nothing you need to hide from me, honey."

That was the first time he called me honey, and it broke through my walls. I swallowed thickly then lifted my arms over my head. Xavier pulled the shirt over my head and threw it to the ground. I started shaking, couldn't help it, and had to fight the urge to cover my body. I feared Xavier's rejection. I didn't think I could live it down if he was disgusted by my body.

For a long time his eyes remained firmly on mine before he finally kissed my mouth, then the tip of my nose, then my cheeks. "I love those freckles," he murmured.

He kissed my shoulder blade, my collarbone, then the swell of my breast. My nipples puckered under his lips. "I fucking love your breasts," he said in a slightly deeper voice.

He touched my waist and got down on his knees. I stiffened when his mouth kissed my ribs, then my stomach, which would never show abs. He dipped his tongue into my belly button unexpectedly, and I screeched with laughter and tried shoving him away, but he was too strong and held on to me as he released that deep, manly chuckle which made warmth pool in my body. He tilted his head up, giving me that wolfish grin as his cheek pressed up against my less than perfect belly. "I love your belly button, and the sounds it creates."

I huffed, then quieted when Xavier pulled back and watched as his hands slid down my waist over my hips to my thighs. He kissed my inner thigh so close to my center that I held my breath in anticipation. "I love your luscious thighs that always squeeze the life out of my head when I'm eating you out."

Heat blazed in my cheeks and Xavier's expression became more intent, hungrier as he regarded me. "I love that blush that tells me all of this is only mine." His hands slid around and cupped my ass, squeezing. "And fuck, I love your ass. I can't tell you how often I imagine having you bent over so I can really appreciate it fully." He pressed a light kiss on my pubic bone, then made his way back up, kissing the same spots he had on his way down before he claimed my mouth for a far less restrained kiss. "I love every inch of you, Evie. Can you get that into your stubborn head?"

"Okay." I smiled against his mouth. "And I'm not stubborn."

He growled playfully and pulled me against his body. We kissed and stroked and finally found ourselves on the bed.

Xavier climbed between my legs and reached for his drawer, but I stopped him. He frowned.

"I started taking the pill." Then I hesitated. "So we don't need protection unless you…" I didn't want to bring up the past, but in this case it was necessary.

Xavier looked stunned for a moment. "I've always used protection. I've never had sex without a condom."

"Would you like to try with me?"

He exhaled, then brought his tip to my entrance and slowly pushed in. He stilled when he was all the way inside of me. "Fuck, Evie, you feel so good."

He made love to me slowly, reverently, until my body throbbed with a deep ache, but he seemed content to keep me on the edge forever. A sound of protest burst from my lips when he pulled back and rolled on his back. "Why don't you do some of the work now?"

I swallowed and sat up. So far I hadn't been on top because it would allow Xavier a good look at my body. As he could see my struggle, he stroked my cheek in reassurance.

"I can't wait to have you on top, Evie."

"Okay," I said despite the flicker of self-consciousness.

I straddled Xavier, trying not to worry about being too heavy, because Xavier was a beast, but I didn't sit upright. Instead I pressed my chest against his as we kissed and his hands roamed my back and butt. He squeezed my ass cheeks, then reached behind us and lined himself up. He shifted his hips and slid in a couple of inches. "Let me see you," he rasped, and I gathered my courage and pushed myself into a sitting position, my fingertips splayed across Xavier's chest as he held my gaze. He didn't look anywhere else and I could have kissed him for it because I knew he wanted to, but didn't want to push me too fast.

He squeezed my hips lightly. "You will have to move," he said with an amused look.

I rolled my eyes. "Let me catch my breath here," I said, feeling stretched and utterly full.

Xavier's mouth tipped upwards. "Take all the time you need. But then I'll enjoy the view while you're at it."

His eyes lowered to my breasts as he cupped them and began kneading them gently before brushing my nipples with his thumbs. I gasped and his eyes flickered up to my face. His gentle ministrations quickly had me relaxed and desperate for more, so I put my hands more firmly against his chest and lifted my hips experimentally. I wasn't exactly sure how to move. "Will you show me?" I asked after a moment, biting my lip, and cocking one eyebrow in challenge despite the blush heating up my cheeks.

Xavier twitched inside of me, his jaw tightening. After a moment, the smile returned. "Next time I see Connor, remind me to thank him for his hairy ass."

I choked out laughter. "You're thinking about Connor while we're having sex?"

He chuckled. "It's to pull the reins a little." His hands came up to my waist, and he began guiding my hips in a slow up and down rotation as he met my movements with his own gentle thrusts.

Soon we established a slow, sensual rhythm that made my toes curl deliciously. Xavier's eyes roamed over my upper body and face as he kneaded my butt, and I didn't feel self-conscious because the look in Xavier's eyes held so much adoration and appreciation that even the nasty whispers in my head were quiet for once.

I let him look at me as I looked at him. Soon I could feel the familiar tugging, like a knot being unfastened in the slowest way possible until it suddenly snapped, and I came with a violent shudder.

"Fuck. Yes, Evie, come for me," Xavier rasped as he thrust harder into me, until I half fell on top of him. He wrapped an arm around my back and brought us both into a sitting position where we caught our breath for a moment. "How about I show you another position?"

I grinned. "You know I love to learn new things, and you are a good teacher."

The wolfish smile, then he flipped us around so he hovered over me, and I had to admit I enjoyed the view of his flexing arms and gorgeous face above me. Xavier cupped one of my legs and as he leaned forward, he positioned my ankle up against his shoulder blade.

"I didn't know yoga skills were required for sex," I muttered at the slight stretch in my leg.

He pushed into me in one stroke, shutting me up effectively. He waited a moment before he started thrusting into me. He kissed my cheek. "Tell me if I'm going too hard or if it hurts," he rasped, his eyes meeting mine to make sure I was okay. I kissed his mouth, so hopelessly in love with the man above me, it seemed my heart would burst from the sheer volume of my emotions.

His thrust became harder, deeper, but I'd be damned if I told him to stop. The twinge was soon drowned out by a deep ache that tugged at my core insistently, compellingly, and I wanted nothing more than to give in to it. As if he could see that I needed a small push, Xavier reached between us to touch my sweet spot, his mouth claiming mine, and I came apart under him.

After a few hard thrusts, Xavier found his own release. Still the most amazing sight I could imagine.

Xavier released my leg from its awkward position and lowered himself on top of me. We kissed gently for a while, with him still inside of me. Then he reached between us as if to hold on to the condom before he remembered and chuckled. "That will take some getting used to." He pulled out of me and wrapped his arms around me.

I relished in his warmth, but eventually a trickling made me shift my legs and my stomach let out an angry growl. Xavier kissed my temple with a chuckle. "Why don't you clean up and I'll fix us breakfast?"

He swung his legs out of bed and stood, then walked unabashedly naked to the stairs. I had to stifle a relieved laugh. I quickly washed up in the bathroom before I climbed back into bed and sat back against the headboard, the blankets pulled up only to my waist.

A few minutes later, Xavier returned with a tray with two steaming mugs of cappuccino and the smoothie bowls I'd grown used to over time. "I have a feeling I'm doing something wrong," he muttered as he set the tray down on the nightstand. "I'm paying you but I am the one serving you coffee, breakfast, and hot hunk."

I snorted. "Hot hunk?"

The corner of his mouth tipped up as he handed me a cup. "Are you saying I'm not a hot hunk?"

"Fishing for compliments?" I said, clutching my mug and grinning. He was pure hot-hunk goodness, no argument, and he was only mine.

He sat against the headboard beside me with his own mug. "Isn't that what girlfriends are for?"

I took a sip. "I think in your case that's not necessary. You have a big enough ego as it is," I teased.

Xavier took a deep gulp then set the mug down on the nightstand, a grin twisting his face. "You have exactly five seconds before I show you that my ego isn't the only thing that's big."

"Five."

I sipped at the cappuccino, then licked foam off my lips.

"Four."

"I'm hungry," I said.

"Three."

"Xavier," I warned.

"Two."

I quickly put the cappuccino away because I had a feeling Xavier wouldn't care if I spilled coffee all over the bed, but I didn't want poor Nancy to find that kind of mess.

"One." Xavier grabbed me around the waist and hoisted me against him.

Thirty minutes later, I finished my cold coffee and ate my smoothie bowl, trying to ignore Xavier's smug grin and stifle my own.

EPILOGUE

EVIE

About two months after Xavier had made our relationship public, things finally started to settle down. Dad had asked Marianne to move in with him, so I hadn't felt bad telling him that I probably wouldn't return to the States after a year. They were already planning a vacation in Australia over Christmas. And Xavier's family? They had accepted me into their family without reservations.

Even the press seemed to sense that we wouldn't provide them with gossip anytime soon and turned their sights on other victims. I knew they'd eventually find something about us they could twist into their own version of the truth, but I didn't let it get to me anymore. I'd adopted Xavier's way of thinking. Why should I care what people I didn't give a damn about thought of me?

Even jealousy wasn't the big deal I'd thought it would be in our relationship. Xavier traveled with his team to away matches alone because there was a no-women ruling in place, but it didn't bother me. Despite his past, Xavier was loyal. He wouldn't cheat. Moreover, he and Connor always shared a room, and I knew he'd be the first one to snitch on Xavier if he ever put a toe out of line.

I smiled at the thought as Xavier and I strolled along the beach hand-in-hand on one of Xavier's off days. It was autumn in Australia now, and I had put on one of Xavier's thick sweaters that made me feel protected and small.

"Why are you smiling like that? It's got a sinister feel to it," Xavier said, drawing me out of my reverie.

I flashed him another secretive smile. "Oh nothing. Just thinking how your family and Connor would kick your ass if you messed things up with me."

Xavier groaned. "They would kill me. They love you more than me. You wrapped them around your skillful fingers."

I tilted my head up and let my fingers slip under his shirt to stroke his chest as he walked backwards and I stalked him.

Xavier covered my hand through the fabric. "I want you to move in with me," he said.

"What?" I nearly tripped over my own feet as I gaped up at him in utter shock. For a man who didn't do the dating thing, he moved quicker than I'd expected.

"You heard me," he said, pulling me to a stop.

"Isn't it too soon?"

"Evie, you've spent so much time in my apartment these last few months. I have never spent so much time with anyone, and it just feels right. With you I don't feel like I need to be anyone but me."

"I suppose Fiona will be happy to see less of you once I'm gone," I teased.

"That's a sentiment I share, trust me," he said.

"You two will have to get along eventually. For me."

Xavier pulled me against him. "Don't worry. We have an important thing in common. We adore you."

I patted his chest with a smile. "I must say I get why you enjoy all the attention. I enjoy your flattery too."

Xavier chuckled. "You deserve it for putting up with me."

"Of course I put up with you. You are the yin to my yang, the Ernie to my Bert, the cookie to my milk," I whispered.

Xavier grinned. "The Batman to your Robin, the Bonnie to your Clyde?"

"The peanut butter to my jelly."

Xavier grimaced. "Disgusting combination. You Americans have strange taste."

"The bacon to my eggs," I conceded. "The Han Solo to my Chewbacca."

"Better," Xavier murmured against my mouth. "The Laurel to your Hardy?"

"The Mulder to my Scully," I said between kisses.

"The Sheldon Cooper to your Amy Farrah Fowler?"

"The Beavis to my Butthead," I got out. "We both know you are the Butthead of course."

Xavier let out that deep sexy laugh. "Oh Evie, I can't possibly beat that." He tightened his hold around my waist and looked down at me with adoration, and I didn't care who saw us and what they thought about us, because we had each other and that was all that mattered.

"I love you, Butthead," I said with a smile.

"And I love you, Beavis," Xavier said with that wolfish grin before he pulled me in for another kiss.

THE END

BORN IN BLOOD MAFIA CHRONICLES

Bound By Honor
Aria & Luca

Bound By Duty
Dante & Valentina

Bound By Hatred
Gianna & Matteo

Bound By Temptation
Liliana & Romero

Bound By Vengeance
Cara & Growl

Bound By Love
Aria & Luca

Read Fabiano's story in the first book of the Camorra Chronicles,
a new spin-off series to the Born in Blood Mafia Chronicles:

Twisted Loyalties
Fabiano

Twisted Emotions
Nino

Twisted Pride
Remo

ABOUT THE AUTHOR

Cora Reilly is the author of the Born in Blood Mafia Series, the Camorra Chronicles and many other books, most of them featuring dangerously sexy bad boys. Before she found her passion in romance books, she was a traditionally published author of young adult literature.

Cora lives in Germany with a cute but crazy Bearded Collie, as well as the cute but crazy man at her side. When she doesn't spend her days dreaming up sexy books, she plans her next travel adventure or cooks too spicy dishes from all over the world.

Made in the USA
Monee, IL
11 March 2022

92696910R00159